I, CHARLES, FROM THE CAMPS

A Novel

Matt;
As you sail your boat,
remember our wars in Africa;
Joel Aug 3/18

JOEL D. HIRST

iUniverse®

I, CHARLES, FROM THE CAMPS
A NOVEL

iUniverse books may be ordered through booksellers or by contacting:

iUniverse
1663 Liberty Drive
Bloomington, IN 47403
www.iuniverse.com
1-800-Authors (1-800-288-4677)

ISBN: 978-1-5320-4773-2 (sc)
ISBN: 978-1-5320-4772-5 (hc)
ISBN: 978-1-5320-4774-9 (e)

Library of Congress Control Number: 2018904648

Print information available on the last page.

iUniverse rev. date: 04/20/2018

PROLOGUE

I never asked to be born Ugandan—to come into the world a poor black African man, here on this, the most terrible of continents. It seems oddly and especially unfair, being hobbled from birth, a chance event deciding whether I will sleep in a bed, find a job. If I will marry, build a life "more abundant," as the white missionaries insist. Whether I live or die of hunger and disease. Ease or suffering, prosperity or that shadow existence that fades away. I suppose nobody ever does accept their fate. I'm sure most people ask themselves in their own moments of angst, *But why me?* It is part of human nature to envy and to seethe. Be honest. If you were given a choice to arrive as you wish, where you wish, would you choose to be who you are? Or would you also envision for yourself something better, grander, with greater significance? With less pain, suffering, and insecurity? Would you not have chosen the life of a prince? A king? A sportsman who dances atop polished wood? Do you not also dream of being one of those celebrated people who I too have watched, though while seated on a broken-down bench in front of an old television in a camp of which you have never heard? I paid a few shillings for the privilege of losing myself in the extraordinary, forgetting my life—my suffering—for so brief a moment.

No, I never asked to be born into the camps, never invited the war, never desired the suffering. Following life's opportunities, such as they were, to Kampala. A thug, only to flee and flee and flee again. Day laborer or rebel warlord. Those were my options, until I ended up here—another camp, another food line in another country at the end of it all, to sit and wait for death. God, if He exists, hands down to His wretched creation what He wills, and it is our ration to bow our heads as we crawl forward and accept the beating. That is it. That is all. While to others across the oceans He gave power and position and comfort and opportunity, we were given only our tribes. Our families—children running naked and unencumbered in the dozens, in the hundreds—our culture, our rituals and rites, and our constipated systems of subjugation. Tradition, those who study us call it, squatting as we have always been on the pounded earth in front of our *tukuls*—our small circular mud-and-wattle homes—drinking the rancid banana wine to forget. To endure. Our destiny, they said it was. Predestination. The big words used by the missionaries to lend inevitability to the violence and the boredom. To attempt to make do on our tiny pieces of land, the rains that rarely come, the seeds that don't germinate. Poverty. Our history.

Ah, but when that is not enough—like it so often isn't when the fabrics of our societies are shredded by one war, after another and another—do we not also have our muscles, the strength of our backs, and the keenness of our minds to understand the danger and to discern friends from enemies? And do we not also have our understanding to see the monumental events for what they are and to seize what we can from an unforgiving world? The will to resist, the courage to rebel, and the strength for the fight? We've been doing it forever, we the black people of tropical Africa. Our entanglements with authority have so rarely been productive. For as far back as our collective tribal memory reaches, ours has been the story of violence and conflict; it's the story of humanity, after all. Why should we be any different? The tales are commemorated in our ritual dances that our leaders ban out of fear and in the sagas told over the campfire by our elders as we defy the boredom of our world. Our battles. We fought each other for the right to our land, to our families. We fought the wandering herdsmen who sought to turn our fields into their overgrazed pasturelands. We fought the Arabs and the Portuguese who sought to abduct us to work in foreign lands for no money. We fought the colonizers who willed that we labor even in our own lands for their comfort, to increase the measure of their wealth, and at their pleasure. Now we have returned mostly to fighting our own people, those put above us by dark forces that we do not understand, much less control. Elections and constitutions and representatives who exist outside of our consent, raiding the coffers and raping the ground to buy their luxury lives in the lands of the white people.

Yes, I, Charles Agwok, dared to rebel against that. Dared to hope. Dared to desire something else, something better. How did I do this? Mine was only to fight with the people I knew and at the moment of my opportunity. I have learned from my time in the bush, under the stars and beside waters both still and raging. I have learned from the training and the battles, the hardship and the suffering and the occasional triumph. I have learned from the brutality, that of others over me and my own brutality over those who challenged me. I have learned the most from my last, final flight, which laid out before me my mistakes and cemented my destiny. Is my story easy? No. You, who sit fat in front of television screens watching movies you did not make and reading books you did not write, who live in worlds you did not form and visit buildings you did not construct and eat meals you did not cook, might criticize me, might stare down your long noses in disgust at my attempts to establish something of my own, for myself and mine. Have I failed? Yes. Because I built in blood? Sure—what other material did I have? Blood is an insubstantial mortar, not favorable for cementing the efforts of man. Was I wrong? I ask you this one thing: If you were born a poor black African, faced with what I have known, would you have chosen a different way? And had you tried, would you have been any more successful than I have been?

I doubt it.

So, such as it is, this is my story. My confession as I reach the end of my life. Not to you, hoping for forgiveness from a world that never considered me. But to God, if He exists. Not that I owe Him any explanations, for I am a child of His camps, after all.

CHAPTER 1

I was born Charles Agwok from the village of Odek in the Gulu district of northern Uganda. My mother's name was Susan, and her life consisted entirely of tending to me and my nine brothers and sisters while my father, whose name was Moses, looked for work. I was the oldest of ten, which became five as our family was ravaged by disease and misfortune and hunger. They were of the old Acholi ways, my parents were—our ancient tribe that had forever possessed that fertile land between the river and the vast desert—before those were corrupted by the camps. Silent, emotionless people trudging heavyhearted through their difficult lives. I cannot even recall a full conversation with my father, speaking to me mostly in grunts and dark glares of admonishment. He was often absent. He would leave with a *humph* and a head tussle for my sisters as he walked away, fading between the tukuls as the periods of his sojourn extended. He tried the fields, but the war forced us off our land, being as they were beside the forest and too dangerous to work, even while others more fortunate slipped like shadows back and forth to plant and harvest. He would go to Gulu, the big city, where he was able to find work for a time collecting garbage and hauling it off to the dump outside of town. For another stretch, he watched the goats of the rich men who were too afraid to leave the city. Then again, he laid bricks to build a new market where others sold food he could not afford, or he served as a night guard for a local charity for whose services he did not qualify. Periodic labor, for nothing in Acholi was permanent except the war and the waiting.

1

The painful truth was that the war had destroyed everything, rarely leaving one stone atop another. The only thing that punctuated the waiting were the comings and goings of the white charity workers, beardless and moist—boys and girls, children really, of loose morals, all who worked during the day and debauched all through the night. They would come for a season to scratch that itch for adventure or out of misplaced rebellion or latent white guilt or whatever makes an adolescent come to Africa—expunging their remorse at having been born middle class by handing out plastic sheeting beside a stinking latrine in the day and lying flat upon the cot with a black savage in the storeroom behind the empty pharmacy at night before returning home to become housewives or secretaries or bankers or noodle factory managers. A brief adventure—fornication in a war-torn jungle. Double up on the condoms, please. But it was something to talk about at dinner parties when they were fat and bald; that's what Acholiland was to the do-gooder army of the West.

We lived in the big camp behind the subcounty offices and walking distance from the makeshift school that had been built for us, construction workers from Kampala trucked in by their cousins to move around Acholi dirt while we watched purposelessly. We were legion, the displaced people of Odek; they called us IDPs—internally displaced people—a term that let the white people think of us without thinking about us. There were tens of thousands of Odek IDPs; I called them neighbors, although nobody has imagined such a neighborhood. Listening to each other fuck and fight. The snoring of the fat woman in the tukul so close to ours that I could touch it by leaning out my window—if I had a window, that is. The grouchy old man's dirty hut that we all avoided lest he grab us unawares and we were buggered in the night, like some of the girls or smaller boys I had known. Outbreaks of lice and fleas that were uncontrollable, passed from one urchin to another and defying my mother's best attempts at cleanliness. The latrines and showers had been built on the outskirts of the war village by one of the charities, painted in their colors—black and yellow—as if they were a work of creation to be proud of. During the rainy seasons, they would back up and overflow, and the smell would waft over the camp, mingling with the corn-soy blend with which we made pancakes or the earthy aromas of beans and rice, distributed in huge burlap bags mixed with rocks and sometimes weevils and stamped with the colors of yet another charity, as if that cuisine demanded acclaim.

Every other Saturday, we "beneficiaries" lined up a thousand strong, hands extended to receive whatever it was that was being handed out that day, our ragged little green punch cards held fast in our tiny hands, cherished more than our Ugandan ID cards, not that we all had those. For the government, we didn't exist; only those who voted for the tyrant were ever graced with cards, and we would never vote for the tyrant.

We were often told about the homesteads of our ancestors, over firelight while one of the elders got drunk, over the din of the camp at dinnertime and the sounds of frying and squabbling and the smells of boiling rice with *linga-linga*—although that spinachy weed has never been my favorite. The old stories were not joyfully proud or even nostalgic. In the camps, all the fruits of our daily bread were seasoned with bitterness. My grandfather, on a visit from the camp where he ended up, would tell the stories of the night.

"Out there, in our lands," he would say, slurring, "you can hear the crickets chirping so loud you think maybe they will wake the babies. There were too many even to eat. Above, the bats spin the nighttime into a vortex while a wise old owl hoots in the tree beyond, a captured snake still dangling from its beak."

"What did you do?" we all would ask.

"Ah, eat well, drink clean water, smell only the food and the land. Go to bed early. These were the luxuries of our people," he said. "Awaking at the break of dawn to welcome the arrival of a new day of expectation and opportunity. To sit in the chill morning, drinking tea and looking out over the vast expanse of our fields heavy with the harvest. Space, to stretch and to grow. These were the birthrights of a free people—the Acholi."

Truth be told, I never really even imagined that life. What it would be like to not have to stand in line to take a crap, squatting atop the filth of my numberless neighbors. The luxury of having our own tukul, just for us boys, where we could chatter together at night without worrying about waking my mother or listening to the drunken snoring of my father when he returned, defeated again. Pens where the pigs were kept, the homemade granary where we stored our seeds first and then our harvest later, the showers where we washed with soap if the harvest had gone well, with charcoal if not. All placed evenly around the clearing, the massive acacia tree overhead protecting us from the open night, while in the middle the fire pit—for cooking, sure, but, more than that, for the rituals. The humming of the elders' voices when they came through for a visit to tell the stories, back when they were proud to be Acholi and the tales did not bring shame. The music that my grandfather would play, which he no longer played. In the camps, there is nothing to sing about. The songs and dancing as we children would run in circles until we collapsed to sleep in the stillness of each other's reassuring company. The trickle of the little stream that was just over the hillock like a soothing melody, clean and pristine for drinking or washing.

Then morning in Africa, my favorite time. When the sun is still just a suggestion on the horizon, the light starts to appear in the east, and the pervading darkness loosens its hold ever so slightly at first and then in greater abandon as it loses its fight against the sun. Slowly the fog is revealed, and for that brief instant between those two forces, day and night, the world is mysterious and powerful, blanketed by mist and the quiet coolness of expectant nature. The animals are still roaming the coolness, clutching their last prey or their final mouthful of grass or water before returning to their homes to wait out the heat of the day. Deer and antelope, occasionally a warthog or a snake, fish eagles overhead. It's quiet, contemplative. Pigs grunting in the early-morning crispness, the embers of the fire still hot as Mother brings them to life again to prepare breakfast. Working the fields that were so close before returning to eat *matoke* and rice and then rushing back to work again. And in the evenings, family, community. Weekends with a goat, a stew. A party. All these were the memories my grandfather tried to pass on, part of the imagined life that was beyond my reach.

Because I was a child of the camps.

As I indicated, our hovel was close to the schools. These had been built near the subcounty offices using white plastic sheeting marked with another logo, the alphabet soup of "assistance," which did not sustain. Hundreds of us would cram into a room with no desks, sharing the used textbooks and the occasional notepad that would arrive on a big truck painted white, also marked with a logo. Inside, a teacher would try to instill in us a love of reading and writing and math, when she wasn't drunk. I was unlucky though; my teacher was always drunk. Not that it mattered. School wasn't for me. I knew I would never escape by a miracle, like some of the special exhibits who the charities toured through the northern camps. Children who had "made it" and were studying in Makerere University in Kampala or even overseas. The odd softball or football star who ventured nervously north of the river, attempting to instill in us some misplaced hope. I have never been that naive. At least that's what I told myself to buttress my cynicism, my constant protection from the despair. Mine would never be the lottery of "discovery," and even if I did go from one class to the next—shuffled upward through inertia that involved no effort on my part—I knew that at the end of the mindless hours listening to the slurring instructor would be only a piece of paper, a ration card, a bag of corn-soy blend, and the right to build my own tukul next to my father's.

Instead, I had spent my time honing—oh, let's call it the art of the deal. Stealing something to sell. Acquiring nuggets of information that were valuable to the right people: when the food trucks were to arrive and what they would be carrying, who was sleeping with whom, who was stealing money, who had an illegal abortion at the hands of the pubescent doctors. The white workers—they liked to call themselves humanitarians—always took for themselves African girls, to make their experience on our dark continent sublime, erotic, forbidden. It was always profitable to make friends with these girls. They had more money, gifted by the guilty, which they would share for news of girls who had come of age who wished to replace them in the beds of their keepers, or of where to buy the best condoms for their paranoid lovers who were always worried about returning to their parents with a mulatto baby or an abortion on their conscience. Who of the new arrivals drank to excess and was easily ensnared. They were always on the lookout for all this—information that was easy for me to find, traded for money and sometimes for pull, a well-timed word tumbling onto a naked body that would allow a sick aunt to move to the front of the queue at the health facility or an extra ration of medicine for somebody's sick sister. Coveted space in the cars that came and went from Gulu; specialty food; advance notice of the next in the endless line of absurd activities concocted by a bleeding heart attached to an empty mind that would require labor or materials or "local knowledge"; the names on the selection committee for the next work program. Then there were the dealers, who always had the drugs that the white "humanitarians" wanted for their parties, or the real drugs when the pharmacy went without—and I knew them too, counted them all as friends for the influence they provided.

All this I sold, back and forth and up and down and across. This made me powerful in the camp, and I soon stopped going to school to dedicate myself full-time to my more lucrative endeavors. That was when the trouble started.

CHAPTER 2

I awoke one bright and sunny morning just after my fifteenth birthday; not that I had remembered it was my birthday, not that I would have been given a party anyway. Expectations in the camps are low, and even so are rarely met. Nevertheless, as I woke up, I thought to myself, *Today is going to be a good day*—notwithstanding the previous night's troubles—and whistled softly as I put on my pants, followed by the faded orange shirt that once had advertised soda pop. I found my flip-flops under the mat and crept outside. It was early, and my parents were still asleep; they always woke late and holding their heads, stumbling to find water or that last bit of drink left over from the previous night to take the edge off. The day really didn't matter; Mondays blended through to Fridays and into the weekend without anything to differentiate them except which line we should stand in. That day promised to be something special, a contact had told me, which I had since passed along—although it was not for me. Feminine hygiene items, but the lines started later. The charity workers too would crawl in to work well after the sun was up, nursing swollen heads and looking at patients through bloodshot eyes. I was quiet as I crept from the tukul, not wanting to wake my father and mother. We had fought again, like we often do when he drinks too much banana wine. It had started the way it always starts.

"You need to go back to school," he had told me.

"Why?" I responded, but it was a snap like the bite of a prairie turtle.

"Because that's the only way you will ever leave this," and he gestured around at the camp. We had been sitting on the hard ground outside of our tukul. The fire was blazing bright in the cramped little porch, around which were cluttered several chairs, while my brothers lay on the ground in the dirt, picking at an old blue fire engine handed down used from some home in the West to we, the poor in Africa, who didn't need new toys. We'd finished eating our dinner of rice and beans with some greens my younger brother had picked from a patch a short distance from the camp that nobody knew about. My father sat on his chair, a rusted metal frame with a precious few remaining plastic strips holding his sagging mass inches above the dirt. He leaned back, occasionally refilling his green plastic cup with wine from a yellow, twenty-five-gallon jerrican.

"How many do you know who have left the schools to work in the big city?" I had asked. "I'm not talking about as security guards or moto-taxi drivers. I mean like lawyers or doctors or bankers or whatever else it is people do in those big offices all day long."

"Well ..." His voice trailed off into a slur.

"How many?"

"They are not like you," he responded, "the children in your school. You're smarter, quicker."

"Not like me? Opportunity knows no Acholi. Smart or stupid, quick or slow is irrelevant for us, from here in the camps."

"You mark my words," he'd said. "This path you are choosing will only lead to misfortune."

"Misfortune?" I had said, sneering, looking at him wistfully. "Misfortune? How much worse fortune can I have? What do you call all of this?" And I had stood dramatically to rotate deliberately clockwise in a full circle, arms held wide, head thrown back and face to the stars above the camp. Across my countenance spread a viciousness that seemed to surprise my father. "I'd say we're all in a bad misfortune as it is, wouldn't you? And nothing we do seems to make any difference," I continued, sitting back down. "Look at you, drunk on banana wine every night. Worst thing that can happen to me: I can end up like you."

"You watch your mouth," he responded, groaning as he staggered to his feet.

8

I didn't even stand, just watching him sway there for a time.

"I am still your father." He stood there for a moment, attempting to sound menacing, I suppose, but came across mostly as exhausted before he collapsed back into his chair, breathless from the exertion.

"My point," I said when he sat back down. I was no longer afraid of him. I could beat him and had once or twice, especially when he drank the wine, which was all the time. Though I was young, I was strong and sinewy. He'd stopped hitting me two years before, when he split my lip with his fist and I cracked open his head with a rock. Since then, we mostly just argued, him staggering toward me and me pushing him back to his chair. I went on. "My point is that, really, we've got nothing to lose. Do we? Bored here under the stars." I'd gestured up. Yes, I was sad, thinking of the time wasted as the smoke from the perpetual fires blackened our lungs and reddened our eyes, as the wrinkles crawled across my parents' faces and their teeth yellowed and chipped. I had looked down at my brothers to underscore my father's impotence. "Look at them, growing up until they no longer even fit into the school desks, as if it matters. You may say it's what everybody does, that it is our fate, our destiny. But this"—I gestured again at the camp around me, at the totality of my portion—"isn't gonna be everything for me like it is for you. I want to take the chance—because only then maybe can I get out of here. I don't know, maybe even move away. To Gulu or further. You could replace this," and I kicked the jerrican of banana wine, and it sloshed up to spill some of its rancid contents on the packed dirt in front of the tukul, causing my father to cry out, "with beer. A television, things that should not be fancy but that for us, the Acholi, might as well be made of solid gold."

We didn't talk about the end of the war, and my fantasies never considered the return to the land. The violence had raged in the smoldering villages of Acholiland forever. We knew there was no end to the evil of the rebels, that they could feed off that malevolence in the shadows until the end of time, and that they probably would. And we knew that the government didn't care, that for them we were all the same. Former rebels, future rebels. Trouble. So we, the mighty Acholi who had fought in great wars across the oceans, had stopped waiting for our own war to end. Now we waited on … well, we just waited.

9

"No, Charles," my father had responded after sinking back heavily into his chair to caress his plastic tumbler. "The worst case is not that you end up like me, although I know it seems that way to you now. The worst case is you do something really stupid and are handed over to the soldiers. You hear the screaming at night coming from the soldiers' camp, just like I do. You know what they do to those who cause trouble. Those screams belong to boys who have fathers too, and I will not sit here listening to your hoarse pleas getting weaker and weaker by the night. So I implore you, my son. Stop your scheming and keep your head down. We'll make it. I am sure we will. Our fortunes will be found right over the horizon. In fact, just yesterday I heard a friend ..." And the old man descended as he always did into speculation, his fogged mind following idle conjecture and lazy rumor of fortune and opportunity while he grinned at me and I just watched and let him speak. Finally, he was finished.

"No," I whispered defiantly. "I can't live my life in vain hope. But neither will I fear them. I'm faster than they are—and smarter. And I know this land. I'm not scared of the soldiers."

"You should be," he mumbled, emptying his plastic flagon and reaching down again to refill it. "You should be ..."

"If the soldiers come after me, I could always just go join *them*," I said, attempting to lighten the mood with an ill-conceived jest. But my father jumped to his feet again, swaying menacingly. He stood there, reeling from the wine, having trouble focusing on me and squinting as he wagged his finger.

"Don't even joke about that," he said. "Even the jokes could get you killed."

I remained seated. "Oh, calm down. Nobody cares what you and I talk about over wine."

"I'm telling you," he responded, agitated again. "Go back to the school. Get your piece of paper. Go to one of those training programs."

"No," I said in a low voice that radiated finality. "You've seen them. Skinny white kids trying to teach us how to stitch underwear or fry a banana. Fuck them. I won't do that, even if it costs me everything."

"The day is coming," my father said, but this time more tired, "when I will no longer be able to protect you, my son. They come around

10

here, the chairman and the police. Did you know that? They look for you, wanting to ask you questions about this or that problem. You've developed a reputation. Someday you'll do something so ill advised that I won't be able to hold them off any longer."

"That day," I said, "well, we'll deal with that day when it comes."

After that, we'd remained silent for the rest of the night. Slowly my father's eyes glazed over. The smells of the night surrounded us: food, tobacco. The comforting fragrance of always. The night sky had darkened, and it was quiet with a chill that had descended from the forests to lay over the slumbering camp. My mother had returned from washing the pots and plates from dinner in the communal pool by the borehole, the one with the shiny silver hand pump that had been installed only two years ago and still spewed enough water that she didn't have to risk getting raped beside the bigger, electric-powered one by the women's showers. *I am trouble?* I laughed to myself. Drunkards fighting. Men beating their wives. Prostitutes spreading AIDS among the desperate. Disease. Early death. Malnutrition. Babies wasting away when the truck was delayed by the rains or attacked by the rebels. Those things were trouble—but I, because I chose to defy those who would consider themselves my betters, had a target on my back?

So be it!

I then had found myself studying my mother in the firelight. She had been a onetime beautiful Acholi woman, and the traces were still there beneath the grime and the misery. She was round in the right places, with smooth, unblemished ebony skin. When she smiled—which she rarely did anymore—her even-set teeth glistened like the kernels of the white corn from a perfect harvest. But slowly, the ugliness of resignation had begun to settle into her eyes, and the bitterness bitten back by pursed lips had replaced the beautiful line of her mouth, though she was still in fact young, not even forty yet. Camp life destroys people. Her curves had become misshapen from bad food; her skin had hardened from working and sitting under the sun; her eyes were bloodshot. The constant lifting of water and wood and bags of food had bent her over like a young tree after the great storm has blown through the valley. It made me sad to look at her, and that night, I had looked away, gazing instead at the night sky above. To not have to consider our collective frustration, if only for a moment. That has always been one of the Acholi's greatest dreams.

Early that morning as I abandoned the tukul, I found several of my brothers, who I had thought were still asleep, sitting on the far side of the open space, playing marbles with three other children from the neighborhood, the occasional clinking of the glass the only sound between them. "Where are you going this early?" they asked me in unison, to which I responded with only a grin, kicking at the collection of marbles as I passed, sending them scattering. "Hey!" they yelled after me as I flashed them a quick grin. Yes, although I am now old, wrinkles lining my face and my sparse hair white as the snow atop Mt. Kilimanjaro, back when I was just a boy in the camps, I was strong and confident, considered even by some to be handsome. Six feet tall, thin, and strong and black as the ancient Acholi warriors, the stories of which I was told by my grandfather before he died.

I walked on, whistling carelessly. Past the hut of the old man who always beat his wife, only barely fifteen; the thumps followed by a whimpering that would last late into the night, especially after the food distribution, which the poor girl would ferment, hands trembling as she stirred the noxious mix. I went past another that sheltered the old woman who everybody knew was a witch, where we would visit when we needed to procure a curse against somebody or somebody else. Life in the camps, rubbing up against other people in the thousands—unwashed and bored—often creates quarrels that at times can be answered only with dark magic. It was secreting an unpleasant odor, and I skirted the small building holding my nose. Beside the latrines were the girls' showers, and I slowed down, hoping for a glimpse of something forbidden before sauntering out into the open area in front of the subcounty offices. On the far side of the clearing, in the center of which stood an enormous acacia tree providing shade for the lazy police and homes for the disease-ridden bats, sat the school and the health center. A distance behind the school and halfway to the next neighborhood in our great unplanned town was a block of five square, cement stalls where those with shillings to spare could procure items from Gulu—toothpaste, pasta, little sachets of *waragi*, Uganda Waragi, that local gin that rots away the mind, the brew of choice for those with limited means who wish to lose themselves quickly. The cinderblock cubes were set atop cement slabs and covered by zinc roofs that during the savanna storms pounded out a dissonant rhythm that represented for so many yearning souls the sound of African prosperity in a land of want. Bats hung too from the rafters, and the occasional rat could be observed poking around the garbage pile on the far end of the block. In the middle, the most elaborate stall was painted yellow and white and even had a tiny generator that powered a TV and satellite dish in front of a dozen orange chairs and a few rickety tables covered by another plastic sheet. There we "troublemakers" would often congregate to watch football games, paying a few shillings for the privilege of not being chased away as we had been as children, as the other children still were. That establishment even sold real beer, which nobody could afford except occasionally.

It was to there that I was headed, because as the makeshift bar and the epicenter of the town's tiny gambling racket, it was also predictably the place to acquire something illicit. Or make a sale. And today I had something special to sell.

"Charles, how are you?" said Henry, the middle-aged proprietor of the establishment. Henry was slightly overweight with a roundness that hinted at success, but that not too great. He had thick, bushy hair over thin sideburns that petered out into a scraggly beard toward the bottom of his chin, framing polished white teeth that were always visible in his radiant smile. Henry was an avid supporter of the overthrown and deceased dictator, Tito Okello, the premature end of whose abortive six-month rule Henry considered the worst tragedy to have befallen the country, leading as it had to the current tyrant's takeover. And Henry hated the tyrant, often embarking upon drunken tirades in the dead of night, which he had been warned against but could not keep himself from engaging in after the third beer had enlivened his tongue.

"Good, as always. Nothing to complain," I responded.

"Excellent. Tusker?" Henry said. He'd recently acquired a tiny fridge after the looting of a charity residence when the old Frenchman in charge had been found to be buggering little boys. The buggering of

13

our women, well, there was nothing to do about that. But our babies? The Frenchman had been lucky to escape with his life. My friend rifled around and withdrew a green bottle of Tusker, popping the cap with his teeth and handing it over.

"Yes, thank you," I said.

"We missed you last night," he said as he slumped heavily in the seat beside me, wiping the condensation down his own bottle with a practiced hand.

"Aja," I grunted, staring into the golden brew with one eye closed.

"The African Cup finals. We did not make it, but a valiant effort was made!" Henry said, jubilantly raising his bottle for a toast, an act left unanswered as I said nothing, still bitter at the fact that I had been unable to locate one of the girls who owed me money for a particularly lucrative encounter I had facilitated. Consequently, I had been forced to listen to the game on the scratchy, battery-powered radio with my brothers, a singularly boring experience absent the camaraderie and the beer. I could not drink my father's banana wine, even if he would let me, which he never did.

"So what do you have for me?" Henry finally asked, perhaps realizing I was not at that time possessed by the jovial spirit of conversation. I had been cradling my beer protectively in two hands, watching the early-morning coolness condense the heavy droplets that seeped through my fingers to run down my arms. There were few people around. Noises came from the schoolyard where the teacher-less children were running helter-skelter after each other. A line had already formed at the health center like an enormous mamba that curved away into the shadows. Beside Henry, the other four stalls in the block remained firmly shut, metal doors fastened with padlocks.

"For you," I said, only to be interrupted by a little boy who approached timidly to pass Henry a five-hundred-shilling note in exchange for an envelope of detergent. Henry stood to extract one from the darkness behind the counter, surrendering it to the child before sitting back down.

"For you," I repeated, leaning forward, with Henry unconsciously mirroring my movement, "what I have is this. There's a new project that has come on line ..."

"There's always a new project coming on line," Henry said, sitting back, disappointment in his voice.

"Hear me out," I said sharply. "You know Nails for Peace?"

"Of course," Henry said. Everybody knew that group. Unbeknownst to them, they were the joke of the camp. When they introduced their program, the camp commanders—enraged—struck back, stacking the "beneficiary" list with the worst whores, trollops, and syphilitics in the camp. Discarded women nobody would touch. Watching these diseased wretches shuffling each morning to the pink-painted building to be pampered and manicured by aging, overweight white women had become one of the central activities of the day.

"So. They are starting another program."

"Okay," Henry said. "I'm listening. What do you know?"

"I know where. I know when. I know how much."

"Spill it," he said harshly.

"One of the Australian volunteers is engaged in an amorous dalliance with one of my girls," I said, finally taking a drink of beer as I looked back and around to assure we continued our subterfuge unobserved.

"And what did she say?"

"She said that they will be bringing in the shillings they require for the full project, six months of work. Salaries, rent, food, supplies. All of it. And they will be holding it here, in Odek."

"Why the devil would they do that?"

"Who knows?" I said. "Who cares?"

"I see," Henry said, leaning back. "So, your friend. She wants her cut?"

"Of course," I said. "Cost of doing business."

"What," said Henry slowly, almost menacingly, "is it you need from me?"

"Not much. The usual. I need a lookout or two. I need somewhere to bring the money, somebody to take it to Gulu and keep it there till the pressure is off, and somebody to pay off the military when they start asking around. It's going to be a lot. They might even search the camp. And you know where they will look first."

"Yes, I do, *troublemaker*," Henry said, elbowing me in the side, causing me to spill some beer on the hard-packed earth beside the stall. "Fair enough. So, what's the plan?"

"Ah, the plan," I said. "So here's what I've been thinking. It seems like the offices of this charity will receive the cash on one of the next few Fridays ..." And we hatched the plot. I had no way of knowing that the small subterfuge we were planning on that bright African morning north of the river would be my escape ticket from the camps. Neither could I have understood as I ambled away from Henry's establishment the dark road I had begun to tread and the grisly places it would ultimately lead.

CHAPTER 3

The weeks went slowly by while I anxiously awaited news, and I passed the time throwing rocks at the children on recess or making the rounds collecting my payments from the various clients of my obscure services. Then all at once the moment arrived. "This Friday," said my friend, the girl who enlivened Australian beds, as she passed me on her way to the clinic while I was leaning up against the Acacia tree, staring obtusely at the charity offices as if the intensity of my stare and the force of my will would precipitate the long-awaited moment. "They are planning a party. It is going to be big. They're bringing in the money in the same Land Cruiser as the beer and vodka. The drugs have been slipping in all week inside cold-chain deliveries with vaccines."

The moment had come—a score, as big as any I had heard, certainly the biggest of my nascent career. Padding beneficiary rosters, registering ghost workers, faking ration cards, and slipping medicines into my pocket for Henry's black market. Those were the essence of my daily bread. Pittances, almost not worth the effort. But finally, my opportunity had arrived. The prospect of leaving and going far away. The dream of a house where snakes did not crawl through the thatch roofs hissing at the rats and the bats; where air conditioners hummed soothingly above pristine cement and tile; an electric kitchen where wood smoke would no longer aggravate my mother's hacking cough. A bathroom, shitting in silence and peace without the incessant banging on the wooden boards of the latrine doors, propping my leg horizontally against the one that did not adequately close. A shower—better still, a bath. I had never had a bath, could not even imagine really immersing myself in that much clean water alone, in private. Water it would take two hours of work at the hand pump to accumulate, as if you could ever have two hours at the hand pump, when the line of angry women behind would barely let you fill a bucket. Slipping into the hot water, covering legs, then knees, then torso, and finally head, letting it soothe away the aches of the years and the layers upon layers of grime I had come to accept as a part of my life.

It was only Tuesday, so I nestled my anxiety in the dreams of the future as the time passed slowly, crawling by like the fist-sized snails that would occasionally traverse my path as I squatted, unmoving, in front of the acacia, seconds turning to minutes, turning to hours, turning the world. Smoking a cigarette, adding the butt to the ever-increasing mound beneath my feet. Drinking an orange Fanta—bubbles tickling my nose. Playing cards or whittling at a piece of wood. Whatever I could do to look busy as I cased the offices, aching for the arrival of that which would set me free. Nobody paid me any attention. I was just another young African adolescent sitting under a tree; even invisibility would not have increased my anonymity.

By the time the night came, I knew every movement, each coming and going. Who guarded the facility, both by day and by night. At what time the workers went to lunch, and when they closed up for the night. I knew how many whites there were, how many locals. When they ate and when they went to the latrine. Everything, that is, except the trysts—the unpredictable urges of the unsupervised.

At long last, my intense vigil yielded fruit in the form of a VHF radio antenna piercing the sky from the other side of the hill. The radios, expensive and arrogant—bravado thin and delicate, the pretense of security, as phony and powerless as the white skin they believed protected them. Then came the shiny white four-by-four, maneuvering carefully to avoid the children who were a ubiquitous part of camp life. Only the previous week, a careless charity worker had run over a toddler chasing a blue rubber ball, and the military had been forced to intervene in defense of the scruffy white man, and only just in time as the enraged clan had already hung a rope noose from the stout branches of the acacia tree under which I had been sitting, forcing me to continue my watch from a different and less convenient venue. As the truck moved ever closer, I scampered up the tree for a better look. The colors decorating the side of the vehicle were bright pink and light green, the sign of a cross advertised by a sticker crookedly slapped upon the metal of the driver-side door. The truck came to a stop in a puff of dust in front of the offices, and they dropped out, the adolescents did, dressed in T-shirts that matched the sticker over new, crisp jeans and leather sandals pulled tight over white socks. One of them had a bulging green backpack thrown over his shoulder, the contents of which were betrayed by the wary signs of hunted prey. They glanced furtively to and fro, their inexperienced eyes looking for danger and finding only boredom. As if we didn't know what they were doing, as if they were outsmarting me, in my camp. I opened a new pack of cigarettes, withdrawing one and lighting it to take a drag, the orange tip bright before me while the pungent smell of unfiltered, old tobacco radiated electrically upward into my head, lending a sense of giddiness to my growing invincibility. One step, two, then three, and they were inside, slamming the corrugated metal door only to reappear after thirty minutes, locking the door with a padlock before retreating to their compound on the other side of the clearing. I lingered and lingered, and then lingered still longer.

Slowly the sun set in the west, accentuating for a brief moment the silhouette of the camp under the explosion of orange and green that ended the day. The smoke wafted from a thousand campfires to accumulate in a haze that spread out above like a blanket. It was almost beautiful, the evening in the camps, observing as I was from on high, as if the problems were not my own, as if the misery was not my ration too. Antiseptic and even exotic, though it was all I had known. The colors creating a metamorphosis, a makeshift community becoming watercolor on canvas; the smells of food and the sounds of family lending a peculiar charm to my prison-village. From all around me, the bats took to flight, shrieking in the night as they began their nocturnal hunt. I sat upon my perch until my legs cramped up and a knob on a tree branch began to dig unforgivingly into my thigh while I waited for the perfect moment, the moment I had planned for, the moment of truth.

It was deepest night. The lights had finally gone out in the far compound where the party had raged. The sounds of music and drinking had abated as one by one the do-gooders collapsed upon each other to sleep away their evening's diversions. The final light—an empty socket looking out onto the misery beyond, window cracked open slightly, allowing the squeals and moans to tumble out upon the poor—at last was turned out, and all was darkness. Under the tree, the pile of cigarettes had grown into a little hill. Finally now was my chance.

I climbed down and moved on the offices, flitting from shadow to shade to arrive under the cover of the corrugated metal roofing, upon the cement walkway beneath the overhang. Nobody had seen me. I was sure of it. First, I tried the door, just in case. It was locked. No surprise there. Unfazed, I crept around to the back, as I had planned, crawling over a pile of cement bricks and a rusted assortment of rebar beneath an old toilet that had been thrown haphazardly behind the building. Behind me was the expanse that led toward the forest in the distance beyond the clearing, which had been cleaned of trees by the paranoid soldiers wary to give themselves advance warning of a rebel attack. On the back side of the building above the pile of refuse was a window high and small but just big enough for me. I pulled a few cinderblocks from the pile and set them atop the toilet, laying them one atop the other, precariously scaling the tower until I was able to reach, stretching, to the window that slid open silently, responding fluidly to my overtures. I carefully hauled myself up onto my belly and then into the darkness, spinning to hang for an instant over the void and then drop to land in a whisper upon the cement floor of the office. I looked around. Inside there were two small rooms, one with desks and files, and the other with a large old safe sealed with a padlock. I crept silently over to the safe to examine the padlock, which was thick and of the variety that I had seen in every stall across northern Uganda for years. That is to say, cheap and brittle. *They think we are even too stupid to steal*, I thought. *I would do this even if only to burn the money later.* I took from my pocket a piece of steel rebar, weaving it through the hole, grabbing one end in my hand and pushing against the other end with my foot until I heard a distinct click. *This is too easy*, I thought as I removed the lock and opened the safe. Inside were bricks of Uganda shillings, fresh and smelling of ink and held together by pieces of paper with the denominations and quantities penned on them. I removed the three black plastic bags I had in my pocket—the kind that dance together in the winds before the summer rainstorms—and filled them with the bills, closing the door of the safe carefully when I was finished.

Click. I froze in place. A sound from the entrance door, keys in the lock.

Jingling, and then the key was removed, replaced by another and then another, increasingly urgent.

"What are you doing?" The voice, a young girl speaking in an American accent.

"Damn it, I can't find the right key." Another voice, this one with a thick Irish brogue. More jingling.

"Come on. I'm horny." Giggles. "And Tom doesn't know I slipped out. He was pretty drunk, but if he wakes …"

"I'm trying," the Irish brogue responded.

I began to tiptoe urgently back to the window. There was a desk a few feet away, and to reach the window, I would have to push it against the wall. I had planned to do this when I departed and silently cursed myself for my procrastination.

"Oh, you're not doing it right." The girl's voice and then a scuffle.

"It's not that one." The brogue again. "See, look." A click, and a little bit of light shone from the keyhole.

I reached the desk, putting the black bags on top of it.

"It's this one here," the brogue said again. And the sound of a key being inserted into the lock.

I held my breath, waiting for the inevitable turning key, but then I heard another giggle. "Hey, don't do that. Stop it." And the sound of a key ring fell on the other side of the door. "Let's go inside first."

I took my opportunity. I tiptoed silently to the door and used a coat hanger that I'd found in a pile to slip under the door and hook onto the key ring, hauling them into the room swiftly.

"What the hell?" the brogue asked.

"Where are they keys?"

"They were just here a second ago."

"Shine the flashlight over there. Maybe they fell into the grass."

21

I thought perhaps my subterfuge had succeeded and they would return to their compound. But I had underestimated their desire.

"Fuck it. There's a window out back. I keep a spare in the desk. I'll go through and pull you up, and we'll look for the keys in the morning."

Damn.

There was nothing for me to do. I tiptoed back to the desk, tensing my muscles. One, two, three, and then I pushed the desk with all my force, and it crept across the uneven cement floor making a shrieking scraping sound.

"What was that?" the brogue asked.

I jumped to the top of the desk, throwing the black bags out of the window and finally lifting myself through. I heard footsteps pounding on the cement as I plopped onto the ground behind the building, grabbing the bags and sprinting toward the forest.

"Hey, you," I heard behind me. It was not a yell but a hiss. I didn't stop, sprinting at full speed toward a hill on the other side of the small clearing, waiting for the yell—the gunshot. As I ran, I ventured a look behind me and saw a figure just turning the corner of the building, starting to sprint after me. But he was less fit and slightly drunk, and he stumbled on an old tree trunk that had remained from the military's razing of the land. I jutted back and forth and back again and vaulted the hill to fall flat, looking back. The adolescent was just flipping over to stare up at the stars, apparently catching his breath before huffing to his feet. He was limping as he moved toward the hill slowly. I ducked down below the crest of the hill and crawled away, waiting for the ruckus to alert somebody. But the cries never came, and the figure never crested the hill to continue the hunt. I had been saved from the soldiers' torture chambers by lust and adolescent fear of, I suppose, whoever "Tom" might have been and whatever he might do to them. I slipped away—another black figure that they would never identify, even if they dared admit that they had been witness to the heist.

I occasionally wonder what the ephemeral companions of our misery are doing now, so many years after they, and I, grew old. Do they also tell stories about their adventures in the African camps, as I am doing? Do they remember the fleeting withdrawal of that boy-thief so long in the past that interrupted their plans? And do they lament the disruption, missing out as they did on forbidden sex in a foreign land? Questions with no answers, I suppose. For whatever reason—fate, perhaps—I was allowed to escape. Looking back at the path I took after this, the first of many bad decisions, I sometimes lament the fact that I was not caught, not tortured and dumped into a shallow grave. But so great an evil as I became for a season cannot be extinguished by the likes of a moistened boy seeking closet intercourse. Mine was too formidable an evil.

At any rate, the whole operation had taken only a half hour or so. I moved steadily and stealthily away from the scene of the crime, arriving at last at the grain storage bin I had carefully chosen as the place to stash the spoils, a building leftover from times of normality when traders came and went from Odek and the farmers stored their harvests to wait for the bulk purchase of the big companies from Gulu. I slipped inside, the bags hefted over my shoulder, and immediately sneezed. The air inside was stale. Something moved in the corner that I assumed was a rat. Two of the iron sheets that had made up the roof were missing, letting in a view of the stars above. A few bats hung from the rotting wood beams, and they screeched at me as I disturbed the stillness of their abode. I found in the corner a pile of old corncobs—the kernels eaten away long ago—where I buried the black bags, throwing dirt and a piece of plastic sheeting over the top for good measure. Finished, I stepped back, looking at my handiwork, and then quietly exited the building, glancing first left then right before stepping out into the night and ambling nonchalantly toward the stall where Henry was serving his last drunken customers. He'd turned the music high, and the final patrons—those most committed to their vice—were swaying in the plastic chairs to the music. Two of them had their heads rested upon the tabletops, presumably in a valiant attempt to stop the spinning, and there they had stayed. They were all passed out, which made the evening's business anonymous.

Upon seeing me walking empty-handed, Henry frowned, pulling me into the tiny interior of the store. "So, do you have it?" Henry asked.

"Yes," I said. "Hidden away."

"Good," Henry said. "Where is it?"

I told him the story, leaving out the part about almost being caught.

"Sounds like it was fairly painless."

"Yes," I lied. "People aren't very careful with money that isn't theirs."

"True. Good work today!"

"So how will I get my share?" I asked.

"Tomorrow I'll go find it. I have to go into Gulu anyways, so I will stop by the bank to make the deposit."

"Aren't they going to be suspicious, all that money at once?"

"I already do deposits every few days. Do you think you are my only client? The bank teller is a friend. In a war, complicity is for sale." Henry smiled.

"And what should I do?"

"You lay low for a few days, and on Wednesday you come by here. I'll tell you how much it finally ended up being, and I'll hold it in safekeeping for you. There's nowhere you can hold that much money without being caught anyways."

"Okay," I said tentatively.

"Don't worry," Henry said, obviously sensing my distrust and slapping me on my back. "You did great. I won't cheat you. Mud flung up from the affairs of men sticks to us all, and we need the companionship in darkness to achieve success. North of the river is a dangerous place to make enemies we don't need, isn't it?"

"You're right," I said, somewhat relieved. We shook hands.

"Good. Then see you Wednesday. And stay out of trouble till then. When the Aussies realize the money is missing, there will be hell to pay."

"Okay," I said again. "I will. See you Wednesday."

By Wednesday, I was already far below the river.

CHAPTER 4

The sun had started to rise the following morning, thinning out the nighttime darkness above the camp as the bats jostled with each other for space to sleep out their day in the crowded old acacia. The sounds of morning life had begun to fill the clearings, people stirring to prepare meager breakfasts. Children screaming. A radio somebody had switched on playing music, competing with another blaring the BBC news about troubles in a faraway land. The news was never about Acholi; our misery had ceased to entertain many years before. Out of the tukuls, the few people who had real jobs emerged, some even with suits and ties, others only with ripped pants and faded T-shirts. Those without agency meandered over to stand in the line out front of the latrines, the first line of a day that would be measured by the length of its lines and the heat of the sun. Little girls were dispatched with big yellow jerricans to stand in wait before the borehole for their turn to fill it with the water that their mothers required for that day; they were the unlucky ones, the ones who had been born to serve as day laborers and who would never go to school. Not that it mattered anyway. I slinked from behind the church where there was a depression in which I sometimes hid, returning home as if I'd spent a night carousing. I'd even had Henry splash me with beer; my father would be angry, yelling and screaming. But he was always mad, and he would be madder still if he knew the true nature of my evening's enterprise.

As I walked, my mind strayed back to the money. Those who have access to money don't often think about it, not really. They think about what they could buy if they had more, or they fret over investments that are not growing as they expect them to, a tall tree in a jungle of wealth. They stew over their neighbor who has more, perhaps. But they don't really understand the nature of need because they have never wanted as we from the camps have. They have never watched their children's fevers spike, staring through that delicate pane of glass to the drugs that would save her life. They have never watched their emaciated son's gaze become cloudy as the pangs of hunger force his little body to double into a ball while the beating music of the charities' parties rage into the night, keeping the child awake—as if he would sleep, as if the hunger would let him. That desire to assault those who stand between you and that which would stay the hand of death—a brief reprieve only, perhaps, but nevertheless pushing to tomorrow the misery of want—that is the world's most powerful force, which expresses itself in a craving for money. It gives us time. Those of us who are poor buy only time, if we can afford it. Want, honest and pure. Most have no idea what this is.

And there is no substitute for the universal language of money. The measure of a pile of it allows one people to place themselves atop others—measurements that do not change with age or disease. The storing of value when all harvests are eaten by mice and all houses are pillaged by soldiers or rebels and all lands lay fallow out of fear. As all beauty that has given a modicum of indiscrete wealth also fades away. Pieces of paper stacked in tiny piles that guarantee opportunity and well-being, especially if they were American dollars. Even the communists, who occasionally wandered through during election time talking about revolution to the vacant stares of the hungry in food lines, couldn't find an explanation of how their violent words would have helped my father acquire the pills that would have turned my sister's eyes from yellow back to white. Except to take them, and that I was already doing. But the violence always creates scarcity, something we knew well in Acholi.

Money.

I hadn't had a good chance to count it before I'd given it to Henry for safekeeping, and I had a gnawing suspicion in the back of my mind. Henry, my friend, my confident—but a hustler after all, like me. Was my money safe with a man such as that? Sigh. I could only shrug; the die was cast, after all. I turned my mind to what I would do with my share. Henry very well couldn't steal all of it, if that's what he would do—there was enough to go around with some to spare. Maybe I would buy a motorcycle or two and start a moto-taxi business. Or maybe it was enough to buy a proper house for my family. We could move to Gulu, and my mother could start a restaurant. She loved to cook the *matoke*, that plantain mash with sauce. Maybe I'd become rich, and I could leave this miserable country that had never given any of us anything but suffering. Go to Mombasa—the beach. Even Zanzibar, an island where nobody knew us or thought to look down at us. Yes, that was it. We'd move there. I'd spend my days lying on the beaches and the nights carousing the bars looking for girls. They'd be easy to find—the girls would. They always sense those with money, attracted like lions to a gazelle. I would let myself be ensnared by two or even three; we can have as many as we want, we Acholi. Muslims are limited to four, but I could have forty if I felt like it.

I walked on, my steps lighter and lighter as my imagination soared, only to come crashing to the ground as I halted midstep before rounding the last neighbor's hut, listening to the escalating voices of an unfolding disaster entirely of my own making.

"He did not," my father was saying forcefully.

"We aren't asking you if you think he's the one. We already know that. We want to know where he is," said the chairman. I knew his voice well from the countless political speeches, the prayers at church, and the lessons in school. And the scolding, when I'd been occasionally caught in any one of my endless schemes.

"He's not here. And he's not guilty."

"Your son? Not guilty? You think we don't see him at night, drinking and carousing? You think we don't watch him as he watches us from the shadows—always calculating? Your boy is a rotten jackfruit."

"No," my father said, patiently and painstakingly. "Perhaps he is bored. I will say that. Life is not easy for an adolescent in the camps, and we must give leniency to the victims of our wars. But he would never do anything like you are suggesting. What proof do you have?"

"Proof? We don't need any proof. We'll find your boy, and when we do, we'll find the money, and then you will have your proof, and us our money," said the chairman.

"Over my dead body will I let you torture my son."

I peeked around the corner at the scene. I saw my dad. He was square and tall, facing down a young charity worker, the chairman, and three soldiers. It wasn't panic that seized my insides as I listened; a boy as accustomed to trouble as I had been develops a sense of invincibility and of inevitability. Nor was it remorse. Survival allows for no moral qualms. It was pride. There my father was, standing tall, swaying a little with age and exhaustion, but the Acholi fire had returned briefly to his eyes as he faced down my pursuers. For a moment, a split second, I was proud of him again like I had been when I was just a little boy and he was that great, silent protector, before he had been destroyed, and before I had realized that in fact he'd been destroyed long ago.

"Um, sir," said the foreigner haltingly. He was different from the one I'd seen last night, puffing behind me in drunken exhaustion. Not that I can ever tell these *wazungu* apart. *That must be Tom*, I thought, smirking. *I wonder what story they told him.* He was fidgeting with his hands in front of him, looking awkward and worried. He was pink from the assault of the Acholi sun on his milky skin. His stringy blond hair was pulled back in an unkempt ponytail, and his shoulders were slumped under a white T-shirt advertising his charity. "We just want the money returned, and, like, we don't want any trouble for anybody," he said. It was more of a whine than a request.

"What money? We don't have any money," my father said. "Go inside and look." And my father stepped aside, away from the entrance to our family hut.

"Not your money," the ponytail said. "Money taken from the people, man. Money we brought in to help you."

"Help me?" My father stepped back into the doorframe, suddenly filling out as he towered over the boy.

"Yes, cuz you know, we're here because of our love …"

"Love?" my father repeated, his voice disgusted.

"Well, yeah. I mean we're here cuz like we love all of humanity. We just want to help. We are, well, disinterested. Which makes our love purer. But we need that money—"

"Yes, you are disinterested. To that I will agree," my father said, interrupting ponytail, who seemed to somehow shrivel or shrink under the withering sun.

"Huh?"

"Let me tell you about disinterested. Did you know I used to have ten children?"

"What does—"

"Yes, I used to have ten children. You, whose families are small, who come from afar, seem to think we cannot love our large families. That the love we have for our children is less intense than your own. But I loved them all! Susan, Carol, David, Stephen, Alexander, Peace, Hope, Blessing, Phillip—yes, and Charles. Each one of them I loved, even those who have died."

"I'm so sorry ..."

"Are you sorry? Or are you disinterested? You can't have it both ways. So I'll take you at your first word. Because, do you know how many children I have left?"

"Well ..." Ponytail Tom looked around, somewhat lost.

"Five. For you, who help disinterestedly, do you know how many that means I have lost?"

"Um ..."

"Five."

"I'm sorry," Ponytail repeated pathetically.

"Are you? You keep saying that. Is it true? Yet here you are to rob me of another of my children. That would leave me with how many?" my father asked rhetorically.

"Well ..." Ponytail was playing with a lump of dirt that was sitting atop the polished earth in front of the hut.

"Four," said my father. I was stunned, I had never heard my father say more than one or two sentences, much less the assault that left the ponytail frail and whimpering. I was at once proud and sad. "Will that make you lose sleep? Will you now mourn for me, you who want to take my oldest boy? Or will you carouse tonight the same as you did last night? Will your party, where you fornicate with our girls, be postponed so you can grieve the loss of my firstborn?"

"Um, sir, I ... well, it's just that ..." Ponytail fell silent.

"That's what I thought," my father said. Then, energy spent, he seemed to shrink.

The chairman had watched the exchange with amusement. He was well known to harbor a hatred for the charity workers, humiliated daily as he must have been by their wealth against his poverty, their means against his incapacity, their preachy arrogance. But this was a situation I knew well would put his job in jeopardy, and for that, he was no ally of mine. He staggered toward my father, his full paunch extending over a sallow visage and bloodshot eyes, his breath coming in ragged bursts, evidently rancid, because my old man drew his head back as though struck. "Give back the fucking money, old man," the fat man said, puffing.

"I've told you," my father, the man I now recognized, defeated and old, responded. "I don't know what you're talking about."

"Then where is your son?" The soldier brushed aside ponytail Tom and the chairman to stand in front of my father menacingly.

"You think I'd give him over to you? So you can torture him? I'd rather die."

"Listen to me carefully." The soldier reached my father, and before anybody could react, he drew his hand up to bring it down across my father's cheek. "Either we take him or we take you."

"Then you will have to take ..." my father was in the middle of saying. But I had heard enough. I filled out my chest and squared my shoulders and stepped out from behind the tukul.

"You, all of you, stand down. Walk away. Leave us in peace," I said.

The five turned to look at me, mouths falling open slightly, obviously unsure of what to do.

"Go! Stop bothering us!" I declared forcefully.

"Ah, there you are," the chairman said, recovering through the stupor and attempting to sound jovial, nonchalant. "We were just looking for you."

"Save it. I heard everything," I spat.

"Just give us the money, dude," said ponytail Tom. "Nobody wants to hurt you. We just, you know, need that money. To pay for things."

I turned to him to size up my foe. His eyes were red with drugs or perhaps a hangover. His breath smelled too, and his pants barely hung on his emaciated frame. Drugs again. Now that I saw him up close, I recognized him. This one, he had a bad reputation with the girls; my girls would never go near him. It was said he liked them young, and he liked it rough. Nothing was hidden from me in my camps.

"You bastard." I realized quickly that I needed to control myself, but try as I might, I could not. The words were coming now, and there was no force in the world that would stop them. "How do you know it was me? Just because you don't like me?"

"We know your kind," the chairman interjected. "If it wasn't you, you'll sure tell us who it was in short order."

"We just want the money back," ponytail said again.

"Back? Your money? It's our money—though you come here playing God. Preachers during the day and players at night when you think nobody is looking." I was screaming now. "But those little girls you fuck? They are my sisters and my girlfriends and my cousins, for you to pay them with 'cash for work' or a place at the front of the bread line."

In the fullness of time, I will admit that I was carried away. Perhaps I was tired. Perhaps I was exhausted by camp life and injustice. Certainly, I was angry at those who thought that a long trip across the big water made them my betters. But the truth is, looking back upon a lifetime of impetuous decisions and bad ideas, I know now that I have a devil inside, a devil who it is best to leave still and unmolested. Whatever it was, what came next was the end and the beginning.

"C'mon," Tom stuttered.

"Just tell us," the chairman said.

"We know that you are involved, or at least that you know," the soldier said menacingly.

"Last night," I said, speaking slowly.

"No," my father, who must have thought he knew where this was going, interjected, shaking his head vigorously.

"Last night, I was drinking with friends out toward the pond," I lied. "I was nowhere near your offices, even if I knew where they were. Which I don't."

"Bullshit," Tom said. "I've seen you watching us from that big tree."

"I have no idea what you're talking about," I said. "And I have no idea where your money is," I said with finality, hearing my father's audible exhalations. "Now I have things to do" I said as I turned to walk resolutely away from the tukul. Each step I took, I expected to be grabbed by the rough hand of a soldier. To this day, I don't know why they didn't. Perhaps it was because I had showed my face, which gave them some doubt. Maybe it was the sniveling of Tom that had caused them to shrink away in disgust from the entire situation. It would not be the first time that a white man accused an African of a fake crime to cover up their own indiscretions. Whatever it was, I walked away, in the opposite direction of Henry's small shop.

As I turned the corner, I saw my father for what I didn't realize was the last time. We had never been close. It's sometimes difficult, the relationship between father and son in the hard lives of the camp dwellers of Africa. People say we don't sorrow, that our women don't feel for their babies like the white women do, that the men don't take pride in their sons. That our capacity for emotion is somehow less, diminished. Let me assure you, now that I am old with children and grandchildren of my own, that this is not the case. We feel more, not less, because of the sorrow. Loving our sons till we lose them, to disease, to violence, to war. It breaks us. The white people can pretend that they can feel more deeply, because they can afford to fall into the desperate pit of despair in the odd event something happens to their babies. Not so for the Africans of the camps. Loss is our daily bread, and we must cope, because while we lose one or two or three, there are still a dozen more mouths to feed, and morning, noon, and night come relentlessly to the willing and unwilling alike.

I spent the day in hiding, avoiding people. My plan, if I had a plan at all, was to get to Henry. By now, he would have collected the booty, and there was still a gnawing in my heart that he was not a completely honest broker. But I knew that I was still under suspicion, that they were still looking. Such a large heist would not fade away into camp history; impunity is too great an incentive. They had to set things right; even in Africa, order must be preserved, and there is nothing more unstable than an African camp. A tinderbox, set alight by the most insignificant of sparks. And for all my faults, mine has never been an insignificant spark.

As night deepened, entering that darkest of periods when the dawn is a suggestion, and I knew that the chairman would be drunk and asleep and the soldiers would be close to their barracks in their eternal fear of the frequent nighttime rebel attacks, I walked in the direction of Henry's small shack. The music was blaring, the pounding beat of the bass drowning out any other sound. The zinc roof was vibrating and the walls humming as I crept around the corner to come upon my worst nightmare. There, seated at one of the green plastic tables drinking cold beer was Henry, and seated across from him were ponytail Tom and one of the girls, one of my girls. I could not hear over the music and the fact that they were hunched close together in deliberations. After watching for a long time, I saw Tom stick out his hand, which was received and vigorously pumped by Henry, all the while the girl caressed the chicken arms of the ponytail. To this day, I don't know what they were talking about, but it could only be one thing. I had never seen them together before. Not knowing what to do, I flirted with my limited options. I could have attacked the conclave, hurling rocks or bottles. I could wait till Henry closed up for the night and kill him in his sleep. But I was young then, though strong—and the wickedness that would become my cup was not yet full.

Without knowing what else to do, I did what I always do—though that was the first time. I fled, turning to march resolutely away from the cement kiosk and toward the forest. It was already late, and I walked slowly, approaching the edge of the jungle as the dawn started to rise above the makeshift village, a sight I had seen thousands of times. The place where I had grown up, now a part of my past. There had been no goodbyes for my mother or brothers or my father. Yet somehow, for some reason I don't understand, leaving was not hard I felt a sensation of which I knew I should be ashamed—relief. I was no longer a problem to anybody except myself. My father, well sons he had, who were just now waking to stagger bleary-eyed into the morning light. They were better students, better boys. Gentler of spirit, less likely to wind up in jail or at the bottom of a well. I knew that my father was not surprised by what had happened, by what I'd become. That I would get him into trouble had been his anticipation for many years, and he had handled that like any man should. With dignity and patience. I had never given him joy. I knew that.

As I left, my relief turned into a new sensation, and I was for the first time in my life immensely happy.

I walked to the edge of the makeshift town, looking behind at Odek. The place that had been my home. The barren land where I had learned to crawl, learned to walk, to run and dance. The school where I had studied for a while. The subcounty offices where I had learned to steal, taking whatever I could from the accidental bureaucrats. The well where we got our water. The lines—the lines for food and for medicine and for water and for everything. The lines at the bar where I drank, where even now in the distance I saw Henry standing to turn off his tiny generator. Henry, who was to be the source of my salvation, who had become instead my destruction. I looked at the tukuls, one after another after another in endless clumps that stretched over the horizon. The place where I had lost my carefree youth to the realities of who I'd been at birth and what that would mean for me forever. And it hit me. Not nostalgia but gratitude. I was finally free. Leaving takes courage, even such a place as this. But my choice had been made. My future, such as it was, was now upon me. And it would be my own.

As I gazed for a last moment at the camp of my youth, a young girl, maybe not more than five years old, stepped from her tukul. Seeing the long line at the latrine, she squatted down by the fire pit where her mother would cook every meal until they all perished, and began to defecate on the hard-packed dirt. I leaned back, facing upward to the clouds, and laughed deeply, the sound of my cackles ricocheting against the trees and back into the camp, and for a moment, faces turned to look in the direction of that sound, and then I plunged into the underbrush.

Hunger.

That was my first sensation as, well, as a boy no longer bound to the camps. That fated morning, I'd left the camps and started moving through the brush toward the forest, heading always south toward the great river I'd only ever heard of. The underbrush was thick, which slowed my pace but also afforded me secrecy and privacy. Branches scratched at my arms, and occasionally I would step into a slimy puddle that sucked my foot in up to my knee, the sludge seeping through my toes. I lost my yellow flip-flops in the first minutes, and then the way became slower as I occasionally stepped on an ant's nest or a hidden branch, cutting open my feet as I pressed onward, dripping blood. The smells around me were of the deep decay of the forest below the sounds of birds crying forlornly, making common cause with my solitary trek.

I went along, and soon it started to rain, and my spirit was heartened by the goodness that washed in rivulets down my face as I crossed through a clearing or that dripped from the green leaves onto my head. I walked lightly, despite not knowing where I was going or how I would survive. I ate nothing and drank only the rainwater. At night, I found a semidry place in a tree that had fallen over and cracked open. That first night, alone, hungry, cold—no fire, no food, and no future—I finally began to contemplate my situation. Kampala, the big city. Of course, that's where I was going. The only place I had ever heard of, where I knew that I would be able to find something for myself, to start fresh in anonymity. I was young then and strong, and I was convinced I could make it work. That night, so long ago, I closed my eyes—the spirit of hope pulsating through my veins. It was the last time I ever felt that sensation.

CHAPTER 5

Kampala.

The first time I arrived in the big city, I must admit I was dumbfounded. Me—Charles, "King of the Camps"—here in this glorious cement and glass world. Oh, you who are probably reading this in New York or Paris think of Kampala only for its mediocre buildings and bad roads, its dirty and worn-down colonial architecture and the slums that extend beyond the seven hills. But for me, from the camps, this was the greatest city in the world. I had finally arrived, although an inauspicious arrival it had been. The flight from Acholi had taken its toll, and I was tired. Down rivers, across bridges, over roads and hills, and beside villages I had walked, stealing what food I could not earn through day labor or begging. Yet standing there on the edge of the city, looking at the buildings that soared so much higher than trees ever did, looking at glass panels that blinded me, vendors hustling about, cars and busses honking, people screaming. Exhaust fumes filling the air. I must admit I was unprepared. I had learned to live in the villages, even after I left the camp, but how would I make my way here when I didn't even understand the advertisements on the huge billboards lit up with bright lights? When I could not even recognize the use of what appeared to be everyday implements of a life outside my comprehension? How would I own this city? My adolescent thoughts of grandeur evaporated like the mists before a hot Acholi day.

Awash with new, exciting but also frightening sensations, I nevertheless stepped into the melee.

36

The concrete and pavement felt rough through soles that had become thick as shoe leather from my barefoot life. My shirt was too tight, and the two buttons that were left did not cover my stomach, which was thin from lack of food and hard from the exertion. I felt worse than naked. There's a certain degree of honor in nakedness if your body is strong and your shape is lean, if you are young. Didn't the Greek Olympians even compete naked? What I felt was not the shame of nakedness but so much worse—the brazenness of my own squalor. My pants were dirty and worn through, the zipper no longer functioning, and too short, ending midcalf. My hair had grown long and was dirty, still with pieces of sticks poking out of it from the forests and the savannas. I stank. I could taste my breath and smell my own odors. Humiliated from the sideways glances by people dressed in suits with polished shoes, smelling sweet, of deodorant and shampoo. Of laundry detergent. I had been accustomed to a certain amount of stench from camp life, but here in the city where all smelled sweet and clean, I realized the depth of my own poverty.

Yet through all this, I put my head down and began to work. Moving dirt around in the construction pits. Carrying garbage from one part of town to the other. Washing the windows of cars stopped at traffic lights. Selling the occasional items that I was able to steal from the unvigilant. I learned to not care when women in skirts crossed to the other side of the street to avoid me, looking down at their feet or across at a sign in a window to pretend that it was not me that they had to see—had to deal with. An unwanted intrusion in their world. I learned to not care when a miser rolled down the window of his shiny car to scream at me for washing the window and I had to restrain myself to not break his taillights as he sped away, a handful of coins thrown at my face, a worse insult than nothing.

"Fuck off, urchin!" they would scream. "Do you know that you stink?"

How could I not?

"Go back where you came from, beggar!" I was an offense to them, dirt that befouled their fair city. A reminder that this, after all, was still Africa.

For sleeping, I explored the darkened corners of the city. I refused to sleep piled up with the other migrants one on top of the other in the slums, packed into a single room. Neither would I take the charity of the missionaries and their poorhouses, which I had tried only once. "Before we eat," they would say, all of us staring hungrily at the mounds of bread or the big pot of soup or the fried pieces of chicken, mouths watering and stomachs growing, "we will hear a few words from Brother Phil on the saving power of Jesus."

"Yes, I'm sure your white God loves black people too, but I'm fucking hungry," I had let slip once, immediately sorry because I was still hungry and my little outburst didn't get me any closer to the plate piled high with food. Instead, I had to endure a prayer session over my immortal soul.

"These are the bunks." After supper calmed the rumblings in my stomach and improved my mood, if only ever so slightly, we were taken to the dorm, and I looked in horror around the foul-smelling room with an assortment of unwashed young and old—the city's lost souls. Despite my best efforts at restraint, I turned and stormed out to spend the night under a bench at the Independence Park. I had slept in mounds of flesh piled high my whole life, and I would be damned if I was going to exchange camp life for the life of a three-story bunk amidst the snoring of the riffraff.

Oh, sure, I knew I was no better, but that didn't matter. I would just as soon die than return to that condition. As I hunted, I stumbled upon the old train station at the center of town, and in my search of the perimeter, I found a place where the fence had been pulled back. During the time of the colonies, this had been the center of trade. The building had been enormous and majestic, huge arches elevating an enormous clock that ticked away the day, proving the British sense of timing as the shiny locomotives came and went from Mombasa. Inside, the floor had been fitted with shiny marble slabs leading the passengers to the tea house at one side where the elites could await their transport in luxury. The benches had been polished mahogany brought in from the forests, and the inside of the domed roof had been painted in a mural of the white God overseeing a railway line construction that powered across Africa. The platform where the steam trains had arrived was broad and had also been polished in shiny brick, with iron benches set evenly between. It was all now broken down and worn by time and the lack of use and maintenance. Off to one side, abandoned and unused, was an old freight car that was rusting alongside a piece of track that had turned orange. There had been rats and a stray dog inside, but it was shelter from the rain, and the door still slid open and closed, so I spent the next night expelling all the rodents into the darkness and sweeping out the inside using a handful of tall grass that was growing in the yard, bound into a makeshift broom using banana fibers. When it was as clean as I could get it, I began foraging for anything soft I could use as a bed. Hay, grass, clothes donated by any charity I could find, until it became comfortable, a place of my own. My first home. The dog had refused to leave and would just growl at me when I tried to push her out the entrance. In point of fact, she probably didn't have anywhere to go either, and try as I might, I could not bring myself to do her harm, so forlorn she looked, the sagging tits a display of a recent litter. With none of the pups around, I assumed the worst. I lay down, and to my surprise, after a short time I felt her warmth beside me, and we slept. During the day, she would guard our home, and I would return at night bringing her whatever I could find to eat that day. She became my friend as I slowly and carefully rescued her from the brink, cleaning her with water I collected and stealing soap to wash down her fur and drown out the fleas.

"Tomorrow," I would say as I returned from a day on the streets to her wagging tail and happy yapping, "I'll bring you a piece of bacon." This as I tossed her some mystery meat from the soup I'd eaten for lunch along with half the bread I'd received. Sometimes I was lucky to come up with food that looked and smelled clean as I rifled through the garbage behind the Chinese food restaurant; or was handed day-old bread from a friend I had made, who was also Acholi and worked in one of the supermarkets; or stumbled upon a party people were having in a park and inserted myself, filling a plate before I was chased away. On one occasion, I'd been walking beside a small grocery store when I'd fortuitously noticed a cart parked outside, unattended. Inside were bags of groceries: eggs, milk, a block of cheese, and meat neatly cut and wrapped in cellophane. I waited for a moment, looking around for the owner, and noticed a red sedan pulling slowly out of a parking garage.

Quickly, I snatched the bags and ran, my bare feet pounding on the pavement as I headed straight for my makeshift home. The yelling behind me slowly faded into the cacophony of city noise as I careened through the alleyways that I had come to know well.

"Like I promised," I told my dog, bursting through the door a conquering hero. With a flourish, I laid out before her a feast served upon the Styrofoam containers. By this time, she was relatively clean and extremely happy, and her joy at my company was mutual. "Here you go." I gave her an egg, then two, then three. Then half the carton of milk. By the time we were finished, both of us could barely move. I had never been so full in my life, a sensation that was uncomfortable in a new and satisfying way. We lay there together, me talking to her and her licking a paw or scratching at a dry patch while the rain fell outside, a moment of contentedness in a lifetime of hardship.

It was this simple solitude that represented for me the greatest of sensations. I, a child of the camps used to the press of human flesh, had finally found a place of aloneness. Not to be confused with loneliness; that emotion I would not feel again for a long time. I had come to realize that the only time I was truly lonely was when I was crammed in unwilling intercourse with idiots. Here, in my container, I had found true solitude. I loved the days when it would rain the whole day long, giving me an excuse to stay in my container, not venturing out to work or to look for food. In the camps, we always had to go out, even in the rain. The charities never varied from their distribution schedules; never did they consider the ease of their beneficiaries. And the wetness always stirred up muck and shit that was lying around and caused a terrible stench for those of us standing, waiting. Inside the tukuls, we would all huddle together to avoid the leaking parts of the ceiling, trying to keep each other entertained while the babies cried and the children complained. Not here! My container home was just for me. I had long since thoroughly cleaned it. The bed was a mattress I had stolen, soft and covered in a sheet I had lifted from a clothesline, and I even had a blanket. There were a few books; I always liked reading, and the variety of books in the big city was amazing, while people were always throwing them away. I was meticulous in keeping a small stash of food stored for these days, canned meats and vegetables and pastas that I could open and share with Dog. So I would lie there hoping that the downpour would abide while I listened to the pounding of the droplets on the metal above, breathing the moist coolness and reading books out loud to my friend. Alone, defying even the memory of others. It was a great luxury.

And for a season, I was calm.

My days were each the same, varying only in the type of work or the quality of food I was able to find and bring to my square, metal home. I would wake early, washing outside with water I had collected from the old faucet that stood in solitary defiance of the entropy that had engulfed the station, positioned in a lost corner of the railyard and that, amazingly, still worked. I would put on clothes. My collection was growing in quantity if not quality, and I was often able to choose something clean that smelled fresh. I would douse my hair in the water, sucking in my breath in the cool mornings as the water shocked me awake while I scrubbed with soap. A quick breakfast, some bread or a piece of cheese; water in the bowl for Dog; lacing up my shoes—and I was off, sneaking back out through the bent chain-link fence. I would sometimes make my way to the Catholic charity house beside the old cathedral, where they served food to the poor and the destitute. Bread, hard as slices of shale, beside thin, watery soup of vegetables, with the occasional piece of rubbery meat inside, which I kept for Dog. Sometimes rice. A bin of clothing—and I would take a few more pieces than I needed for my nest. Then I would move on. Mostly I would walk to the warehouse district to wait with the crowds of men for the odd jobs of manual labor that came up. Unloading bags of rice from off a truck. Sweeping out an empty warehouse. Hauling tires or car parts from old wrecks from one place to another. On the rare, lucky occasion, construction projects that lasted a season, not only a day—pouring cement and laying brick.

"Today, I only need five," said a driver of a truck full of tiles that had arrived from Kenya. "You five over there." I was not in the group, and after milling about for a few more hours, I walked back to my container, defeated but only for a day.

"Here." On another occasion, somebody approached from behind, handing me a broom. "We must sweep the highway between the airport down in Entebbe and the city. The president is hosting a summit." There were many summits; I'd noticed over the time in Kampala that there were always comings and goings of expensive black cars flashing blue and red lights, going to and from the airport, followed by soldiers and police cars and motorcycles as they sped through lights and over curbs, ignoring laws and bystanders. Crowds would gather, gawking and chattering to each other excitedly. Spice for their tasteless lives. I saw once a famous face—a great man who I'd seen on the front page of the newspapers I'd sold for a time beside a café. Some of the papers called him a despot, a distinction without a difference in my limited experience with authority. My heart skipped a beat, and I was irrationally excited for a second before remembering that catching a glimpse through armored glass would not put food on my table or help Dog, who was struggling with a pain in her leg that I could not identify. I could only comfort her as she whined in the night. My lot would not be changed by the travels of men with loud names. They never came to the camps anyway, the men who traveled in convoys, offended as they must be by the dirt and the smells. Never mind. A great man I would never be, although sometimes in the dark silence of night, I still harbored illusions that somehow something would change for me. I was young, and though my pants were not always clean and did not match my shirt, neither would I bow to those who seemed to wield power so naturally. "Get to work." A command breaking through my reverie because my broom had stopped going back and forth across the cement. "I'm not paying you to daydream." I spent the week with a hundred others sweeping garbage off the streets and shining up light posts to hang images of the latest in the endless parade of despots come to serve themselves of Uganda.

And so it went for several years. I left my adolescence behind and donned the figure of a young adult, my body sculpted not through carefully planned exercise but by the hard work of African poverty. Cleaning, sweeping. Picking tea or maize or chopping sugarcane. Unloading crates of beer or slaughtering cows and goats. Painting buildings, washing the windows on the buildings that seemed to reach right into heaven. A few hundred shillings a day, the going rate. At night, lying in my container in silence; when it rained or on public holidays, curled up with Dog, reading aloud from books that I swiped from vendors or took from the Catholics at no charge. Sickness, shivering in the quiet, afflicted by some disease. Malaria, dysentery, typhoid—coughing or bleeding sometimes from an orifice in fear that this time there would be no recovery. No care, of course. There were no doctors in the cold city who would give of their precious time to touch, much less treat, the ratty sojourners from the northern camps.

"Today I need some help," said a greasy Indian with a mouth full of tiny white sores that made me recoil when he approached me, emerging as he had from behind one of the big iron doors of the warehouse and walking purposefully toward the gaggle of workers milling about. "You, you. And you," he lisped, pointing to me last, and I walked hesitantly over to the side where he had gone to a pickup truck full of wares. As I got closer, I noticed that he smelled of curry and too much cologne. "We are going to Jinja." Without a further word, we jumped into the bed of the pickup, an old Toyota with muddy wheels and scratched olive-green paint around an interior of worn-out seats and a gaping hole where the radio should have been. We sat where we could, on the wheel bumps or on one of the boxes. Barely settled, the truck careened onto the street with the three of us gripping tightly, bouncing down the road that leads out of Kampala to the east.

I had never seen much of the southern countryside east of the city and was quieted by the rolling tea plantations, workers hunched under immense bags of shiny, bright green leaves as they picked them one by one in a fluid motion, depositing them over their backs into the rucksack. Small villages beside the highway, naked babies staring vacuously at the moving traffic. Banco mud houses under construction. First, sticks taken from the forest, tied together with the sinewy parts of banana leaves in a roughly square shape. Followed by mud, mixed with excrement from cows and straw, pushed between and then over the sticks until they were fully covered, a makeshift vertebra, and then smoothed over using a trowel and some water and dried in the central African sun until it was a shiny brown that looked almost slick. Following this—for the poor—the houses were covered with thatch, elephant grass harvested at just the right time of year and replaced yearly at the same time. For the richer, metal zinc roofs that did not provide sanctuary to rats and snakes. All around, through, and over the villages were the smells of burning word, smells that permeate clothes and embed themselves in our nostrils until we cannot even sense them anymore. We drove through trading towns with huge open markets full of squawking chickens and bleating goats beside piles of tomatoes and cucumber and the occasional shack selling cheap electronics, a radio, some movies. Little skillets of boiling oil with mamas selling deep-fried dough to passersby as they shopped. The buildings of these towns were made of square, cement blocks or the dark orange bricks fired in the makeshift kilns that dotted the landscape between Kampala and Jinja; bricks piled two stories high, covered with mud to hold in the heat, holes at the bottom filled with offerings of burning wood looking ever like religious shrines on a pilgrimage to nowhere. In some places, a church was in session, one of those that never seems to recess; there is very little to do for poor Africans, and worshipping Jesus is free and occasionally even leads to opportunity, but I'll get to that later. The sound of hymns floated out over the road, of which I caught bits and choruses while I sat in the back of the truck.

Then suddenly we plunged into the dark, almost forbidding shadows of Mabira forest. The trees reached four stories high on both sides, dark emerald greens that leaned over the highway blocking the sun. In the high branches, red-tailed moneys chased each other through the treetops in their eternal games or on their constant search for lizards and the big tree cicadas we could hear screeching above us. I had just settled in, finding a place to lay my head on a piece of sheeting that cushioned the bouncing to stare above at the virgin forest—imagining I was somebody else and this journey was one that would lead me somewhere, anywhere, as long as it was a place of opportunity—when we suddenly braked and turned sharply right, the old Toyota shifting into low gear to navigate the muddy, single-lane path into the forest. It became immediately quiet as the greenery muted the sounds of the outside world; only the truck engine, an unwanted intruder into the solitude. Butterflies flitted over us. Birds, blues and greens like I had never seen before, watched warily from the trees above. It must have been an hour when at last we turned into an open spot under the clearing with a few Land Cruisers parked beside the back entrance to a facility.

"Grab those boxes," the Indian said, exiting the truck to march empty-handed toward the brown wood double doors, "and follow me." We each seized two, stacking one on top of the other as we hurried to follow the fat man into what we soon learned was a hotel, a lodge of sorts. We entered the back door into the lobby.

I had found myself in a resort—luxurious and opulent in a complex mix of simplicity and excess. Not like through the screen of a movie, white women dressed in sequins sipping Champagne. Nothing like the commercials for hotels or vacations beamed into a poor Acholi camp lost in the vast northern expanses of central Africa. But here, all around us, was a resort for the world's wealthy who came all the way to Uganda to frolic in a place I would never know—would never be invited. The entire building was built of lustering wood, polished until I could see my face reflected everywhere I looked. On the far side, through a set of crafted double doors with stained glass windows was a vast veranda that sat in easy observation three stories above a clearing beside the deepening jungle beyond. In the clearing had been dug a man-made pond with enormous orange and white goldfish meant to attract the jungle animals, who were frolicking in the shallow waters. A tiny jungle elephant with her tinier calf was standing beside the trees, sucking water into her trunk to wash off the baby who was caked in mud, dirty as all babies become. There were several red-tail and one black-and-white colobus monkeys sitting one in front of the other, their tiny fingers searching the fur of their companion to find fleas or lice and eat them quickly. A pair of crested cranes stood upon one leg, staring into the clarity looking for guppies, minnows, or baby trout. Above in the trees around, all manner of life unmolested. We would eat all of it—we from the camps—if given the opportunity. But here it was the luxury of protected life for the rich to enjoy at their leisure. Atop the veranda were chairs where white people were sitting, watching the pageant of Africa play out while they enjoyed a campfire that crackled in the dense jungle air, black people in black suits with bowties and tails bringing them colorful drinks one after the other from the bar that was on the far side of the interior of the building. That too was something unheard of, never seen before—especially in Acholi. Individually carved stools tucked neatly under a gleaming flat surface of the wooden bar made

45

of a single tree, in front of a towering display of jewels. Reds, greens, blues, oranges, all in distinctive bottles that refracted the lights from the chandelier onto the wall beyond. The bartender looked just as polished as the surface in front of which he stood, elegant, without talking, smooth and perfect.

On another side was the reception, beautiful girls the likes I had never seen, rounded out in the right places, their breasts, hips, and thighs. I had seen many, many breasts in my life. Hanging listlessly above a newborn, tired and old and worn. Being washed down in the communal shower facilities. Nakedness is not uncommon for the poor of Africa. But here they were carefully packaged beneath tight, matching dresses below the perfect smiles and flawless complexions of these girls. Secrets hidden away from view—teasing, forbidden, unattainable. Beauty as a ticket to luxury, with no utilitarian function whatsoever but only for the attainment of the ultimate extravagance. My gaze pulled reluctantly away as I continued to examine the lobby. The floors were carpeted with a lush rug, thick and red, that led from the main lobby doors and down to the restaurant waiting expectantly through the next set of double doors—it too overlooking the jungle life below—for its nocturnal work to begin, emitting smells that made my mouth water. Sweet and spicy and delicate, so unlike the boiled egg and warm milk I had enjoyed only last night, which I had considered a feast. From the roof hung a chandelier, cut crystal that threw multicolored pieces of light around carelessly, frivolously. And the people, white people, yellow people, brown people all walking back and forth dressed in new clothes, neatly painted, hair carefully prepared while they looked at expensive watches or took pictures on elaborate cameras.

"You, stop staring." I was jolted back to reality. "Go put that box in the kitchen. We don't have all day." And the cocoon of opulence was burst by the fat Indian man with the pimply mouth—it was over.

I hazard to mention this brief anecdote, so many years afterward—something that you certainly would have forgotten but that has remained indelibly imprinted on my consciousness—in an endeavor to help you to understand the way of the world for us, the Africans from the camps. So I ask you this: Do you remember the precise moment when you first comprehended the resolve of your restraints? When you looked down at your hands and feet and realized that you were shackled in place and that you would never, ever move? If you are anything like Ugandans born into money, I'm guessing the answer is you don't. You see the natural limitations of humankind—intelligence, beauty, quickness of wit—as grand conspiracies by which you are somehow denied your birthright of superiority over others. You complain, you assault, you rage, you cry, you wage war through your lawyers and your judges, all to prove that it is not simply a result of your station, the limitations of who you are nestled in an unlimited world that are your downfall.

You do not understand, cannot fathom the weight of true powerlessness. It is for this reason that you who are reading this will not appreciate my first reaction to the opulence. You have lived it all your lives. It is second nature to you now, even if you do not consider yourselves wealthy. You are accustomed to options, opportunities, places. Air-conditioning, varied and delicious meals. Night enlivened with bright, colorful drinks in company, without the bugs crawling over you. Vacations you don't even remember; boats and planes and pools that blend one into the other in an endless pageant of extravagance. But for the poor of Africa—for a child of the African camps—admitting that a place such as I had entered could even exist within the confines of the national geography that I called home was difficult. It wasn't that it was worlds away from my understanding. Nor was it a representation of the inequality that is wrong with the world, which you who read this complain about all the time as you sit in your large homes, drinking imported coffee and typing indignantly into your new computers. Or even that it was a visual demonstration of the power of the white man to colonize, control us even in our own lands. Like the rich black people say, who are as much a part of the system that they decry as are the shoes and shirts that they buy in expensive chain stores in Europe, to have us polish away the dirt from the African streets. None of these are what we feel, because they are all facile assertions by people who are innately other, different from a black man from the camps. It isn't powerlessness, because that requires an awareness of the power in the first place. It isn't inferiority, for that that emotion requires a recognition of the fundamental equality of people. It isn't anger, because anger grows from comprehension and then impotence. It isn't even hopelessness, as hopelessness needs the belief in hope itself to give that emotion power. This experience—for me—was like a movie I had seen in the camps about an astronaut walking on a red planet and encountering life; one is not jealous of the Martians who have specialized instruments that would make life so much easier. It is accepted that they should, that they must. How they got them, how they sustained their superiority? Conjecture. Doesn't even cross our minds.

That is the way we feel, we the children of the camps.

The trip to Jinja that followed saw me returning to the world that I recognized. We are all most comfortable with what we know, aren't we? Or are we? Even if what we know is shit? After dropping off the boxes, we rode along the bumpy highway for several more hours, finally cresting over the last hill to look down at the source of the White Nile. On my right sat a great brewery that took advantage of the waters of the lake, the river, and the road to transport their golden treasure through the country and beyond. The whole countryside smelled sour and hoppy with the fermenting wort. Big trucks loaded and unloaded bottles into the immense building, green with a gigantic elephant painted at the top, an elephant I had often contemplated as I sat with Henry talking late into the night about the future and what we would make of it. We drove slowly the remaining length to the bridge that crossed the Nile, over a power plant that supplied electricity to the entire south. Nobody cared that it never made it north beyond the river. The Acholi had never been considered in the national planning process.

We had arrived in Jinja. We passed the memorial for the King's African Rifles—that famed unit in the British military, the black terror of the Nazis—killed in the Second World War when Uganda mattered in the great issues of our world. Still well-kept, manicured grass beside polished stones emblazoned with the names of men who fought a great evil across the ocean, not lesser evils beside a squalid camp when nobody was looking. It was hard for me to imagine Ugandan soldiers being glorious; the only ones I had ever known were skinny and angry, vindictive and often brutal. They used our women and sold our food and medicine and ordered us around as lords in a land that was not theirs. Their occasional violence was accentuated by the reputation of what went on in the square brick building with no windows that sat at the center of their camp, from where the screams often emanated in the dark of the African night. I've often wondered what it is about the heart of soldiers that makes them capable of such good when called to sacrifice for a cause, but whose penchant for blindly following authority, and seeking it out themselves, so often appeals to the sadistic, especially when nobody is looking. I have not forgotten that even Amin—yes, Idi Amin, the dictator whose presence is still a spirit that haunts the hills where the blood flowed and the caves wherein his tortures were enacted—was also a King's African Rifle. Even he had fought against the Nazis. Even he had the mantle of a just fight draped over him, if only for a time till it all went terribly, terribly wrong. Epic fights and grand coalitions of men fighting the darkness were only the ghosts of memory, juxtaposed as they were against our soldiers standing guard over our food, telling us how to vote. Locking our leaders away and disappearing our sons, the sons of Africa too. It's harder, I suppose, because we Acholi have always been fiercer. Didn't the most recent dictator—cursed be his name, one that I will not even mention—didn't he even ban our war dances? So afraid he must be that even the thought of we Acholi, strong as oxen, tall as grown cornstalks, thick as the trunks of trees, and black like the starless night, makes him tremble in his palace on the shores of the great lake. Didn't he betray our great leader, Tito Okello, and send him to his death? The treachery of the sniveling little man with his child soldiers who now calls himself our leader has never known any limits.

Dishonor.

We didn't expect it because we are people of honor who understand the truth of our words and say what we believe, what we mean, what we will do. He betrayed us because we are not people of betrayal and are not ready for men for whom honor comes second, third, even fourth. Haven't all the great men who ruled this country been from the north? And isn't that because the northerners know that the nexus of strength and honor is where Africans are at their best? Not in putting little pieces of paper into boxes every few years, permission slips to continue to rob us, to brutalize us at the hands of these, their soldiers, and at the behest of the old man by the lake.

Then we were past the graveyard and heading up the road beside the Nile. We hugged the river until it curved right, and we stopped. We were picking up fish, I learned, from the fishermen who were harvesting the waters before the rapids—Nile perch mostly, some tilapia and the occasional catfish. The spray from the crushing water drenched us all to the bone, refreshing after the hours under the sun. The healthy fishy smell of our cargo reminded us of life—life that in Africa is so much more closely connected with the waters and the lands. The water dripped through my hair and down my face, into my mouth as I spit and sputtered, occasionally breathing some in as I heaved the heavy boxes of fish from the rock-strewn shores of the river up to the waiting truck. And then back again, passing by the place where the placid bust of Gandhi sat elegantly. Yes, I know who Gandhi is. You probably think we Africans are stupid, or at least ignorant if you are more kindly inclined. But I've had nothing to do except read for my whole life. It is my only escape. My only travel. My only freedom. I cannot fill my days with technology and diversion. Did you consider that? That perhaps I am better read than you are? Because I can't hurl quotes of famous authors at you across social media does not mean that I do not know them. Did you, who read this, know that Gandhi's ashes were brought to the source of the Nile and sprinkled into the raging river, emerging finally into the Mediterranean in Egypt? Did you know that the place is marked by a quiet bust with the words "Universal Apostle of Peace" written below it? Then you, who know nothing of Africa, should not call me stupid.

When the truck was full, we made the trip back to Kampala, retracing the road but faster now because the fish sold fresh fetched the greatest prices at the elegant hotels of that city. Up the hill and careening back beside the tea plantations and the villages and markets and forests until the haze started to appear above in the distance, marking that metropolis that had become my home. I was still reflecting upon what I'd seen—the luxury. More than everything else, the images of opulence would stay with me like the worm when you eat uncooked pork that burrows into your brain, erasing all else. The vision of the girls, the drinks, the luxury. The quiet. The rest.

For now I knew I had never rested.

CHAPTER 6

Back in Kampala, I was dropped off at the same place I'd been collected. Pocketing my handful of shillings, I walked back to my container with my head full of new ideas and my heart heavier than it had been. Knowledge is a terrible companion, especially when it feeds a bitterness that has already been growing like cancer.

"Hello." Dog greeted me at the entrance of our container home, wagging her tail. I'd purchased a half pound of cooked meat with my earnings, along with a loaf of bread, some cheese, and an apple. Finally, I'd pocketed two eggs when the vendor wasn't looking. Those were for Dog's coat, which had become full and resplendent, product of decent sleep, a steadier diet, and the love of companionship that we all need. I gave her some meat and cracked open the eggs for her, which she licked enthusiastically from a bowl that I had found discarded in a garbage pile in front of an expensive, walled compound. The rich lived behind fifteen-foot walls topped with razor wire and cameras, which made home invasions of the wealthy hard, not that I was much of a home invader, at least not yet, but their trash bins were always a source of treasure for the container dwellers of the city. I broke the bread into chunks, eating it with the cheese, and finished off with the apple. All the while, I wrestled with the day's images, thoughts of beautiful women sipping crystal drinks beside a bonfire, the smoke floating overtop of the jungle. I imagined the people—I guess they were people, as I was, despite all evidence to the contrary—staring out at the monkeys, eating dainty pastries, or rising to enter the restaurant to pick at their elaborate dinners, laughing delicately at each other before a slumber both quiet and deep found them nestled in crisp, clean sheets over a firm bed. Their world but not mine. Two different planets, and I began to think.

You may be wondering why I homed in on this particular short anecdote in the months, years of scrapping and clawing for life from the unforgiving city. Though I had been in Kampala for years, though I was now an adult, albeit a young one, the camps never really leave us. Like I said, oftentimes we from the camps don't even realize another world is possible. But that day, a seed was sown in my heart, the seed of doubt and hope and rage that led me to make decisions I might not have before, which in turn maneuvered my path to what came next. A dark place, for sure you will say, but how can I see the greatness of what life has to offer and not make my play for it? To grab for something that is not my born right is wicked, you say. I didn't care—still don't, I suppose. Wickedness is a complicated word that belongs to those who have varied and good options to choose from, and which all might likely lead to prosperity. I had none.

Now, every day on my way to look for food and work, I would walk in front of an ice cream shop. I had never eaten ice cream before. There was none in the camps, even on the days that the charities threw elaborate parties to try to help us forget that we were their prisoners. We'd had cakes, clowns, balloons, piñatas. Music sometimes, big speakers beating out the most recent tunes, powered by a generator on the back of the truck where the speakers sat and belched black smoke above the melee. Food, rice and matoke and beans, and we would butcher and eat several goats and even one time a cow. Gifts, donations of used underwear, clothes, and toys from the West, that arrived by container trucks to be distributed to us grateful beneficiaries. Hard candy. Soldiers standing around the perimeter lest the rebels see it as a recruitment opportunity. But never ice cream; it's too delicate, cannot be transported, cannot be preserved in the unforgiving African sun. As I walked by the establishment, I would slow down to stand by the door to the store—it even had a beautiful name, *parlor*—and as it opened, the cool waft of air-conditioning scented with gentle smells of strawberry and vanilla and caramel would roll over me until the door closed again. Inside, everything was clean, pastel colors of pinks and yellows and light blues. Neither had I known food could come in colors like that, with cream and chocolate sprinkles on top. Gentle music played, and the girls behind the counter were dressed in special uniforms, white and red stripes with little white hats over their heads. I learned quickly that if I passed on Friday, right at the time when the local high school let out, I was always greeted by the caramel-colored smoothness of a girl like I had never seen before. Not black like we Acholi, charcoal and big as trees. More of a brown sugar. She was shoulder height. Her teeth were perfectly straight and somewhat rounded, the color of ivory. Her lips were just a little bit pursed, and she liked to wear shiny pink lip gloss that made them glisten like candy. Her eyes were round and golden, set inside alabaster white, and her cheeks were full and led into her neck, which was long and straight. Her breasts defied gravity as they stood at attention under T-shirt and school clothes alike, when all the others I'd seen swung like bags of beans. And there, under the sun, glistening through the tight, thin white shirt. Her body was a study in curves. Not the white people's women; why the wazungu prefer their girls to look like little boys, straight as an arrow and flat as a board, is beyond the understanding of us here in Africa. A girl should have curves. Her little feet poked out from under her jeans—with her toenails painted a light blue. I imagined touching her. Gazing into eyes that were the golden color of a lion in the bright African savanna. Saying things; having her say them back. I would gaze for as long as I could stand. She would never look up, never look out the window. Even when she did once, she didn't see me. I was part of her city, like a potted plant or a street bench or a beleaguered tree where the storks built their nests. I had never felt so poor—green flip-flops on my feet, teeth unbrushed, my hair matted and sometimes full of lice that drove me crazy in the quiet of the night when they crawled around and around unceasingly, shirt with only two or three buttons, and pants stained with fish blood from a hard day's work. I knew I was a pauper. I knew I was wretched. I knew that I was like so many others in this city that was such a hard place for those without a past and denied a future. I knew that I did not even exist.

That didn't stop me from looking, wondering, and imagining, hoping that something would happen for me that would free me from my life of insignificance.

Then, finally, after years of working and waiting and watching, something did indeed happen. One day I was standing on the street corner of the industrial part of town, looking like I needed to look for people to know that I wanted some work, when a car rolled up and stopped beside the curb in front of me. It was a shiny new Land Cruiser, jasper in color with the windows blackened. I had been milling about with a group of fifteen or twenty other young black men, all of them just like me. Talking and occasionally laughing, running up to the cars that slowed down as we jockeyed for the rare day jobs thrown our way. Smoking a cigarette as we waited under the shade of a wall. So I was surprised when, as quickly as they saw the car slow to a stop, the other men took several steps back, some even frowning and appearing to snap and snarl like dogs sensing danger. I stood still, intrigued. The window lowered, and a woman looked out at me, standing—as I was—alone. She was wearing sunglasses, hair extensions, and what looked like diamond earrings. I could smell the perfume as it wafted from inside the shiny new vehicle. I'd never smelled anything like that. There was no perfume in the camps. I stepped toward the open window.

"You," she said, not needing to point.

"Yes, ma'am?" I answered.

"I need some help," she said.

"Yes, ma'am."

"Can you lift things?"

"Yes, ma'am."

"Are you from here?"

"No, ma'am," I said.

"Can you keep your mouth shut?" she asked, threateningly.

"Yes, ma'am," I answered, unfazed.

"Get in," she said, rolling up the window while the back door of the shiny SUV popped open. I climbed inside, ignoring the hissing behind me, and found myself sitting with two other men who I had seen before on the street corner on various occasions but not for a while. I didn't know their names. Nobody asked anything. Nobody spoke at all. The atmosphere inside the cabin of the vehicle was stifling, tense as we picked up speed and the tall buildings were left behind in favor of residential areas with elegant houses and manicured lawns that also were left behind for the slums of the day laborers, nannies and gardeners and cooks of the rich. I spent my time staring out the window as the city thinned out and gave way to the encroaching countryside. Thirty minutes, an hour, longer, and finally the vehicle slowed, turning left onto a dirt road that wrapped around a hill and field as it traversed several kilometers into the farmlands. Standing around upon their tiny parcels of land were farmers tending beans and corn, little boys herding goats, and little girls with the large yellow jerricans on their heads, ferrying water from the communal hand pump back to their homes. They all stood to stare at the new car— as out of place in their daily lives as a speedboat—before returning without even a shrug to the unchanging tasks that occupied their lives. We bounced over the road, approaching at last a cement block building with a rusted iron fence around it, adorned with multiple signs that read *Keep Out*. At the front, there was a gate that was closed, and the vehicle slowed to stand purring while the driver got out and pulled the gate open, returning to maneuver us expertly through the opening to come to a halt in the front yard. There was knee-high grass around the building, which had a tin roof over it. Cement cinderblocks lay strewn haphazardly around the front, and a medium-sized mango tree, heavy with fruit and providing shade, grew on the west end of the small compound.

"Get out," said the woman. We three disembarked.

"What now?" I asked, standing in the grass.

"You wait," she said, slamming the door closed. The vehicle drove away, wheels spinning up the dirt in a cloud behind.

I shrugged, grabbing a cinderblock to pull it under the tree, close enough to lean back against the trunk. Then I walked around the tree, identifying a mango that was ripe and not worm infested, which I pulled from the branch and teased open with my teeth, peeling away the skin as I sat in the shade and biting into it as the sweet juice ran down my hands. After waiting for a few minutes, standing there in the sun and staring blankly around, the other two men finally grabbed blocks as well and joined me in the shade.

"What are we doing here?" I asked through a mouthful of mango.

"Making some money, I suppose," one of the young men said,

reaching out his hand toward me. "Edward," he said. "This is Vincent." He pointed to his companion.

"Charles," I responded, looking at my sticky hands and then pushing out my elbow, which he grabbed onto and shook with a grin. As I repeated the overture to the larger man, he made a gruff sound that was like a growl and turned away.

I was left staring at both of them, elbow out and feeling foolish and not a little intimidated. While Edward was roughly my size, though somewhat older, with a goatee below a polished bald head and a scar on his cheek, Vincent was roughly a head taller than I was, and half again as wide. When he smiled, which he rarely did, his chipped teeth were evident, with some of them having been filed down to increase the menace. His eyes were dull and lifeless, and his chuckle was ominous. I immediately felt like an adolescent back in the camp.

"So you've never been here before?" I asked, attempting to fill the space.

"No, not here." Edward gestured around. The smallish building had no windows and was made only of square cement blocks. Weeds were pushing up around the yard. The lot was empty, fenced in, and crowned with concertina wire, beyond which were the bald hills of Uganda that marched toward Kenya anonymously. It was dry season, and the landscape was a study in tans, beiges, and browns. The smell of wood fires wafted over the little scene, coming from where I could not guess.

"How long have you been working for, well, whoever the hell that was?"

"Several months," Edward responded.

"And what do you do?"

"Not much, really. Pick things up, drop them off. Pick up packages at the Kenyan border. Take something to the border with Congo and hand it over."

"But you've been in that car before?" I asked, gesturing toward the plumes of dust that remained in the air long after the vehicle had disappeared.

"No. First time," Edward said, reaching into his pocket to pull out a package of cigarettes. "I usually find my own way. They give me an address, and I just show up. Want one?" he asked. I nodded, and he extended the packet out to me. I wiped my sticky hands on my pants and reached out to take it, and he lit it with an old purple lighter in his other hand.

I took a deep drag, letting the buzz go to my head and making me a little dizzy for a second. I exhaled and said, "I haven't seen you around for a while."

"Oh, I don't work for anybody else anymore."

"What?"

"Yeah, I'm exclusive," Edward said, grinning. It was only then that I noticed that his shirt was not missing any buttons, his jeans were clean and pressed, and he even wore a pair of sunglasses. "They call," he said, lifting a simple cell phone, "and I go. No more standing out in the sun for me."

"So," I said, "if that's true, why didn't anybody else back there jump at the chance of this? I suppose they know. They all sort of scampered away like scared mice."

"Yeah," said Edward. "Well, some of the stuff we do, well, isn't exactly—how to say this. Legal."

No shit. I hadn't stayed alive as long as I had by denying the reality of things. All this time, Vincent had not said a word, sitting for a time under the tree with us until he finally stood and walked over to inspect the back side of the building.

"I figured," I said nonchalantly.

"One time," Edward said, evidently convinced that I was a partner in crime, "I was given a package to take over to a big house down by the lake. We're not supposed to"—he leaned in, and I followed suit—"but one of the corners had come open, and so I sort of picked at until I could see. It was a solid brick of American dollars. One-hundred-dollar bills."

"Wow," I said.

"Yeah," he responded, winking. "Must have been tens of thousands."

"And you didn't consider taking it?"

He jerked back. "Are you fucking nuts? You know what these people are capable of?"

"Ha," I said, immediately sorry. "I'm kidding."

"You better be," Edward said, looking at me askance. "It's not a joke. If you want to make this job work, you learn one thing quick. Do what you're told and don't ask any questions."

We drifted into silence.

With nothing left to do, we just waited, and waited, and continued to wait as the sun made its journey past midday and headed toward the horizon. Finally, as the sun was descending toward the horizon, a worn-out pickup truck with no license plate drove down the beaten dirt path, its brakes squeaking as it maneuvered through the still-open gate and came to a stop in front of the three of us, Vincent having returned from his perimeter search, still silent. Out of the truck stepped a burly man with a beard. He was brown, not black but not mulatto either, and had a scar on his cheek. His arms were thick as tree trunks. "You, there." He pointed at me. "Come with me. You too." He pointed to Edward. "And you," he said, pointing to Vincent, "get up in the back of the pickup."

Together we went to the cement building, and the bearded man used a key he withdrew from his pocket on the shiny padlock that held the metal door in place. We entered the dark interior. It was square and without any windows or other openings or furniture; a concrete cinderblock box, dank and smelling of urine, and empty except for a big potato sack in the center. The sack was moving slightly and moaning as if in great pain. "You each grab a side," beard said.

"But …" I started to say but was cut off.

"Shut up. I don't want to hear it. I don't care. Grab the sack," he responded.

There was nothing for me to do. Oh, I suppose I could have just walked out of the building and kept walking. Looking back in hindsight, I realize of course that I should have, that everything would have been better had I done that. Nevertheless, I did not. Choices are extremely limited for those of us from the camps, and Edward's words still reverberated in my head. *"I'm exclusive. No more standing in the sun for me."* I wish I could tell you that my soul struggled with the decision, that I fought and raged, my good angels against my darker demons, that the moment represented for me that sort of crossroads people talk about as a before and an after and over which their souls journeyed to hell and back again. But, for me, I must say that I simply picked up my end of the sack, and together we hefted it to carry it back to the truck where Vincent silently guided it to the center of the pickup bed. Then beard mounted the truck, and we hopped onto the bed to make the trip back into Kampala. We sat there, the distance of the drive, while the bag moaned and moved, and occasionally when we hit a bigger bump or pothole, it would emit a squeal. "Don't ask and don't open the sack," the man had said before starting the car. Again, I had no intention of contravening those orders, although I knew deep down that I should. "Do you know what these people are capable of?" Edward had said, and I had no intention of finding out. Wasn't I in enough trouble already? A damaged soul rarely even looks for excuses. Back through the slums, then the houses and toward the tall buildings that signaled the center of town. We finally left the main road to come to a stop at a construction site I had never paid attention to before. The billboard at the front announced a future high-rise apartment complex.

It had become night while we had worked, but there were no night watchmen, and the gate to the construction area had been left open. We drove around the base of the structure to stop at a scaffolding beside a large hole in the ground that would be the foundation of building. The blazing lights that had always illuminated the site at night, which I had seen sometimes when I walked home late from an odd job, had been turned off. Only a smaller one still burned, a single bulb hanging over the expanse below. "Grab the bag," beard said. Like the zombies that haunt the hills at night beside the battle sites that riddle the landscape of the north, we obeyed, Edward and me with Vincent standing on the other side in the truck bed, pushing at the squealing bag—unthinking, unfeeling, unknowing. Denial is a powerful tool, especially for those of us who have nothing. Because we are afraid of nothing. We seized the four ends of the great burlap bag, which grunted and squirmed and fretted while we walked toward a wooden board that extended kitty-corner over the abyss below, just far enough out to reach well above the cement that was still wet from the day's work. "Walk the bag carefully to the center of the plank," said beard, "and then wait." Again, I knew exactly what I was going to do. I am not stupid, and I have no excuse. But again, the allure of easy work, of which Edward had spoken with a wink. Or maybe just my wickedness, the desiccation of my soul from too much suffering. Who knows?

At any rate, we obeyed, carefully walking across the board until we were standing thirty feet above the wet cement below. Suddenly we heard something strange radiating from the guard shack that had been erected within sight of the place where we were standing. The small building was shrouded in darkness except for a few candles and echoed with the voices of what must have been one man and one woman. The chanting was vaguely familiar, and I recalled some of the sounds that had come at night from the witch's tukul in the camp. An unknown language, rising and falling with rhythm and power, lulling even me who had never visited the witch and didn't believe much in what she pretended to offer. For minutes, we stood there as the bag became heavier. The squirming resumed again after a short time of stillness, and a muffled mumbling that was thick with panic emanated from inside as the thrashing became more extreme. I was starting to lose my grip but didn't dare to say anything, holding tighter and tighter as my knuckles turned white. Standing there for as long as I was, I began to grow afraid, coming at last to grips with my precarious situation, without a ready solution. What could I do? I weighed the options carefully in my mind, of course realizing what I'd done, what I was doing. But also knowing that there was in fact nothing to do. That my decisions had been made, inertia mostly but also carelessness and a sense of inevitability that stems from poverty and powerlessness. Then the bag gave a fierce jerk, and the corner I was holding with my left hand ripped loose. I lunged for the slipping bundle, but it was too heavy, while the sudden shift in the weight caused Edward to be thrown off balance and almost slip and fall himself. Slowly—almost in slow motion—the bag escaped our grasp and dropped, shaking and twirling to plop into the soft cement below.

"God damn it," said a voice I did not recognize from the shack. "You were told to wait for my signal."

"Don't yell at me. It was their fault," said beard.

"No matter," the voice said. "It will suffice."

We had both scrambled back onto land from the board to be met by beard, who was angry. "Next time, do only as you're told," he said.

"Next time?" I started to say, panic boiling the bile in my stomach, but before the words began to flow, they were immediately arrested as he withdrew two large wads of shillings from his pocket and handed them over, one to each of us. Shillings, not in the hundreds or thousands but in the tens of thousands. I hadn't seen this much money since the day so long in the past that I had robbed the safe—but this time it was mine, free and clear. I filled pocket after pocket with the bills, no subterfuge or deals to be made for my share. I trembled as I thought of what it would buy, of what I would have done with this in the camps. Maybe my sister would not have died of starvation. Maybe my father would have been able to afford a tukul closer to the water and my mother would not have been raped that dark night that nobody wanted to talk about. Maybe I would have been able to afford the schoolbooks, which would have allowed me to pass that one class that I could not pass.

Maybe.

The bundle in the wet cement that was still squirming below had fled from my imagination, replaced by ice cream, shoes, a shirt. A shower. Images of things I had never had. "Remember," said beard, "you will tell nobody about this. If you don't think that could be you down there"—he pointed down into the blackness—"just ask yourself who would care, or would even know, if it was. And this," he said, handing me a simple Nokia telephone, "is yours. We will call you, and when we do, you will answer."

As I left the construction site, I heard the sound of a cement mixer beginning to turn.

So that is the story of my first murder. Not out of anger or hate or jealousy. A body in a potato bag. I didn't even know if it was a boy or a girl. But a child it was; must have been because it was too heavy to have been a dog. And if it had been, who would have cared? Why the secrecy? Holding tight to the wad of money in the pocket of my dirty pants, I tried to fight the feeling deep within myself, the realization of what I had just done, of what that made me, of what I had become, and of what it meant. People are not born to murder. Most people, that is. Most people experience it as an escalation; stealing a loaf of bread, hotwiring a car, breaking into a home, slitting the throat of a dog. Not as a decisive act of wickedness but the momentum of a thousand tiny decisions leading inevitably and tragically to their final results. Each decision made existential—me or them—to justify the violence. Until that final decision, which is more easily made because over and over and over again I have chosen myself over them, put my interests, my needs, my anger over that of others.

Incidentally, for those who don't know, what I had inadvertently participated in—a ceremony with which I became intimately familiar as time went along—was a blood sacrifice. This one to bulwark the foundations of a new structure so that it would stand the test of time and bring the owner prosperity. It is an old ritual, from before the colony, but it does endure because it continues to live in the imaginations of our people. Minds who still believe a rebel leader is born of the tail of an alligator, or where a King's African Rifle can become a cannibal.

After that night, the night I helped kill an innocent, my life changed in subtle ways. You might say I became part of something bigger, and I liked that. I began to do jobs for the woman with the strong perfume, the woman with all the money and the Land Cruiser that was always clean and cold. "Hello," I would say, answering the ringing telephone as I sat on the simple, cheap rocking chair that I had bought as my first act with the blood money and set out front of my container, with the intention of truly reveling in my newfound leisure. "Take a package from Masaka to Mbarara," she would say, or "Deliver this message to an address in Mbale." Once I was asked to go to a certain warehouse in Entebbe, by the lake, at night. There, I found myself with another dozen men and was given a bat and a machete. I stood a ways behind a man who I would come to know only as Amin, but that story comes later. I guess it was a shakedown, because the dozen of us stood well behind our leader, who was mumbling something we couldn't hear to a fellow in a suit who started crying and pointing before handing over an envelope. I didn't care. Because after each job, I would get a wad of money that seemed to grow in my hands as I walked back to my container. It was looking clean and polished now, my old metal home was; I had bought a fresh new mattress and a little table, and my sleep was longer and deeper. I had a battery-powered lamp that I would turn on at night in order to read the books that I was able to find on the streets of Kampala. Anything I could buy for a few shillings from the salespeople sitting on plastic sheeting with an assortment of random books in front of them. Stories about heroes; tragedies about people who did not make it; tales about knights. I liked these last most of all. I loved to think that one day I would be a soldier against a great evil, that my life would count for something and I would be considered among the great men. Some sort of antihero maybe, who was wicked and hard and violent but who in the end turned his particular skills to a feat of such significance that all in the past was forgiven. That I was preparing for something and that all I was becoming was to serve a purpose in the future. Didn't all the dictators do terrible things when they were fighting in the bush? How was that different from me? I bought a little radio I would play during the days off that I forced myself to take, or when there was no work and I returned home midmorning to wait for the next day, the next call. I even bought a painting that I hung on a jagged nail stuck into the metal wall. Home—that meaning is relative, and I suppose a solitary container unmolested is better than a mud tukul full of screaming children beside a thousand others.

Dog had become healthy and strong, her coat lustrous and with spring in her step. Good food and the companionship of man. I was looking better too, I suppose. I had bought a jerrican, soap, and shampoo and finally rid myself of the lice and fleas that had been my constant companions throughout my life. Deodorant. I bought a toothbrush and paste. Africans have good teeth, but even we need to care for them. I had a few pair of new pants and several shirts that did not come buttonless and with broken zippers from a charity container—as well as my first pair of sneakers. Learning to walk on them had been hard; an African from the camps uses his feet to sense the land and the earth, to give signals as to what to do, how to balance, when to run, when to fight. Sensations, vibrations; the shoes made my feet mute and dumb, causing me to trip often in the first days of wearing them. But I became quickly accustomed to the luxury of feet well cared for, walking as I was on little mattresses.

Notwithstanding all this, I could never truly escape the knowledge of whence my good fortune had come. I knew very well that my path was far from my visions of a knight fighting evil, books I had read and games I had enjoyed pretending, using sticks from the forest as swords, after watching this or that film on Saturday Magic, our monthly evening of entertainment in the camps when the charities briefly acknowledged our humanity. I didn't want to admit that, in point of fact, I had become part of the dark bands that graced the opaque corners of the screen, against which the hero had to prevail. Thuggery, murder, extortion, these were the crumbs of my daily bread. While the work became easier, the reality of what I had become did not so easily fade, and my stark visions of being an antihero became more and more muted as they were layered over by sin. After each act of violence, the victim's face would return to hover above my mattress at night, haunting my sleep, peeking around corners as I walked from here to there, throwing rocks or lewd gestures from windows as I went about my business.

As an old man now, I can say that the spirits are still with me. Oh, we Acholi are accustomed to the spirits. They never leave the battle sites of our homeland, haunting the fields or perched in the trees until their skeletons are found, wrapped in white and buried, with the requisite sacrifice to the four powers of nature for the untimely death and improper burial of one of her own. A goat beaten over the head to simulate the pain and shock of the illegitimate death, the belly slit open and its contents thrown to the four winds to pacify those spirits. The words of the paramount chieftain, the most senior of our Acholi elders, to calm the ire of the spirits; all this lest they gain strength and return for revenge. They have clung to me, despite the many rituals I have performed over the years since I fled—in an attempt to set them free, to set myself free. Guilt is an easy emotion for those who sit in comfortable chairs drinking good beer. It's hard to find the time for that particular feeling with the knowledge of "it's me or him." Nevertheless, though I hoped that things would settle down in my mind, the truth is that I never was able to make peace with the demons, especially the host of them that came after, when the measure of my wickedness waxed full. Perhaps it's because I began to hate them. I never became accustomed to the pitiful end of the average man. Fear, yellow and stinking. The pleading "Don't do that" or "I have a family" or "Oh no, why me?" The pictures of daughters and wives extracted with shaky hands from empty wallets to prove what I was doing was doubly wrong and for it I would be doubly damned. Seeking to appeal to some part of me that also had loved ones—or so they assumed—so that I would not carry out the task that I had been assigned and for which I was so well paid. Weeping, sometimes the stomach-turning smells of a powerful man who had shat himself upon the vision of his own mortality. It all sickened me, and my revulsion against humanity swelled, drowning my heart. And I persevered. What else was I to do? An African with no education, no friends in government. Where was I to turn if I let my conscience guide me?

And then, as always happens, I found a measure of acceptance.

I found guilt in the men who I punished and the families who I robbed, making the case that their victimhood was their own damn fault. The justifications were many, creative, and varied. They had done this to themselves, hadn't they? Nobody forced them to gamble, to take that loan. If they hadn't done business where they were unwanted, if they had listened when they were warned, and warned and warned again. Yes, I did the warning too and made sure that I made myself clear. If they had not been rich, serving themselves of the poor to become fat and arrogant. I was really a warrior for social justice, maybe—wasn't I? That strange concept that the pimpled white people would lecture at us, seated as we always were on plastic chairs, waiting for the lecture to end and the handout to begin. As if there was anything just about a poor man's life in Africa, social or not. As if there was anything they could do about it anyway. And as if berating us would help.

Then the final justification—the assertion that, at any rate, it was none of my affair. Willfully forgetting that when I picked up the iron pipe, it became my affair. The reminder that I too was poor, forgetting that money obtained through bloody means is quickly lost. That this was the way the world works, knowing that was the problem, that I was in fact the problem now. I thought of the politicians, becoming powerful. Did I think they'd followed all the rules? This is Africa. Things are hard here; hunger and starvation are specters that haunt even the fat. If I'd been born rich already, I would have had what I needed to behave good and true, but we do what we have to, to build a cushion between ourselves and the horrible hunger. This is not necessarily a mea culpa many years after the fact but a sober admission of what life is like for the poor and what limited choices we are afforded here.

Nevertheless, the ghosts came.

One afternoon, I was walking back to my container from a gratifyingly easy job and feeling fine about myself. I had money in my pockets, my jeans were new, and I had on running shoes and a polo shirt. I was clean shaved, heady shiny as the glass that reflected my image back upon me as I strolled. I smelled good. I felt like a paramount chief. I was walking purposefully but without hurry in the direction of the ice cream shop—an act of boldness. My heart fluttered a little bit as I arrived to stand in front of the window and looked at the crystal inside. Because this time, for the first time, I was going in. I reached out determinedly and pulled open the door, entering the establishment with what I desperately hoped was a sense of property and confidence.

"Hello," the pretty, striped girl behind the counter greeted me.

"Hi," I said. "May I please have a strawberry cone?" My voice cracked, and my tongue was dry.

"Sure," she said, scooping it out and handing it over in exchange for the bill that I passed across the countertop, eschewing the change.

It was a Friday, of course, and I went to sit within earshot of the girl. The one with the pressed school uniform under which rested the object of my desire. She was seated beside another girl of unequal beauty, and they were talking about their day. I slowly licked my cone as I listened to snippets of a life I had never known.

"How did you do on the leaving exams?" her friend asked.

"Oh, I think I did fine, not that I studied much," she responded, and they both giggled.

"What will you do this summer?"

"Maybe travel some, Nairobi or Zanzibar. The beach! Maybe London if my father has the time, to look for a university and to shop!" More giggles. "I can't wait. Real people, with real money, going real places. Sitting around this jungle is getting boring."

"You're lucky," said the ugly girl.

Nairobi, Zanzibar, London. I had only seen these places in the occasional movie or television series, crowded around a small television with a hundred other children in the camps. And university? In London no less? What a world that must be!

"What are you thinking of?" she asked.

"Oh, I don't know. Oxford or Cambridge maybe," she said. "Wherever the boys are cuter." And they giggled again.

"When do you want to go?"

"Well," said the pretty girl. "I suppose I could go now, but I didn't get my papers in in time. No matter. I'll take some time and maybe do some travel. So next year, or else my daddy will get angry. He says I have to study. Oh, sure, I know he's right. But it seems like a lot of work right now! I only just finished—and I want to have fun!"

I got up, scraping the chair around the floor to draw attention to myself. I swaggered over to the counter to buy something, anything, in order to walk back slowly. There was a wall mirror covering the entire far side of the parlor. It made the room look twice as large, the pristine reds and crystal whites of the cleanliness glistening back upon the three of us. I have perhaps not said this yet, but I had become a good-looking man. The hard work under the sun had thickened my shoulders and arms, carving out my chest, my abdomen, and the V of my back into an ebony wood structure. My shaven head made me look older, accompanied as it was by a thin goatee. My complexion had never suffered the frustrations of adolescence, pimpled and bumpy, but instead remained clean and smooth without blemish. I was tall like the Acholi of old who stood like a baobab tree under the African sun. My teeth were white and strong, and my eyes were bright and clear and full of hunger, of yearning for knowledge and experiences of things beyond the understanding of the camps.

I swaggered back to flip my chair backward with one swift motion of my powerful arm and thumped down, small acts of disregard as a hint of my contempt and defiance. It worked; for as I walked back to sit at the little round table a few back from the girl, she looked up casually from her conversation, and our eyes met through the reflection at the far end of the restaurant. And just as I knew it would, from the way she talked and the way my stomach tightened up, the way I held my breath to listen to her words, the way my hunger melted away like the ice cream I was unable to eat, our gaze held, and it was electric.

CHAPTER 7

Ruth. That was her name. It had not been easy, wooing the paranoid little rich girl. But as an operator from the camps, a thug from the nasty underbelly of Kampala who dressed slickly and spoke with enough malice to be able to pass it off as a forsaken refinement, she didn't even see me coming. At least that's what I thought then. That day, that fateful day when our gaze crossed, I knew I would have her. It was inevitable. My experienced eye had held her gaze for just too long before turning to pull out the chair and sit. I could feel the lasers of her eyes burning a hole in the back of my sleek bald head. I ate slowly, deliberately. I savored the flavors. I crunched the cone, sweet molasses and strawberry sugar mixing to explode upon my tongue and slip smoothly down my throat. I ate carefully—every bite an audition, every move a private hearing, for her. Nobody else existed but her. Until the last drop. I wiped my hands carefully with a napkin, and then I stood suddenly, overturning the metal chair I'd been sitting on, and the tangy clang ricocheted around the quiet parlor. "Pick that up," I commanded the serving boy, not unkind or in malice but with what I hoped was authority and some bravado. Then I marched toward the door without giving her another look and walked out into the sunlight. I could feel her gaze still boring into me as I walked around the corner.

It worked, because it became she who made sure that every Friday at the right time, she was at the ice cream parlor. School was over for her— that building just across the road, an institution that had been founded by the British during the occupation and colonization and appropriated by the Kampala elite to continue to pretend that they could be both British and free, shuttered for her forever—but still she came. She was a new adult, free and independent. Ready to taste the world. I could see it in her eyes. I didn't know where she lived; that far into her world I would never be allowed. I was exciting, a summer adventure, forbidden and secret. Fridays, I would do my best to finish my tasks early in order to be sure I was walking by the parlor when I knew she would be there. But not inside, never again inside. That was too obvious. She would come to me. I would make her come to me. I made sure she saw me passing, and one Friday became a second and a third, and then finally, for a reason I still don't know, courage or a fight with her father or the feeling of youthful invincibility or whatever, she rushed into the street.

"Hi," she said, squirming a little bit.

"Hello," I responded, stopping.

"So what's up?" she said, fidgeting with her short skirt.

"Nothing," I responded.

"Where you going?" she asked.

"Nowhere. Just finished for the day," I said.

"Finished with what? I see you come by here every week," she said.

I ignored the first question. "Yes, I like this walk, this street."

"Hmm," she said, obviously searching for conversation. I let her stumble around, not initiating any dialogue but also not leaving, the corner of my mouth slightly upturned. "What do you do?" she tried again, eying my new clothes.

"Odd jobs, this and that," I said, and gave her a little shrug and a winning smile.

"Kinda hot this week, isn't it?" she asked.

"Indeed," I answered. "It's nice to have a place to go." And I gestured into the parlor.

"Yes," she said.

And we would continue on that way for a few minutes, banal questions and abrupt answers until I would excuse myself, "Must go now, busy," and I would walk away, throwing a "Take it easy" over my shoulder.

Slowly our engagements became more protracted, the lingering more expectant. I took to leaning against the wall carelessly. Acting uninterested. Not really pursuing but neither denying. Always making the conversation last just a little longer than was natural. The pauses became pregnant. Until finally the moment was right. I had gotten paid, and my pocket bulged with bills.

"Listen, I'm not doing anything right now," I said.

"Neither am I," she responded.

"There's a movie theater down this way ..." I gestured, and she nodded shyly.

There is only one movie theater in Kampala. It sits at the intersection of the two major roads that run through the city. One goes up to the National Assembly building and on to the Sheraton hotel where Idi Amin once forced all the diplomats at the soiree—including the British ambassador—to pick up his chair on their shoulders and parade him like a long-ago Nubian Pharaoh around the pool, which at that point was filled with naked women, white and black. It had been one of his legendary parties, and as the evening went along, the increasingly unstable dictator had become increasingly and violently drunk, finishing with this act of humiliation. That had been the final straw, after which the United Kingdom had broken diplomatic ties with Uganda. The other road led down toward the train station, my home, and on over the hill to the lake. Both roads boasted great sidewalks, legacy of the British who so much enjoyed tropical Africa, away from the smog and mists and the damp chills of London. That every evening, they would don their finest outfits and place their toddlers in elegant strollers before embarking upon long walks in the cool, clear Kampala evenings. Grand trees, knotted and old, reached high above the sidewalks, their roots breaking the pavement beneath them, while in their creeping branches lived the gigantic storks in their enormous nests, diabolically ugly beasts that released their droppings on the pedestrians below in huge globules. It has been said that these storks soared nightly to kidnap the babies of poor Africans and deliver them to richer families elsewhere, and poor families were advised to keep the wooden windows of their hovels fastened tight during the dark hours to discourage the nocturnal predations. Doing what I have done, I know the real reason the children go missing, and it still makes me shiver and sorrow.

Right there where the two roads meet is the city's finest and only mall: food courts; stores selling expensive dresses for the brides of wedding parties that cruised through town every Saturday blowing their horns and generally making such a ruckus that laws had to be passed to keep the noise levels down; pet food for those who could afford special food for their dogs while people starved in the camps up beyond the river. The first time I visited the mall—a child from the northern camps—I hadn't been able to believe something like this existed, a place dedicated to extravagant excess, purchasing things that were not needed for daily life but that nonetheless people bought, when all the Acholi had ever known were the banco huts and big black bags of soiled, ill-fitting clothes brought from over the seas. That was long ago, it seems now, and I realize just how naive it was, pretending that one thing had something to do with the other. I have since become used to the incongruity, even somehow comfortable with it; it is the way of the world. It's the way things have always been. Why fight it? Just do your best to try to move upward. That's all we can do. In point of fact, it actually provides motivation. Sitting around the camps, there was nowhere to go and hence no need to work, innovate, or invent or dream; *pure socialism* some politicians who came to the camps to berate us called it. As if we had another choice. It had made us Acholi lazy and complacent. "The poor you will always have with you," was something we were told quite often by the priests to make us feel better and keep their churches full. But why did we Acholi always have to be those poor? I digress.

I took Ruth's hand. Ruth—yes, it was a lovely name, lovely like her face, but I didn't want her for her name but for what was underneath her dress. For what she represented. For the places she would go that I never would. For the things she could say with property, with legitimacy and fluidity, for the ideas, the names that rolled off her tongue while all I thought about was food and shelter and the white panic of poverty. Unlike the other boys from her school, ambitious boys who were well aware of her last name, who knew where she lived and what a match like that would do for them, she wanted me for other reasons.

I didn't care.

We walked hand in hand down the wide sidewalks, beside the pillbox with the sleeping guard and up into the mall. There is a pizza place selling the Ugandan version of American pizza on the ground floor, and we sat down to order peperoni and cheese. Then we walked up the steps to the top floor where the small theater was showing the latest American movie. Action, sex, humor. Fairy-tale lives with white people's problems: who slept with whom, a comedy about a party gone awry, fictitious problems for which I could only yearn. Or maybe it had been gratuitous violence and blood for those who don't know what the violence means. For those of us from the camps, who have grown up with the violence, with the blood covering the ground after a night squatting sleeplessly in our mud tukul, hoping a bullet didn't rip through the mud and end our meaninglessness once and for all, watching the violence on the big screen was both traumatic and somehow tedious. Traumatic because the memories were still fresh; they always would be. Memories like that don't ever diminish, despite what people tell you. The screams, voices you know—playmates with their lips sliced off—girls you once fooled around with raped, their screams and moans juxtaposed against the cackling of a laugh without mirth. Wanting to stand, to grab your machete and charge into the night because at least that would be a noble end, but huddling in the tukul nevertheless, fear and that basic impulse for survival overpowering the desire to fight. Humiliation. And tedious, because for those of us who know, the blood was unreal. Explosions do not sound like that. Nor does rifle fire. Cars do not explode when shot at. Because we know how grenades, assault rifles, and explosives look, sound, and smell.

"Did you like the movie?" she asked. The lights had come on, and I was brushing popcorn from my shirt. We exited the theater into the back side of the mall.

"Of course," I lied.

"What should we do now?" she asked.

I suggested we go to the rooftop and have something to eat at the Indian restaurant that overlooked Kampala. Sitting there across from her as the sun faded into the west and the Central African mists crawled slowly from their caves and started to wrap themselves around buildings or lay across the golf course, I started to feel almost at peace. Africa is lovely just twice a day, in the early morning and just as the sun expires—those times when the hostility of the day, with the heat and the misery

72

and the poverty, releases a little bit of its anger. The lights started to twinkle from Kampala's seven hills. On one sat the great mosque, on another the Catholic cathedral, on yet another the new hotel—recently completed and glistening like an ivory hippo's tooth above the valley below. The bowl under the vigilance of the hills was also coming to life; the hum from the traffic of people rushing to and fro in the heat of the day had turned into a steady stream of those returning home to settle in for another night, watching television, eating dinner, fighting. Fucking. Drinking the night away in silent acceptance that this was the meaning of life. Not too different from the camps, I supposed. Exchange the boredom of the camps for the boredom of life in an office, shuffling papers around a wide desk to return home, sit in front of a table with a big plate of matoke, watch the nightly news about important people doing important things—what rich people were saying, where powerful people were traveling, what beautiful people were wearing. Slowly let the stupor fog the brain until sleep overcame. Only to wake up and do it all over again. In the camps, we were told that if we studied hard, we could get a job inside. Seated, not standing. In the air-conditioning, not in the sun. Watching the years go by as our stomachs pressed more firmly against the desk in front of us. Letting the fingernail of our pinkies grow long to prove to others ours was a job inside. The most important thing, or was it?

I sighed.

"You've never told me what you do," she said after a period of silence, during which we both ate our chicken tikka masala with naan while looking out over the darkening city.

"Oh, it's not that important," I responded.

"No, I mean it," she said. "I'm curious."

"Why?" I asked gruffly.

"What do you mean why?"

"I mean why does it matter?"

She stared at me blankly.

"Whether I push papers in a bank, or in a law office, or in a doctor's office. Does it matter to you really? As long as I can afford this?" I asked, throwing the piece of naan into the little copper pot heated by a candle beneath.

"Well, when you put it that way," she said, "it's not that it matters. Those are all good jobs that people can be proud of. Are you a doctor? Are you a lawyer?"

"Why?"

"Huh?"

"You said those were jobs to be proud of. Why? Why should people be proud of some jobs and not others?" It was nasty, I know, but I was annoyed.

"Because, well … I suppose that, you know, like, doctors—they help people. Right? And lawyers? They do important work, I mean like protecting the laws and stuff …" She trailed off.

I realize now how I must have come across to Ruth, my love, my lost love. But how could I tell her that the only doctors I had ever known were the white ones in the camps? Teenagers looking for an adventure. Or old. Washed up, faces red from too much alcohol, thinning white hair long and collected in a ponytail. Maybe on the run. Who knows? Maybe nobody would trust them back home, so they came to practice on us. Africans. Who gives a shit, right? If they fuck one of us up … How could I tell her that there were no lawyers in the camps? No judges, no courts, no juries. No rules. The only law that was exerted was through might—power over others—strength to stand and not perish, to survive and not die. How could I tell her there were no banks in the camps? People passed around grimy, crumbling bills that were received from what the charities self-importantly called cash transfer programs, to not have to say the word *handout*. As if we didn't know that's what it was. Or the "food for work" programs. As if they would work for a bag of beans or a potato instead of money that they controlled the world with—but no, no money for us. They had to make sure we didn't use it to buy booze. As if they didn't drink. As if their nocturnal rampages didn't end in drunken orgies, people vomiting all over the front of their tents—running naked through the camps. And as if we didn't deserve to drink real booze as well, hiding out for a time from our lives. Yes, I was cold and hard—and getting harder. The irony is not lost on me either that it's probably because of the mystery, the intrigue, that she stayed with me as long as she did. Until that fateful day, but that comes later.

"You still haven't said," I said on the rooftop that day, through tight jaws and furrowed brow, "why those are nobler—better than a garbage collector. A teacher. A bricklayer. Why? Tell me."

"Well," she said, thoughtful. "I suppose those jobs are important because not just anybody can do them. The folks who work them, they had to study a lot. They, well, they dedicate their lives to something bigger than themselves maybe. They have read books. You know, they see the world and not only the neighborhood; they look beyond the Nile to the Rift Valley, the beaches. They know about other things—"

"What you're saying," I say, cutting her off, "is that they have more money, that they don't have to lay sleeplessly in their shacks every night, worrying about their children dying of hunger or disease. That they can pretend that they are not part of a world where people work hard, eat little, and die young. You say they think beyond themselves, to something bigger than they are, but all you describe is money. Knowledge, horizon, leisure, cleanliness—all these are the by-products of money. But they can't have it both ways. They can't tell the world they love something beyond themselves while with their every action they are only seeking after money. Because that is not truth. Love of something bigger is a mama going hungry so that both her children will eat and perhaps live. Love of something bigger is not sending others to their deaths but picking up a machete yourself to defend your family. Love of something bigger is not some grand idea discussed over Champagne; it is a neighbor sharing half of their bowl of matoke with the family who just arrived next door dirty and bloody and hungry." Love of something bigger certainly wasn't throwing children in burlap bags into the foundations of buildings, but it seems there was no end to my hypocrisy, especially where Ruth was concerned.

"But ..."

"So let me ask you, you who say you love study and knowledge and selflessness but describe only privilege. Let me ask you this. Who cares where the money comes from, if with it you are able to read and learn about what interests you? As long as you smell nice, why does the source matter? So long as you are able to travel, to get the fuck out of here when you want—why does it matter how?" I asked. I was not speaking loudly but quietly and deliberately. Not angry either. It wasn't her fault. I knew that, but neither could I stop myself.

"I guess ..." she tried again.

"Let me save you the effort of guessing. It doesn't matter. You ask what I do. Not because you care whether I am a doctor or a lawyer or a banker but because you want to know where my money comes from and whether I'm of your world or not." I took the large wad of shillings from my back pocket, slapping it down on the table, upsetting the little copper pot filled with chicken tikka. "And you want to know if that source is permanent. Sustainable. To be trusted."

"Oh, I didn't mean to imply ..."

"Of course you didn't. Let me ask you, though. Isn't it enough that there it is?" I asked, signaling the wad that was blowing from the table, bill by bill flitting over the ledge into the darkness beyond while we both watched. The Indian waiter had rushed over to pick up six or seven stray bills to return them awkwardly to the table, placing them atop the pile and then setting a pepper shaker on top, while we were just silent, staring at each other.

"I'm sorry," she said simply. We ate the rest of our meal in silence.

That should have been the end of our tryst, I know. I hadn't reacted well. I don't even know why. Simmering rage, the violence always only a layer or two down. Nevertheless, girls can always be trusted to make poor choices. Show them an upstanding young man from a good family who has a diploma on his wall and a silver spoon in his mouth, and they will yawn. But give them somebody who is angry, vengeful, deliberately duplicitous, and secretive, and as long as he is handsome and with a hint of the dangerous, they will throw all their father's careful nurturing and admonitions aside and rush headlong into the unknown.

It was after this date that our affair began in earnest.

CHAPTER 8

For a season, she and I carried on our clandestine liaison. I was still living in my container; for a boy from the camps, even the idea of attempting to navigate the complications of life on the grid was too much for me. Rental agreements, reference checks, bank accounts, electricity bills, water and garbage and neighbors. Especially not for people like me who made our living on the dark fringes of society.

I sometimes thought of the slum on the far side of the hill, up the road a ways, the one on the back road to the lake beside a tremendous resort where presidents visited and rich white people ate poached eggs in the morning served by nice, clean black men in suits. Men like me. For a time, I thought about moving from my abandoned container to that place, but every time I found the courage to take the moto-taxi to inspect this or that house that I had seen advertised by a phone number scrawled in marker on a piece of paper and taped to a light post, I could barely find the will to enter the teaming mess of humanity. For those of us from the camps, exchanging the tukul life in the great plains of nowhere for these houses, trading mud for cement, and firelight for stolen electricity—shimmying up the posts, looking ever like a spider's web—to string wire down into the one-room hovel is never very appealing. Sitting there stupidly, watching cable television stolen from a neighbor, listening to the neighbors fight and make up—the moans and the knocking replacing the smashing of glass and screams of rage. Children screaming; babies, babies, more babies; crapping in the alley, yelling at the tops of their little lungs. Cats, rats running around.

No. Never again.

Returning from my expeditions to the slums would remind me with renewed appreciation just how livable my container was becoming. Each time, after the slum visits caused my blood pressure to rise and my breathing to shorten, I would sit on the wooden rocking chair I had purchased. I had hung a tarp above the entrance of my container, fixing it in place with a few metal supports I had found lying around. There I had put a small barbeque beside my chair, not one made of a stolen hubcap but a real one bought with real money from the large Game store on the other side of town. After difficult days at "work" or an afternoon with Ruth, I would often return to sit in the chair at the opening to the container and stare out—the lighting chasing the thunder around the valley as if beholding a great battle of the angry gods. Above me hung a lightbulb, which I would turn on and off and on and then off again, enjoying the power. There was another bulb inside the container, electricity stolen in the way I had learned from the slums; at least my visits there had been useful for something. Dog at my side in a special plastic container I had also purchased. She was fat and happy now, and she barely left the container. Why would she? A bottle of red wine in my hand—no more banana wine or fermented millet for me. I was developing a taste for South African wine, the most readily available in the little markets of Kampala. Filling and refilling a hard plastic cup as I rocked, occasionally standing to turn the steak or the chicken drumsticks and corncobs that were cooking slowly on the grill beside me, releasing perfect smells of delicately cooking meat as I entered that special place when one is most lucid.

Alone, not a person in sight.

Sometimes, when it wasn't raining, I would walk a ways down to the little buffet on the other side of the tracks where the railroad workers ate. Nobody asked about me or talked to me even; I figured they assumed I was homeless or a day laborer. My container had once been discovered by a night guard, but he was a good man of family, also from the north, who had understood. He would sometimes stop by at night, when he saw my light on, to share a glass of wine or a cob of corn, and we would talk in our language—not about anything specific but in generalities, as people do who only want to forget. After a time, he would stand and bid farewell, and as he left, I would hand him a few shillings, and together these secured his silence.

Silence.

The best part of my arrangement. After a lifetime of chatter, noise, crying—screaming, orders. Directives. From the military, from the white people, from my drunk father and my destroyed mother. From the schoolteachers, from my occasional girlfriend, the camp commanders, and every other idiot who saw their place above mine. Drunks fighting, occasionally the moans of a girl being raped in one of the abandoned tukuls. The vulgarity of humanity, the terrible fastidiousness of man. Here, in my place, I had none of it. I would sleep deeply, a second mosquito net hanging from a chink in the metal roof above, protecting me from the humming menace just beyond that impossibly thin lace. Drifting off under the pounding, the refreshing scent of the storm filling my nostrils. It was, well, it was good.

Like I said, Ruth and I had begun to see each other more frequently. During the days, I would do my work, no longer standing on the street corner—that was for those who were still at the service of the highest bidder. My new employers would not allow for that; the nature of my new employment required the utmost loyalty and discretion. Early every morning, I would receive a phone call on the cell phone they had given me, telling me where to go. Often it was back to the industrial part of town, over destroyed streets that after each rain looked more and more like ruins of war. I would arrive in front of the same warehouse where I had met my employers on that fateful day. But I would not stand with the others, nor even acknowledge them—instead turning the corner to a small café where I would order a hot tea and sit and wait. At times they came right away, in different cars but always stopping to honk twice and then a third time and then once again. I would pay, rushing over to fold myself into the cool interior of the vehicle. There would be others inside, some I knew, others who were new. All soldiers of fortune, like myself. We would not speak. There was nothing to say; the industry in which we were partners was one of the silence of complicity, mud that stacked up layer upon layer, the comforting coat of shared guilt a wall between us, keeping us all safe. From there, we would go about this or that task—the devil's errands.

One day it was to visit a bakery. They had not paid for the service that we provided, keeping the thieves away in what was becoming a very dangerous city. The owner saw us coming—and he paid. Later, it was to pick up a package from a village on the outskirts of Kampala and take it via moto-taxi to a small warehouse on the lake, where I was met with a dozen other moto-taxis in various stages of coming and going. From there, I was to wait for the other moto-taxis to hand off their products—dozens of other large, tightly wrapped cellophane packages—and take them through the Ugandan waters into Kenya and deliver them unseen on the other side. They were always my favorites, those tasks that got me out of town. The lake. As far as the eye can see, a mammoth inland ocean. When the little dingy with its diminutive outboard motor pulls away from the land far enough that the shores become first a blur, and then a dot, and I turn off the motor for a few minutes to sit there in silence in the midst of the immensity. The famously voracious Nile perch, big as sharks, would arrive to poke at the fiberglass of the dingy, and in fear, I would hold my breath as they bumped the bottom, again and again. Like many Africans, I can't swim. Overhead, the gulls squawk and swoop, looking for the little fishes that we see by the bucketful in the markets, dried and salted and sold by the mamas as the only meat most Ugandans can afford. The air is different in the lake than the ocean—I suppose. Not that I've ever smelled the ocean, just the descriptions from my books. The lake has the fishiness without the salt that refines the odor and makes it glorious, or so I'm told, making the lake seem just a little fetid—despite its size. The water is not clear but murky and brown, especially after a storm, which kicks up the waves high when it comes. It's best to watch out for this, for those of us who make the dingy journeys frequently. And I did—make them frequently, that is. I took the trip enthusiastically and efficiently, with the hopes I would get reassigned the same task, which I was—over and over. It is glorious, the water, the solitude. Water. In the camps, we would wait for hours, lined up with our yellow jerricans as the sun climbed into the sky, the charities forming us into committees, picking their favorites or the girls they were fucking to receive the stipend and be the arbiters of the water. As if we didn't understand the value of the water and how to manage it. But here, the endless expanse—out of the vastness would emerge islands, some with trees and even monkeys on them, screeching at me. I wanted to stop, to spend the night there alone without hearing anybody or considering another soul, but I was worried what they would do to me if they thought I had made away with the cellophane bricks. At very least, I would be on potato bag duty—and that I never wanted to do again.

I would see Ruth often. No longer at the ice cream parlor beside the street; we had begun to trek further afield, always seeking that elusive place away from the prying stares of others. Not my container—how could I take her there? Sometimes under the bridge where the refuse floated atop the water. Other times in an abandoned sugar mill that was quietly disintegrating into the Central African rain. At the center of a banana plantation on the west side of town, on the road to Fort Portal, where there was a little hut in which the banana workers would sit in season to eat their meager lunches. But never did I deign to imagine she would be mine—in that way, in the only way that counts. Not until she came to tease me with the prospect, an idea, to speak of her desires and open for me a door that would never close again. It would change everything, because it could change nothing at all.

Do you remember a single day? One trip, one meal, one talk, one sleep—one night and one morning? Does your universe revolve around one moment, nothing before and nothing after? Just that one blessed day when you are exposed to the fullness of joy and opportunity. Although you know it will never be, can never be forever—not for you. That brief glimpse into a room before the door is closed and you are left standing outside in the cold? That brief sensation when your belly is full, before you head back into the hunger? Isn't that how the Christians describe hell? To see the face of God and then be thrown from His presence for eternity? You never really experienced the warmth, the light—the feast, the peace. But you can imagine that you had. Stealing a glimpse from high in a tree that you have climbed. I know what that is like at least. "It's better to have loved and lost," fools say. But they don't know what loss is.

The week after she suggested it, I asked for the hardest jobs, ones I usually resisted. Blood work, death—it's the screaming that I can't abide, that haunts my nights. Their voices—pleading, begging; pathetic really. But that week, I didn't care. I would welcome the demons coming as they did in exchange for the hope of something magnificent. Naturally, this was because the blood work paid more. Threatening, cajoling, beating. Bodies to be dumped in the lake. That week, I asked for all of it and kept the sweaty wad of shillings growing under my mattress in my container protected by my dog.

Ruth had convinced her father that she was to stay the night at a friend's house, an elaborate deception that included the hint of a camping trip lest her father sense a rat and wish to call. When she had told me, she was breathless—flushed with expectation. Lust, I know. Wealth knows no consequences and is also carnal in its own way. I was a part of her world for a time, like a stray cat upon which she would lavish attention, a fling, daring and brazen. An act of rebellion. I didn't mind. Oh, if I thought about it, which I didn't, I would have told myself I could win her over. That love conquers all. Some such bullshit; melodramatic, stolen from a movie. Truth is that those of us from the camps have become experts in pushing off the thoughts of tomorrow: of next week, next month, next year. What career will we choose? A question we ask ourselves less frequently than the real question: What if the food trucks stop coming? And that is a question we never allow ourselves to ask. When Ruth had told me that this night would be mine, I was shocked—had never imagined that we could go away like real people. We had not made love yet, only fooled around a little. I assumed that moment would never arrive, and I understood. Under a bridge that smells of garbage? Beside a putrid pond? In an abandoned mud hut? That is good enough for those of us from the camps. But not for her, not for Ruth. She was, nevertheless, anxious lest we be discovered—and had told me, after that one time we had carelessly gone to the movies. Never again. No big restaurants, no hotels, no bars. No upscale clubs. I had asked occasionally, but she was unmovable. "They can't see us." But she would never answer when I asked, "Who are they?" An Acholi knows he is not the same, somehow inferior. They usually don't see us, but when they do ... I know, I should have asked who she was, who her family was, who her father was. Truth is I didn't really want to know. I never found out.

In my comings and goings, I had heard of a place a few hours outside of the city that was both private and pristine, perfect. Luxurious. Not the jungle lodge, although my heart yearned for that. It was too close to the capital, too public—meals in that immaculate restaurant and then to the deck to listen to the night sounds. I ached to go there, to take her there. But I knew I had no chance; she would not accept. The morning arrived early, and we met where we usually did beside the ice cream parlor and walked side by side through the early morning to a matatu that left west from the town center, crammed in with a dozen other travelers, rucksacks of pots and pans, burlap bags of rice, live goats and chickens all tied to the back of the listing little bus. She was wearing a ball cap pulled over her face, making sure nobody would see her and report back to her father. "He can never know," she had said the week before, panic tinged with excitement. "He would not approve." Of course he would not approve. Even she didn't know the truth, and if she did, would *she* approve? I didn't much care. A boy from the camps with a girl like this? I considered myself lucky.

"Hi," Ruth said, meeting where we had agreed at the bus terminal. She was carrying an overnight bag, keeping with her ruse.

"Hi," I said.

"Where's your bag?" she asked, looking at both my empty hands.

"Bag? No, I never carry a bag. Slows me down," I said, not wanting to tell her I'd forgotten, never having gone anywhere before, that I didn't have one anyways.

We boarded the bus, which started moving slowly, jostling through the morning traffic. Thick fumes filled the air. The sun had only just begun to sting a little, and the cacophony of honking was maddening. Through the traffic walked men, missing one arm or one hand, victims of this or that war, a grenade that hadn't gone off, until it had, gangrene from a wound that didn't heal. Scars across their faces, arms held aloft, hawking their junk. Yellow, black, and red ties with the crane at the center. Self-cooling hats with little fans that blew air at the crown of your head. Big pictures of the president, of Che Guevara, of Mandela. Little yellow cars for the kiddies. Cold baggies of water atop round metal platters perched on the heads of little girls. Anything that had fallen off the back of a truck or that the desperate vendor believed would turn them a profit. An occasional brown face selling cell phones. A look of desperation in their eyes, pleading, victims of a great war beyond the sea, so anxious to get out, to leave, to go *anywhere* that they found themselves here. They all had the same look in their eyes, pale yellow of disease and desperation, hoping against hope that somebody would lower a window. Running down the street after a sideways glance or a hint of interest. Through it all, a crippled man, atrophied legs curled up under him as he used his hands to push along his skateboard from car to car, reaching up his emaciated arms, selling nothing but his own misery. I reached down from the window to give him a few shillings, and he smiled at me, not with hope, which had abandoned the man long ago. But definitely with gratitude for a meal that would preserve life for another day.

Then we were through it, and as the road that went out of town cleared of the traffic, we started to pick up speed. The smog of the Kampala daytime began to dissipate, and the blue sky beside the greens of the fields to one side and the dark canopy of the jungle on the other were clearer, closer. Up above in the trees, parrots played, squawking their warnings as the monkeys crawled closely in the hopes of ensnaring one as a pet. Few know that the monkeys too like the company of pets, and if they catch a bird, they will hold it close until it most likely is suffocated. For this reason, parrots especially are on the lookout for the red-tailed or colobus monkeys, lest they be ensnared and perish from an excess of love. By this time, it was an hour outside town and we were reaching a place where the jungles had withdrawn to make room for tea plantations. Vast expanses of green, the dark green of the leaves on the lower branches, old and mature with time making its way up in an ever-gentling pallet to the bright yellow-greens of the new leaves that were reaching high for the sunlight. It was now midmorning, and there was nobody about; most pickers know to get their work done in the early morning and late afternoon, leaving the plants alone during the heat of the day.

Down the Mbarara road to Lyantonde we continued, and as we arrived, I gave the order, and the bus screeched to a halt for us to disembark, and then in a belch of greasy smoke, it was on its way again. I looked around for a moment, getting my bearings. I had never been here. It looked like every Ugandan highway town. The single paved road ran down the center with boxlike shops on either side selling airtime or canned goods behind open stalls with ladies selling produce neatly stacked in little piles in front of them. The oily smell of cooked chapatti, too thick and greasy, wafted over the market overlaid by the smell of kerosene. I took Ruth by the hand, flagging down a green taxi and giving him the directions and the few shillings. Another thirty minutes down the highway, then off to the side and south, following the road southwest toward Rwanda, before turning off on a side road of dirt and with potholes and ruts washed out by the rains. We rode in silence, leaving the tiny town quickly and into the underbrush where there was nothing nearby, just kilometers of rolling green hills making the countryside look like a great manicured palace lawn. The puffs of green floated up and down the hillside in perfect lines, between which were barren rows brown and free of weeds. The road turned from asphalt to a hardened red marram dirt to eventually just a muddy rut. Beside us, the tea plants gave way to unclaimed land; animals, wild and tame, sharing a patch of dirt. Then, just over the ledge, a rocky outcropping. "We're here," the cab driver said. I paid, and we exited the vehicle, walking slowly up the trail.

It was still midmorning, and we meandered slowly, unhurriedly. Beside me, Ruth said nothing. The sun beat down on us, causing her caramel skin to glisten. Over the hills we went until we reached the top, gravel paths framed by rocks with lanterns placed equidistant up the trail as we climbed toward the top of the highest rock. There, two unpretentious structures stood open to the elements. One had a few tables, elegant in their simplicity, carved from the wood of African trees and brought the distance. At the back were hard banco walls washed in the browns of the rocks, nooks in which were held pieces of rock art found at the location, vases and pottery from the first inhabitants of those rocks. On the walls hung two-hundred-year-old maps of Africa, those from the times before the great lake had even been discovered. A mounted telescope pointed at the watering hole far below where the animals would come to drink and rest, shining polished bronze in the African sun—all below thick thatch roofs that preserved the cool inside. A pool had been nestled effortlessly into a crevice between the rocks looking out onto the savanna below.

"Welcome," said a pretty lady with a British accent, dressed in khaki shorts with a brown button-down shirt, as we walked into the dining area. On top of her head was a ball cap emblazoned with the logo of the lodge. She looked for the name I gave her—a false name—and picked up Ruth's bag to escort us down another path that twisted and turned as it descended closer toward the savanna that stretched out below beneath the outcropping. We arrived at last to an expansive tent the size of a big room, nestled quiet and alone in a crevice, surrounded by other rocks and some trees. The tent was covered too with thatch. A bathroom had been built behind it, elegant with running water from a well and an oval tub open to the elements under a clear plastic dome. Out front, an expansive deck hosted two chairs on either side of a squat table with two wineglasses and a bottle of white wine chilled in a metal container in front of a view of nature undisturbed. Inside the tent, a double bed, two chairs, and a lantern for the night. Rugs covered the floor underneath, which was a wood dais that had been erected ten feet above the ground below as it tapered away from the rocks. "Thank you," I told the woman.

"Lunch is in two hours; dinner at six. The bar is open until ten." And with that, she was gone.

We looked around, both of us, our eyes landing at last on each other. Quiet. Solitude. Luxury—not the luxury of expensive multicolored drinks and chefs with white hats. Luxury of the pristine, the perfect, the solitude when the world mostly clamors for company; rubbing together on the beaches or crammed one on top of the other in little boxes. Like the camps. But here, aloneness, when everybody wants to spend money in places where they can be seen by others, needing the envy of their betters to ratify their importance. We had not said a word to each other since the bus. We didn't need to. I turned to her, and she to me. It was cool here, but we were still hot from the walk and the sun. I pulled her white T-shirt up slowly, and she raised her arms for me. Unhurriedly, her perfect bosoms appeared. The caramel of her skin was flawless, as I always knew it would be. She smelled of soap, with only a suggestion of perfume, not overpowering but self-assured and confident. She looked at me, eyes wide open, golden eyes unblinking. A bead of sweat that had been growing on her forehead slowly began to run down her face, over her chin, and down her neck. It paused for a moment over her right breast, as if choosing which path to take, and then drifted inward, slowly making its way between her breasts and over her tight abdomen to lodge in her navel, leaving a moist path, which I bent over to lick away. Then, slowly, gently, and with great purpose, I removed the rest of her clothes: jeans, open-toed sandals, tight pink underwear. And then I laid her down on the soft blanket, the mosquito net still tied in a knot above our heads.

Our love was slow and deliberate, an exploration of life more than a quest for satisfaction. I lay atop her for a time, and then she atop me, changing places, turning over and over and over and over again in that ancient dance. I tasted her, sweaty and salty, musty and primal and perfect. I do not know if I was her first, although from her familiarity, I expected I was not. I had not had any others except the wretches from the camps, their breasts sagging and their breath stinking of banana wine. Hurried and worried in a tukul or out behind the latrines, not an act of love but instead scratching something that itched. Never looking back, never looking at all, eyes closed lest I see something that would torment me as much as the massacres I witnessed occasionally.

We made no sound, even during the climax, and when we were finished, we lay together looking up at the inside of the tent. When we had caught our breath, she spoke.

"What do you want to do with your life?" Ruth said.

"I want to live it," I responded.

"But aren't you living it? You know that's not what I mean."

"I know," I said, without offering further insight.

"For me," she said, to my relief. I'd learned that if silence abides for long enough, people will return to talk about themselves. "I want to be a doctor. But not here, dealing with the horrible diseases of poor people. Or of those filthy unfortunates who sometimes cross the river from the north." I grimaced. "No, I am going to study in London or maybe Canada. Working in a neat clinic. I want to be a plastic surgeon. You know how much they earn? Making people beautiful—that is so much nobler than just keeping them alive."

"Life is not a beautiful thing," I responded carefully after a time. "It's dirty and dark and violent."

"It doesn't have to be," Ruth retorted. "I've seen the magazines. Lovely people. Grand hotels. Crystal beaches. Vacations, castles, restaurants with Champagne and food too beautiful to eat—chefs in white with those tall hats. Fields of flowers, painters and writers talking about the great ideas. That's the world I believe in, but I can't find it here. Kampala is too backward, lost."

"Camps. Food lines, lines for water and for the next idiot know-nothing nurse. Dysentery, disease. Stench. Boredom. Poverty. Death. Those are the conditions for more of humanity than the Champagne," I said but mostly to myself. "And nobody writes novels about the misery."

"Yes, I know there are those places too," Ruth said. "And I see the people standing beside the street, bored and hungry. But we can't let that define us."

"Why?" I asked, but not harshly, and Ruth, who was used to my caustic reactions when the theme of poverty emerged, turned to look at me. "Why can't we?" I repeated. "It defines them."

"I know," Ruth said. "I don't know. What can we do—be miserable all the time?"

"No, of course not," I said. "But what are our responsibilities? It can't be to ignore. It can't be to flee to places far away that are cold and clean."

"Maybe not, but they are bigger than we are—those problems. Destroying our lives because their lives are already destroyed doesn't seem to make sense."

I knew she was right, that there was no answer. But that didn't make it any easier, because she was talking about random people she saw through bulletproof glass of her four-by-four, while I was talking about myself. My brother and my father and my mother and my friends. "No, it doesn't," I said finally. "But we're here now," I said, "and we should make the most of it."

We both watched as a gecko crawled down the inside of the tent canvas, slowly and painstakingly stalking a fly that had come to rest upon a strawberry, which had been left as a welcome by management in a basket of other strawberries surrounding a sliced pineapple. Slowly moving above the creature, carefully descending down, down, down until at the last moment it released a burst of energy and fell upon the insect, chewing it and swallowing quickly as the fly struggled for its life, until finally it ceased—the life-fight finished. In its primitive, tiny brain, it accepted the fate it knew was part of the order of things.

"Yes. You know, I think that there is beauty in even ..." Ruth started to say, but I stopped her, my finger on her lips, and then I leaned in and pressed lips against hers. At first haltingly, gently, tenderly. Then she met my mouth more firmly, her lips pressing against mine. I was hungry now but also somehow angry, and I turned over to lie atop her as we became lost in each other, our lust, and youth. Alone under the great expanse of the African skies, we explored each other, finishing together in an explosion of passion that required no words. Afterward, we lay beside each other for another time, not saying anything, only reliving the moment, the experience. The lack of shame, not needing a future, not acknowledging a past—just together, there, natural and animal and perfect. We must have fallen asleep, because when we came to, the sun had moved closer to the horizon and we could hear voices, other guests making their way on the paths above to dinner. We rushed to dress, Ruth covering herself with her blouse as she threw on her clothes, and we hurried up the hill, fearing being late and missing the last meal.

Three courses. The first, a salad, fresh and crisp dressed with lettuce and nuts and black olives and soft white cheese I'd never had before. This was served with soup, green and refreshing—cold, which was new for me. Cucumber, I think. Then a plate of wild rice beside chicken covered in mustard sauce and asparagus. The fresh burn of the mustard against the pepper was remarkable. Followed by ice cream over a cake so light I thought it would float off the plate. Never had I had anything like this, living as I did in a container and saving every penny to ward off the terror of tomorrow. Champagne to drink, and we watched as the sun set over the national park. Slowly the bright yellow sun turned to orange and then blue and finally purple before the pinpricks of the stars filled the sky like diamonds. Bats swirled overhead, and we were moved effortlessly by our hosts to the bar, collecting our next crystal goblet, red wine to deepen the experience, and down again to a little platform beside a timeless tree in front of a controlled fire crackling in an outdoor fire pit. There we were met by another man who was playing guitar, sad ballads of longing and suffering and sacrifice as we drank one glass, then another and yet another. At the apex of the evening, we heard a squeaking and three tiny bush babies, those little marsupials who are territorial and would never give up their tree—even to tourists from Kampala—as they descended curious and hungry from above for their nocturnal hunt to empty peanut bowls and overturn fruit cups while we all laughed.

Then back to the tent and to sleep. That night, I slept the greatest, grandest night's sleep I have ever had. The sounds of the insects, the occasional squeak of a bush baby finding a cicada, rustling around in the thatch above the tent. The neighing of one of the zebras we had seen prancing around the watering hole at dusk. A light rain started to fall, pattering against the grasslands below and the rocks around us. None of this kept us awake. We were exhausted from our time together, from our walking and the anxious tension of the previous weeks, months. We lay in each other's arms and drifted away. Even today, at such a distance, with so much time having passed, I still remember that night's sleep, that evening together, when I again struggle to make it beyond the next minute, the next hour of camp life. When I think I cannot bear the darkness anymore, it serves to remind me that there is light out there, that it does exist and that I have known it, even if it was not for me. What is time, anyways, for us to consider it? Whether something lasts a day, a week, a month, a year? These are all fleeting, to be looked back upon in nostalgia or bitterness. During the terrible days of my violence, that night was a constant beacon, an ever-present glimmer of the goodness, tiny as the tiniest of stars, soft like a firefly in a great field, lighting nothing but proving that the darkness is not all-consuming, that it can in fact be challenged by so small an act of defiance.

Yes, that night I slept.

The next morning, I awoke early, with Ruth still sleeping by my side. I delicately extricated myself from her embrace to go and stand naked on the wood terrace, watching the early-morning comings and goings of the animals. A herd of fifteen zebras was milling about, looking anxiously at a lion lying under a tree, asleep and paying them no attention. The tiny little deer that looked like medium-sized dogs were jumping to and fro, chased halfheartedly by a leopard. A hyena laughed in the distance, and all the animals looked up nervously. The melee was invigorating. I felt the delicate touch of a silken hand on my lower back as Ruth glided noiselessly to my side, wrapped only in a sheet. A pot of coffee had been delivered in the early morning, and she brought me a cup, with milk and sweet with sugar, and we watched the sun rise over the African plain.

"How did you sleep?" I asked.

"I always sleep well in these places," she said—and the barb went deep, deeper still because she didn't mean it, didn't know that what she said would be a wound that I still feel today.

"I'm glad," I responded. "So did I."

"Breakfast?" she asked.

"Of course, but first ..." I grabbed her sheet and pulled it away, throwing it over the wooden railings of the terrace and onto the rocks below.

CHAPTER 9

I t was during this time—these years that had gone by, taking me into my early twenties—that I also started to feel something wholly unfamiliar, a feeling that I could only guess was guilt or perhaps shame. This is not a particularly welcome emotion for a poor Acholi man from the camps. Taking what we need when the opportunity arises, eating too much and getting drunk when food and drink are at the ready, sex with whomever when a willing partner presents herself. When death is visited indiscriminately, those of us who know do not have the luxury of that emotion so many people seem bothered by. The call of conscience is unwelcome for those without a cushion from the misfortune.

I would spend the days doing the tasks I was assigned. Beatings, robbery, armed and otherwise. Threats. The occasional abduction. Those paid more because they were fraught with risk. Whenever I was able, I would find moments to see Ruth. A stolen kiss under a tree or a movie at a popular cinema, one where her friends did not frequent. Dinner somewhere, pizza maybe or shawarma. Just talking, finding a place where there was not too much noise, eating corn cooked over hot coals, worrying the chewy, tasteless grains from the cob one by one. But I was not at ease. Sure, I was better off than any Acholi I had ever known. I had money in my pocket, new clothes. I was well fed; no longer did my ribs push through into the sunlight when I ran from a job gone bad. But each night, sleep eluded me. Lying awake in my container with Dog by my side, the faces of those I had wronged would appear one by one in a gruesome parade.

"Who the hell do you think you are?" one would ask, followed by another. "I did nothing wrong." And still another—"I had a family. Who will feed them now?" I heard their pleas through the long, silent nights, cries to save their legs, their eyes, their lives—whiny voices demanding more time. The worst were the images of the children, young faces staring down at me with uncomprehending eyes.

On Sunday mornings, I would often awake late and crawl from my container to the little latrine I had dug for myself. As I squatted there, I could often hear music floating atop the African morning mists. Hymns, I was to learn they were called. They sounded joyous, filled with a sense of longing and of yearning that touched something deep in my soul that was chafing after a lifetime of hardship. One morning, I decided to see what they were all about. I put on my finest clothes from the makeshift dresser I had fashioned out of some boards and an old piece of rebar I had taken from a construction site some time ago, or some time before that. Polishing myself up beside the piece of mirror, I walked in the direction of the singing. I found that the sounds were coming from a grand building, two or three stories tall with wide, rounded double doors and stained glass images depicting what I knew was Jesus surrounded by a group of men in a garden, below a massive bronze cross. I poked through the double doors and was instantly greeted by a jovial fat man, dressed in a cheap but clean and pressed navy-blue suit, a red tie, and shiny black shoes. He smelled fresh, and his smile was contagious. "Welcome to the house of the Lord," he said excitedly. "Is this your first time with us?"

"Yes," I answered timidly.

"Great!" he said enthusiastically. "Please follow me," he said as he escorted me into the main hall from the foyer. It was immense, even bigger inside than it had looked on the outside. The benches were placed in a semicircle around the rounded amphitheater, facing the podium where an enormous woman was glistening in sweat as she bellowed full-throated the music that I had heard from afar. Behind her, a group of thirty other women and men were singing backup, and around me in all the pews, people were standing, gyrating, singing along with the music that was being played by a band beside the podium. Some people had spilled into the aisles to fall over themselves, some people were on the ground rolling around like they had some sort of illness, while others mumbled gibberish to each other and smacked each other on the heads. "You may sit here," the man said, and I slipped into a back bench beside a few others who must have been newcomers, because they were all sitting uncomfortably on the benches with a similar dazed expression in their eyes.

I settled in to observe. Off to the right under a painting of Jesus flying above a crowd, a group of young women had formed a circle and were busy yelling the songs at each other. Up in front under the podium, one man holding the biggest Bible I had ever seen was laying hands on a child who appeared to be disabled or paralyzed, while a group of others danced around the duo in a circle, hands held high in the air in a grasping motion; what they were grasping for, I had no idea. Just in front of me, somebody had collapsed and was convulsing, ignored by the congregation. I almost got up to see if they needed me to call for a doctor when they popped up of their own accord and started singing again at the top of their lungs. At the front, the choir was reaching full orgasm—hands flying, twirling and screaming and bouncing and kneeling. The cacophony was in fact something that I had not expected, and I considered slipping out the back, but the fat man with the shiny shoes was watching me intently, making me feel self-conscious. I stayed. Mostly I think it was because of the smells. They were so good, when all the people I worked with stank of shit and blood and body odor and the mercurial pongs of evil. Not here; air-conditioning, flowers, and cologne. I decided to just sit back, nowhere else to be really, and observe the experience.

After what seemed like ages, the music began to wind down. The crowds started to pick themselves up off the floor, the spinning choir sat down to catch their breath, and the fat woman with the wig at the front who had been belting out a version of a song "Jesus Loves Me" became quieter, and quieter, and quieter still. An enchantress skillfully bringing her disciples down from their frenzy. The frothy mouthed wiped away their drool. Those strewn across the ground like in the aftermath of a battle picked themselves up delicately, straightening their Sunday dress. At the front, the people who had been healed hobbled back. I assumed that the healers' work took a while to kick in. Together they all folded themselves into the pews to await the sermon.

Then he came, the man I only assumed was, well, the boss I guess. Dressed in a robe black and purple, covering his entire body and held together by a massive golden cross that hung from a thick chain around his neck. His smile was radiant, white, and perfect, his hair neat and short cropped. He was broad chested and strong, his gut containing the force of his power as he berated the assembly.

"You, who say yourselves to be Christians," he said, looking at each of us directly in the eyes. "I have seen the sin in your lives. I have seen the grime that you wish to hide from each other—which you wish to hide from God. But let me tell you—there is nothing that you can hide from God. He sees all, knows all, and watches all. Small, insignificant things, you may think. Like when you did not return the change after being overpaid"—he stared down in blistering anger at a young man far at the back—"to big things, like those who fornicate with your neighbor's wife." He was then looking at a man in the fourth row, who seemed to shrink beneath the withering gaze. "And even up to grave sins—when you murder the innocents for money." Was he staring at me? I looked behind and around and then back to the pulpit, where I met again his wrathful eyes.

"None of that can you hide from God. He sees it all and knows it all," the pastor repeated. "But there is a silver lining. He has seen everything, so nothing surprises Him, and nothing is beyond His forgiveness. Even the wickedest of you," said the pastor, looking at me again, "can be cleansed of your darkness and can find healing in God's perfect mercy."

The sermon went on, and I listened intently. Quotes, reading from that enormous Bible on the pulpit, stories and exhortations, waving hands around in the air, screaming, only to return to a whisper. I found myself leaning forward, enraptured. Never had I heard anything like this. Sure, there were the Christian charities in the camps who would force you to listen to them preach before they would give you food or allow you access to the clinic. Oftentimes there was a mass that the Catholics would orchestrate for some high-ranking white priest on his way through from somewhere to somewhere else, and if you participated, you got paid the following day. But this, the energy and purpose—well, I guess it all had a ring of truth to it. It felt not like the charades of the do-gooders but instead like something with innate power of its own, more akin to the witches' magic than the pubescent white missionaries who would come through every summer for a week, bright T-shirts sporting a cross and a logo that said "Mission Uganda" and handing out tracts to the illiterate and candy to the malnourished. Puppet shows for the impoverished.

Then all of a sudden the sermon was over, and people began shuffling from the colossal sanctuary back out into the hot African noonday sun. I stayed for a time, seated, staring at the now-empty dais, wondering what to make of that pastor and his strange but perhaps exceptional church. I had never been a man of faith. "God loves you and has a wonderful plan for your life," the missionaries to the camps always repeated, driving up in their shiny new Land Cruisers and walking delicately over the piles of shit in their shiny new tennis shoes. A plan for my life? A plan for their lives. Perhaps their refrain should instead go "God loves white people and has a wonderful plan for the lightly pigmented." He obviously couldn't give a shit about Africans. The proof is, well, pretty obvious. If this, what I have lived, is a wonderful plan, I'd hate to see what happens when God is pissed. Not that I had much frustration with God either; He was an entity without any earthly allure for me. A foreign body, a deity who may or may not be but whose existence had no relevance to my life whatsoever. Besides a little entertainment, of course; that's why African churches are always full. White money, brought over from America to make clean churches, air-conditioned with great music and oftentimes even cafeterias with free food. Who wouldn't want to be a pastor when the benefits were far beyond anything else an African could achieve? All you had to do was convince the next gullible mzungu of your sincerity and come up with a cogent salvation story, starting from such a level of depravity that it was incontrovertible proof of God's saving grace, and you were in.

Maybe this is why the pastor picked me.

"You look thoughtful." A voice came from behind me in the instant that the powerful preacher appeared at my side, sitting in the booth to my left. He had concluded the sermon while I'd been lost in thought and had left the podium, handing it over to the fat woman again, who had started where she left off—only with a new chorus this time—while people filed out of the building.

"Yes, I suppose I am," I responded.

"What strikes you about this place? I've never seen you here before," he said.

"No—it's my first time. I heard the music, and I came. I enjoy music."

"We Africans are good at music! And my choir is the best in the city," he boasted.

"Well deserved. They must practice a lot," I said.

"Every evening."

"Well, keep it up. It's working for you," I said, and the pastor bellowed a powerful laugh.

"Dominic," the pastor said, reaching out his hand.

"Charles," I responded, taking the outstretched hand. The shake was firm, not like the limp fish of the foreigners in the camps who always looked nervous about any physical contact with us and hurriedly slathered sanitizer all over after a handshake, hoping we didn't notice. We noticed.

"I sense that you have questions," Dominic the pastor said.

"Well," I responded, "this is all new to me. Not that I disagree or anything—but, well, I was just curious. It's just that, well, this is my first time, and you know ..."

"Spit it out," said Dominic the preacher, smiling.

"All that, well, mayhem," I said. "What was that about?"

Dominic laughed deeply, and the mirth was genuine and charming. "The Holy Spirit works in each of our lives in different ways. Some people prefer to sit and contemplate the greatness of God from the back—soaking ourselves in the Spirit's presence. Others experience God through acts of service, and still others with acts of abandon that allow the Spirit to fill them without trying to control Him through their mind and their reason. They prefer the pure power of His presence. The apostle Paul in his letter to the Corinthians talked about 'the tongues of men and of angels' that had been ratified when the Holy Spirit took over the bodies of the first Christians during Passover, as it says in Acts, in order to allow them to give the message of Jesus to people whose languages they didn't even know. The Holy Spirit's power is real—and beyond our understanding. We do not judge it. We provide a safe place for people to experience it."

"It was quite a ruckus," I said, trying to not sound judgmental.

"Yes," he said, "I know it can look that way to the outsider. You'll get used to it. Who knows? Maybe the spirit will fill you one day and you will also commune with God through tongues."

"What were they doing up at the front? I couldn't catch it. It was far away."

"Those were acts of healing," Dominic said. "We have a healer here—and today she was healing people with physical maladies."

"Does that work?" I asked.

"It is not the healer's power that makes it work or not; healing is given by God based upon the measure of the faith of he who is seeking intervention. The healer is just a conduit of God's power. Here at this church, she's a woman who is especially sensitive to God's energies moving around the world and has given her life to be God's implement to show a hurting world His love and continued presence."

"In the camps," I said, letting it slip before I realized what I'd said. I decided to continue anyway. *Who cares if this man knows where I am from?* "We had a witch who would make potions from the bark of trees and berries she found in the forest, mixed with frog's legs and egg shells and other such stuff to cure our maladies. She charged only a few shillings; but then again, she wasn't very effective."

"Our healer is not a witch," Dominic said, frowning. "The traditional healers are children of the devil, doing his bidding for their own benefit—for power on earth."

"Oh, I didn't mean to offend. Just thinking out loud I guess …" My voice trailed off.

"And the camps, huh?" he said.

"Indeed. Okay." I stood swiftly. "Well, I'd better be moving on." And I vaulted over the pew and rushed out of the hall without even saying goodbye.

I started showing up at the church more regularly. I would slip into the back when nobody was looking. I came mostly for the music, but I would stay to listen to what Dominic said. It was often about forgiveness and mercy but also about responsibility to repent and the blood of Jesus that would wash my sins clean. Wash my sins clean? That sounded to me especially unlikely because, well, my sins were particularly egregious. Even I knew this. Even an Acholi from the camps knows that the price for death is, well, death. "An eye for an eye," as Dominic had said once from the pulpit. But I couldn't stay away even if I'd wanted to. I was drawn to the glorious stories of how God responds to hurting souls. Not that I ever admitted that I was hurting, but it was good to hear, that message was. And slowly I started to become involved. In a bold act of abandon, I joined the choir. Pastor Dominic gave me a blue satin robe and a songbook all my own that I practiced sometimes in my container, my dog watching me quizzically and perhaps wondering if her master had finally gone mad. I would collect offerings, showing up early to help distribute the Orders of Worship to the incoming parishioners. I would stay late, cleaning up, sweeping, collecting the tiny plastic cups used for the communion once a month, straightening the hymn books. Vacuuming. Odd jobs. It made me feel useful, like I was doing something, somehow, to make up for—well for who I was.

One Saturday night before church, while I was practicing belting out "Are We Like Sheep," my cell phone rang.

"We need you," the voice said.

"Yes," I responded. No was never an option. I got dressed and went to the rendezvous.

"Get in," a voice said. A different voice, a different group. We drove quietly toward the lake, down in Entebbe. As we approached the airport, we took a right-hand turn onto a bumpy dirt road that was tree-lined. But just as we were arriving at the whitewashed house, I heard gunfire. For the life of a thug, you learn quickly that gunshots always mean things are going wrong.

"Stop the car!" one of my companions yelled, and the truck brakes slammed, causing the truck to slide into the ditch. All of a sudden, the gunfire arrived close, a few of the rounds hitting the side of the truck, and I jumped out of the door on the left side, which was sticking up into the air, and started to run, hearing the gunfire behind, the occasional bursts around me and the sound of feet pounding on the road. I threw a furtive glance over my shoulder to see if it was me that was being chased, and I saw not the police, which I had expected, but some of the military who had been guarding a house. One of my coconspirators was running beside me, and I puffed out, "What ... the ... hell ... are the ... military doing here?"

"We were going ..." my friend puffed, "to steal weapons ... from a weapons depot."

"What?" I asked, and looked back just in time to get the full beam of a flashlight in the face, but only after the burst of light had illuminated our pursuer. I had seen him, and he had seen me.

This didn't matter so much, although I usually operated with a mask and had forgotten it at home in my rush to leave that evening. What mattered more was I thought I recognized my pursuer. Being in better shape, it didn't take me long to outpace him, and as things went, it wasn't even very problematic. Except that it weighed on me. Was he from the choir? The man who had looked at me from behind Pastor Dominic with curiosity? Or was I making it up? I did not want to stop going to that church, it being the only wholesome thing about my life besides Ruth, and the only one that was not a complete lie. But if it was him, he'd seen me.

All this put me in a foul mood, and I arrived back to my container in a blackness that presaged bad decisions, as it always had in the past.

"Good morning!" Dominic said after the sermon and as the people were clearing out. "We missed you in the choir." I had spent the sermon with my hand over my face, looking up to the choir in an attempt to decide whether or not my pursuer was about to ruin both my life and perhaps my job. I hadn't wanted to come, but damned if I was going to let fear interfere with my life. At one point, I had to know one way or the other anyway.

"Good?" I sneered.

"Well, bright and cool at any rate." His joke that fell flat. I only glowered before standing up.

"Well, I better get going." Confident that it had been my imagination, but my heart still beating heavily, I made to head toward the exit.

100

"What are you doing now?" Dominic said, perhaps sensing something was wrong.

"Nothing."

"Why don't we eat something?" he asked.

"Okay," I said, still angry but also hungry. Chinese, I hated Chinese food. I hated everything Chinese. Add that to the fact that our meal was constantly interrupted by people coming up to Dominic, telling him how much they appreciated the sermon. How happy they were about a memorial service for their father who had passed. How grateful they were that their son had been healed. All the while, I sat there looking stupid, feeling stupider.

"I've been watching you," he said between interruptions.

"Yes? And?" I said between mouthfuls of noodles.

"You seem hungry for something. Like you are looking for a way out."

"A way out of what?" I snapped, putting my fork down and leaning back, throwing my arm across the back of the booth behind me.

"I don't know. Some mess you're in. Your life maybe. Your past, your future. How can I know if you don't tell me?"

"Don't you people read minds?" I asked sarcastically.

"No, my son," he said, without smiling. "We are not psychics, beholden to the devil like the people from your camps—of which you refuse to speak. We are simply men and women who believe in the power of God in our lives, are on the lookout for the messages He wishes to deliver to us, and know that the world around is His vessel. That He can do as He wishes—He is not constrained by the laws of the physical universe. He wrote them after all, didn't He? Yet we also know that God is not duplicitous and does not seek to confuse His children. He merely knows when to show Himself, when He is sought after."

We had both finished our meal, and Dominic had paid, leaving a generous tip. We walked down the street beside shops selling electronics: TVs, computers, sound systems—things I had never owned. In the camps, there is no electricity and no power outlets to run any of it, unless you have a generator. Only the white people have generators, behind their ten-foot walls with razor wire where we who are from the camps can hear the pounding music, the laughter, and the occasional splash as somebody jumps into the swimming pool while we wait for hours for water or our women go further afield to save time and risk being raped by somebody or somebody else. The television that broadcasts the football scores as we crouch around a battery radio listening to a world beyond our grasp. The whirring of the air-conditioning when all we know is sweat.

Dominic was looking at me curiously and then back to the store. "God loves you ..."

"... and has a wonderful plan for my life?" I said, filling in the rest.

Dominic smiled sadly. "I know it must not seem like that could be so. I don't know your story—you won't tell me. However, I do know many, many stories. So few of them are good."

"What do you want from me?" I asked.

"It's not what I want. It's what God wants. I'm not trying to be flippant or facile. I'm not a white man. I don't have to pretend that I believe everything just goes away when you make the choice to follow God. But I do know that with discipline, finding your faith, and starting to make one good decision after another and another, and then another, pretty soon your life begins to straighten out as well. Do you want that?" Dominic asked.

"Your God," I said, knowing I was about to say things I would regret. "What does He think about death?"

"Death is not the end," Dominic said. "He hopes people believe in Him in order for them to cheat death."

"No, I don't mean that. I mean little babies with bloated bellies and flies crawling out of their noses. I mean women dying of AIDS because they were raped by a soldier. I mean a man having to choose which son will live and which son will die, because he only has one cup of rice."

"God does not promise it will be easy ..."

"No, that's pretty fucking obvious." I said. "What I do know," I went on, "is that your God, whatever His motivations, really hates us Africans."

"No, that's unfair," Dominic said. "It's unfair because all those things, He lived them too. He made common cause with humanity not by coming to live in the suburbs and eating in fancy restaurants but to be poor and bored and angry and, in the end, murdered. That's all I can say, Charles, my friend. That you can't one up him in the misery department." And the preacher grew silent. "So do you want a better life?" he asked again.

"I suppose I do," I said, a little deflated and knowing full well I really couldn't imagine how that would even be possible.

It wasn't like the movies or the stories you hear about people's conversions. There was no weeping—at least not yet—and there was no great laundry list of my sins in front of the crowd. Not even was there a prayer, Dominic saying, "Repeat after me," and me mouthing words like an incantation that would somehow transfer my accounts from Satan's to God's. We just agreed.

"You must renounce the things that I see in you, just behind your eyes. Whatever it is that gives your eyes that look of both predator and prey. That you must surrender."

I knew what he was talking about, even if he did not.

"Will you?" he asked.

"Yes, I will," I lied. I liked to make people satisfied and happy. Besides, we from the camps are taught at an early age to open every door that you come to, because you never know what could be behind it, and if it was more misfortune, well, we already had that in spades. Who would even notice? I opened the door, entering into my new life: star-crossed lover of a poor little rich girl, born-again believer, and thug. What could possibly go wrong?

Naturally, despite what I told Dominic, I had no intention whatsoever of renouncing my sole source of income and what amounted to the greatest power I'd ever had. People feared me. When they saw me coming, they would run. Sometimes grown men—men of industry or position—would kneel before me and grovel, looking up, hands clasped in front of them as they whined. And money such as I'd never had, never imagined I could have. It was really more about the money than the power. I could give up the power, the fear, the respect, but deny the money? Walk away from a world without want to return to a time when hunger was my constant companion? I was no stranger to the hunger. I had lived with it for many years. The gnawing in the morning. The pangs of my stomach, even after "eating." Looks of longing and thoughts of violence as I saw bread or bags of chips, wondering if I could steal them yet knowing that everybody knew who I was. These days, I can't remember the last time I was hungry—the last time my belly rumbled and I had to fill it with dirt in order to sleep. Give that up? For what? "The Lord will provide," Dominic would say confidently. Easy to be confident with a thousand people turning over their own money freely every Sunday morning; it was quite a scam really, if you could make it work. The Lord will provide? What am I supposed to do in the meantime—starve? And what if He doesn't? He never has before, so certainly His track record could be found wanting.

"You must also renounce worldly pleasures," Dominic had said.

Renounce worldly pleasures? Renounce Ruth? She was the only pleasure in a life of deprivation. The only itch that had ever been scratched. Oh, sure, there had been sex in the camps. The girl from the neighboring tukul—lying together bored and dirty in the grasslands. The occasional white charity worker who wanted to go native in order to make her African adventure complete—thin, limp, listless, paranoid love. Making me wear two condoms out of panic at who I was. But there had never been anything like Ruth. Those who are accustomed to refined sex probably don't know what I'm talking about. Sex is sex, right? You huff and puff, tussle, tumble until you finish; a little explosion and a brief feeling of release. Satisfying hunger pangs, right? Does your stomach really care whether that hunger is satisfied by a filet mignon steak perfectly cooked or a piece of day-old bread? Naturally, that question itself is foolishness; despite what white people say, they who can afford both and choose the latter out of convenience or laziness or their great cloud of uncaring. Nor is it the correct metaphor. The pleasure of sublime sex is closer to that slippery slope of intoxication. For rich white people, they don't understand that either. "A distinction without a difference," I'm sure they say. They get drunk on local beer—or a bottle of expensive wine bought from a store in Kampala. It's about getting wasted at one of their parties, "working hard and partying harder" as the justification for their debauchery. But for a boy from the camps, the contrast is extreme. Because exalted sex is not the difference between a bottle of eight-thousand- or ten-thousand-shilling wine. It is the difference between sitting under a tree getting drunk on banana gin fermented with gasoline and a bottle of South African red wine atop a rocky outcropping, gazing at the setting sun.

The first is an attempt at escape, the second to embrace. The first is quick and violent, while the second is slow, an act of love—self-love above all but also love of life and love of humanity. The first is harsh and bitter; the second is smooth as silk. That moment of release, under the tree, comes as an act of violent unknowing until the next morning when you walk shamefully away, head splitting and body aching from the toxins. For the latter, the realizations are a growing awareness opened by the bouquet of a life more abundant.

Renounce Ruth? Hell no.

Now, I'd never given much thought to my own duplicity. It had come naturally, keeping my own counsel and telling people what I knew they wanted to hear in order to get what I wanted. But this was more complicated. The stakes were higher. My employers were unforgiving. I knew that very well. Ruth, well, she knew nothing, and I don't think she even suspected, not where I came from or who I was and certainly not what I did. When pushed to the wall, if she became too inquisitive as to the source of my reckless wealth, I would tell her about a job as an entrepreneur. She often asked about my past, my family, but I made insinuations about personal tragedy that had cost me everything, and she backed off, nodding in understanding. Dominic the preacher was harder still. Though not clairvoyant, he certainly did have a sixth sense about things and would often grill me about my life. I suppose religion gives people the belief that they have the right to pry, but he was relentless, forcing me to come up with ever-more creative means of deceit.

And so I lived like this for a season. Engaging in the only work that I knew, the violence now a part of my soul, still tormented by the faces so that I could barely sleep. The only time I was at peace was when I was at church, singing hymns and carrying out the service that I came to know well, and when I was in Ruth's arms.

Every Wednesday night and on Sundays, I would work the flock with Dominic. Cleaning the sanctuary, ordering the hymnals, counting the tithes, refilling the communion wafers and wine, ordering the papers. It was quiet work mostly, with a lot of time to think. I would rehearse for the choir two or three times a week. I would engage in the social work: food kitchens that Dominic had set up to feed the poor; building houses for church members who were without. But never once did he ask me to lead a service or even pray. I would find him watching me carefully at the oddest moments. When I returned from the office behind the sanctuary, while I was polishing the brass cross at the front, I would turn to find him there—sitting in the front pew, eyes locked on me. Not frowning but certainly not smiling either. Just staring.

The rest of the time I spent with Ruth. This was hard. She had graduated the previous year and was receiving increasing pressure from her father to commit to the field of study of which he approved—namely being a doctor, a plastic surgeon specifically. But, much to his chagrin, she told him that she wanted to take a year off to "find herself" and to work to earn some of her own money before committing to another decade of study. Little did her oblivious father know that she really just wanted to spend time with me. We met as often as our circumstances allowed, between her job—she had taken a position at the ice cream parlor—and my duties, "managing my multiple investments" as I told her cryptically. We would go to the movies, eat at restaurants, and sometimes even go farther afield to find places for us alone. Swimming naked in ponds in the hills, climbing the great trees in the forest, making love in the branches with the monkeys. Talking quietly, always about the future, a future that in her mind was clear and bright, and my future, which was an ever-more-sophisticated work of fiction.

We never talked about us; it was assumed still that we were engaged in a fling. She knew quite well she could not avoid university forever, and as for me, a boy without a past does not need to concern himself with the future, does he?

A delicately balanced life.

Then in a giant blast of fate, it all broke down.

CHAPTER 10

"Ah, there you are," said Amin, the great mountain of a man with the scar running down the left side of his face, across his eye, which had become milky, who was my minder. He had no name; there were no names among my colleagues. Slim and The Chino were the only monikers we needed. I was The Boy or sometimes Junior. Amin: because he had no soul.

"I'm right on time," I said as I walked through the side door of the warehouse in the industrial section of town that served as our nerve center and as such was open day and night for our particular brand of industry. There were office rooms at the back, padlocked reinforced bunkers with different types of guns—a miniarsenal, really. Cars, a few benches and tables where people could eat lunch, a dirty kitchen with a big hot-water dispenser and some blackened spoons beside big, industrial-size cans of Nescafe and moth-eaten boxes of tea and sugar. At the far end, silent and ominous between a grubby bathroom and a rusted machine, the use of which nobody even contemplated, were nestled several cells used for holding people, people that needed holding, or something more gruesome for the repeat or the serious offender. The place stank of confined air, body odor of too many unwashed men, and sorry fear. "What's going on?" This was the way it worked—that is, when they didn't call me. I had moved up in the organization and gained trust, I had been introduced to this place, Guantanamo as we liked to call it, snickering at our own cleverness. I would show up and receive my orders from Amin, who had received his orders from somebody else, who in turn had received his orders from another. The higher the chain, the greater the anonymity, until finally the orders were delivered by a masked voice on the other side of a cell phone call that our senior commander—a man named The Hook, because he had a hook for a hand—would receive each day or two. I myself had only once met The Hook, when I had surprised him by returning late in the evening to Guantanamo for something that I had left on one of the tables. He had not been pleased, and I had spent the next several days looking anxiously over my shoulder.

"Received our assignment this morning," Amin said, eschewing the small talk. Anonymity doesn't breed confidence. We were all expendable, and the less our colleagues new, the safer we were if something went wrong.

"And?" I asked.

"And ... it's a little tricky."

"Isn't it always?"

"Yes, but this time it's trickier," Amin said.

"Just spill it," I said, sitting down on a bench in frustration.

"Do you know who Emanuel Bamweyana is?" he asked.

"Of course I do," I said. There was nobody in town who didn't know who Bamweyana was. He was one of the rich businessmen of the city; he owned a soap factory as well as the city's abattoir in the hills behind the town, on the road toward Entebbe, which provided the fresh meat to virtually every restaurant and supermarket in the capital.

"It seems Bamweyana is up to something and needs to be brought down a peg or two," Amin said.

"Oh," I replied. Amin was right, tricky. Because Bamweyana was also the city mayor.

"Yeah. Oh indeed," Amin said, grimacing. "We were told he needs to be taught a lesson."

"A lesson? Right. They let us come up with the plan so they can leave us hanging out to dry if it goes wrong," I said, flustered. "We're getting screwed."

"I know that," he snapped.

"How the hell does the mayor end up borrowing money from us in the first place? Can't he shake down some contractors? Steal money from the public pot? Double dip a little? Something is wrong."

"I don't think you understand, Junior," said Amin. "Bamweyana is not a client gone missing. Do you recall his campaign slogan, 'Emanuel will clean up'? Seems he's trying, and we need things to stay a little dirty."

I did remember this, of course. It had been painted in green on every kiosk and bare wall and hung from every traffic light in the city for months. "Clean up" referred to doing away with the syndicates, fighting corruption. I'd always assumed it was posturing; every African politician since the beginning of politics promised to fight corruption. The ones who were the most vociferous were usually the ones caught with the biggest piles of cash in the trunks of their cars as they tried to flee the country.

"So what are we supposed to do? We can't very well break his leg with a tire iron," I said, chuckling a little. I had done this many times in the past and was imagining the look of shock on the esteemed mayor's face.

"No, we can't."

"So how do we go about this? I'm sure he has bodyguards when he is out about town," I said.

"Yes," Amin said. "He does."

"Well then? Did the telephone give you any advice?" I asked, gesturing at the phone in the corner.

"Yes. They did."

"Well?"

"They gave us his home address," said Amin.

"Listen, slow down. Now hold on a second," I said. "I thought rule number one, and for our own protection, is 'No houses and no families.'"

"Yes, that's true."

"So?"

"So we have our orders. It is not a suggestion. It would seem he is sniffing very close to our interests and must be stopped quickly and definitively."

Late that night found Amin, myself, and three other coworkers walking slowly up the steep sidewalk in Bugolobi neighborhood. As we walked upward, the houses around us became increasingly upscale, larger and more prosperous. Three stories, dozens of rooms. The sidewalks were almost polished, the streets free from potholes. The gnarly old trees a reminder of the days of the colonialists who loved to plan their cities with their comfort in mind. One, two, three houses upward, past the residences of foreign ambassadors and the occasional tiny garden-park meticulously manicured for the luxury of the oligarchs. Then up ahead it appeared, a huge, sprawling estate surrounded by a wrought iron fence ten feet high, above which was attached a double circle of razor wire. There were floodlights facing outward and a police squad car sitting at the entrance, no police officers to be seen except for one foot that was sticking out of an open window. "Asleep," I whispered and was immediately shushed by Amin.

We cut through the alley beside the sprawling estate, looking through the iron as we walked. It was huge, several acres of greenery ending in the mansion on the top of the hill. There were ponds where early-morning crested cranes stood on one leg. A large land turtle was chewing on a bush, while several of those tiny antelopes wandered around elegantly. Flowers, birds of paradise and roses and banana plants heavy with fruit, lent the heavenly scents of opulence, while the peaceful tinkling of a trickling stream enveloped the estate in a sense of peace that was belied by what was about to occur. There wasn't a sound except the occasional screech of an old owl that was standing atop one of the iron bars, looking for a rat or a lizard or a snake. The house was every bit as imposing: huge ornamental white pillars holding up the roof above a veranda that wrapped around the house. Balconies jutting out of second-floor windows like teeth. Tall windows locked fast against the night. The main part of the house had two wings extending from the carved wooden double door. A separate building was set back a ways from the roundabout that circled a fountain to deposit visitors at the front of the building. It housed several cars as well as what seemed like the servants' quarters.

"Here." Amin pointed at two iron bars that had been bent outward, creating a narrow opening through which we squeezed one by one. When we were all in, we flitted from shadow to shade, approaching the back side of the house to poke and prod for weaknesses in the armor of the mansion. It was obvious that there was going to be an alarm on the compound and that there were probably cameras around the exterior, so we had pulled the masks over our faces, not that anybody could make out our black faces in the black night. We went window by window, looking for the telltale signs that one had been forgotten, and were rewarded with a sliver crack in a back-pantry window by the kitchen. We propped it open using a branch and one by one shinnied through the opening. I went first, dropping onto the tile floor inside the pantry. On both sides of the little room were shelves of canned goods and other dried foods—tomatoes and vegetables, pasta, rice, bottles of imported beer, spices, and all other manner and assortment of ingredients. We snuck through into the kitchen, an expansive, pristine space with a six gas-range above a double oven. There was a double-wide refrigerator that hummed quietly in the night. An island made of wood and tile sat resolutely in the center, under which rested pans and pots of all shapes and sizes, and over which hung knives magnetically stuck to a strip that was hanging from the ceiling. There was a waist-high wine refrigerator in the corner, upon which sat elegant wineglasses that glinted in the light of the moon pouring in the double windows on one side of the room. They looked out toward the back of the house, which hosted manicured bushes in the shapes of animals and five or six goliath trees that looked like prehistoric monsters staring into the house. A bowl of fruit sat on the countertop of the island. We made our way slowly toward the inside of the building.

The next room was a sitting room of sorts, expensive paintings hanging above carpets imported from Central Asia, purchased probably from the large Indian community of the city. The furniture was Victorian, overstuffed, and at one end a mammoth television hung from the wall. I'd never seen the size of it before. Then came the living room, which had a grand piano set decoratively in the corner, couches facing each other beside a fireplace, over the mantel of which hung an old painting that might have been purchased from an auction house in London. End tables with vases sitting atop them, fresh cut flowers giving the room a sickly-sweet smell. There was a winding staircase to the upstairs rooms on the left, while on the right, double doors headed out to the front driveway and the fountain.

We were headed upstairs.

We had decided that the best way to deliver a message to the mayor was through roughing up his one of his children. Specifically, Amin had found out that the man had two sons, one still in grade school and

111

another who was at university. The son was back from university. It was summer, and we were going after the firstborn. Not to hurt him badly, not necessarily, a little bruise here or there, visible but not damaging, for effect this time, mostly to scare his father away.

We crept down the hallway, our footsteps muffled by the long hall rug of oriental design. On the walls were family pictures that we couldn't see in the darkness, not that we were taking the time to look at the rich man's memories. Doors opened off the hallway at intervals, and we had no way of knowing where the boy slept. The first door was ajar, and I looked in and found it empty, elegantly furnished for guests. The second door on the left was a bathroom. There were three more doors down this hallway, and I—still leading the little expedition—opened the next door on the right. It was pitch black, but I could hear muffled breathing.

"This must be it," I whispered.

We waited beside the door to the room that was now slightly ajar. Inside, we heard voices, giggling, and the occasional bump.

"He's awake," I whispered to Amin.

"So?" the ogre said. "We go in hard and fast, like we planned."

One, two, and three, and we pushed in, walking deliberately into the room. It was a simple creak and some muffled footsteps, but to me it sounded like an advancing army. Amin was carrying a crowbar. I had a knife tucked into my belt, while my other colleagues had a bat, a croquet mallet, and a handgun respectively. Behind me, the door closed with a definitive click.

"Who the hell? What the fuck?" A voice, a young man's voice, strong and confident echoed through the room. Then more rustling, and the bedside lamp clicked on, and a gentle light flooded the room.

He was sitting up in bed staring at us, shock morphing slowly to anger as his rage ignited. "What the hell are you doing here? What is this about? Are you thieves, sneaking into my house at night? You will rue ... You will pay ..."

"No, boy," Amin said. "Actually, you will be the one paying tonight. Be quiet, and it will go better for you, and then you can tell your daddy about your night's lesson. When he asks what it is, you will only have to tell him, 'Look the other way.' He'll know what that means."

"Wait," the young man said, regaining a little composure. "You must understand." He was obviously hiding something. He was sitting straight and bending his torso as if he were covering something, protecting something. "Give me a minute. I will do as you wish. Just meet me in the hall."

"You think us fools, just because we are not *university* students?" Amin said, knocking his crowbar on the dresser and the chair and the door.

"I promise," the boy said. "Just please."

And then there was a whine that came from behind the boy. Amin leaped forward and yanked aside the blanket. And there she was, in bed. Behind the impossibly thin protection of the mosquito net, lying flat, nestled up against her lover, lavender and lilies covering the lower half of her body, her other hand over her chest protectively. The boy did not move, not knowing what to do. The first thing we all saw were those magnificent breasts, black nipples, pools accentuating the smooth obsidian perfection of her skin, her belly tight and supple at the same time, leading up her neck to her mouth, opened in fear with the beginnings of a scream starting to organize itself in her lungs, her perfect teeth exposed under the black eyes that watched the five intruders in terror.

It was of course Ruth, as you all have guessed. At that moment, I suppose I could have done a thousand things differently. Honor the love that I said I possessed for her, the jealousy that bubbled as I looked at her skin. But there she was, nestled up against the man I would never be. Her future, while I, a thug behind a mask at night, a fling during the day when she was bored or feeling rebellious. Impotence, the raging impotence of the camps, the flights, the humiliation and the degradation and the panic. She was mine, and I would have died for her. Then that betrayal. So you will not be surprised about what happened next either, though it should not have been so.

"Boy, this lesson just got a lot more fun," Amin whispered, putting down the tire iron.

I found myself calm, collected. In hindsight, it seems odd, but at that moment, the world slowed down, and I became surgical and precise in my decisions. I took the three catlike steps to the bedside, while behind me the four thugs were gathering their confidence. Rape does not come naturally, even to evil men. It requires some internal convincing. Rape. The word rattled through my mind, filling me with rage and impunity and a demonic sense of, well, jealously again. I pulled aside the mosquito net and pulled my knife from my belt, slamming it into the chest of the college boy before he could even respond, before he knew even what had happened. And I held it there, whispering the words, "Easy, easy, easy," until he stopped moving. I then withdrew the knife, wiping it on the bedsheets, and turned around to face my crew, who were looking at me in confusion, except Amin, who was only eying Ruth.

Amin was approaching. "You first, or me?" he asked.

"Now we must go," I whispered.

"What? Why the hell would we do that?" he hissed back.

"Just trust me," I said. "This won't go well for us."

"Get the hell out of my way," Amin said, walking to within arm's length of me, starting to fiddle with his belt buckle.

"No, I won't," I said.

"Junior, you better. Look at her." I hazarded a glance. Ruth's eyes had filled again with fear, white-hot and perfect. She was hunching over, caressing the body of her dead lover, tears flowing freely from her eyes. I felt myself raising my hand, bringing it down to smack her across the face at the same instant as my other hand, with the knife held in its vicelike grip, flashed upward in a glint of steel from the lamplight glistening off the twelve-inch blade and found the soft part in Amin's upper abdomen below the ribs. It had been a wicked blow, but I kept pushing. The knife, sharpened over bored hours in the warehouse and anxious moments of uncertainty, slipped effortlessly upward through the stomach and lungs to lodge itself in Amin's heart. An explosion of bright red blood covered me, the blanket, the mosquito net, the rugs on the floor and the polished wood under the rugs, and Ruth, joining instantly with the blood of the other man in a bizarre eternal union. He slumped over the bed and finally tumbled to the floor at my feet.

The other three intruders just stood for a second. The confusion that had filled their simple eyes was being slowly replaced by uncertainty and fear. "Now we leave," I said as I stood, seizing the moment of leadership that Amin's death at my hands had provided.

"But … what the … how … why did you …?" the one with the bat chattered.

I just ignored them, grabbing them one by one by the collar and pushing them toward the door.

"But what if he's not dead?" said one of them and made to turn back until he received a blow from the hilt of the knife just over his ear.

"Maybe we should kill her?" another offered before I also cracked him on the skull.

"No, you fools. Don't make things worse. Flee.

"Go. Go. Go," I just kept repeating, an order whispered firmly. They had no understanding of what had just happened; all they knew was they would obey the man who had proven himself, like a stronger alpha male in a pack of wolves. Things had gone very, very wrong. The lust had vanished from their eyes, replaced by the flight reflex, and they stumbled to open the door to fall over each other into the hall, with me herding them ever away from Ruth.

My Ruth.

I knew it was all over. Of course it was. Like the lifeblood of Amin, of her lover, my love for Ruth had boiled over, flowing from my veins onto the floor, forever mixed with jealousy and inferiority in a toxic potion that I still drink today. If I had it to do over again, I don't know what I would have done. No passion has ever recovered from a betrayal so cavernous with such abominable consequences. Sure, nobody had touched her, but she would live forever with the presence of those five men in her room. I saw her in all her nakedness as she sat unmoving, a nakedness that would remind her always now of them, and me always of *him*. I didn't know if she'd heard my voice—if she knew it was me. I didn't care, although I would have liked her to know that it was me who ended her tryst, her forbidden tryst. Except of course that what I always knew, the truth that I never wanted to accept, was assaulting me even as I fled the house: *college boy was her love, and I was her forbidden tryst.*

My mind was a blur as we raced back through the house back to the pantry and through the window into the darkness beyond, frantically scrambling to identify any way that I might be able to salvage the situation. Unfortunately, any plan started with the murder of my three confederates, which I realized immediately was impossible. They were on guard—naturally—and while I was running in front, leading the retreat, they were refusing to even approach me. It was clear that they were also in the process of figuring out how to save themselves when the questions started about our epic failure, and all fingers would point to me. I would be tortured.

We sprinted across the lawn toward the bent fence and had just shinnied our way through to the sidewalk beyond when they came for me. They'd been whispering behind me while we ran, their voices coming through in ragged bursts, and I caught the gist of the plan, which was no plan at all really. Grab me, knock me unconscious, return me to the warehouse, and hold me until somebody more important than the dead Amin came to find out what the hell had happened, at which point they would tell their story, which would be the truth mixed with a dose of conjecture, and then hand me over to the knives and car batteries. Taking them by surprise, as soon as I was through, I sprinted in the direction of the lazing police car at the front of the mansion we had just violated. I could hear the pounding of their footsteps on the pavement of the sidewalks behind me as I careened around the corner and headed for the front of the mansion. There were two policemen in the cruiser—a donation to the municipality of Kampala from the Japanese government, still emblazoned with the flag of Japan—and I ran up to them with a look of innocence and fear.

"Help me," I said, feigning panic.

"What seems to be the problem?" they both responded in unison, instantly alert and reaching for their sidearms, seeing the blood splattered all over me as I came beneath the streetlight. At that time, the three thugs rounded the corner.

"They are after me. I don't know who they are," I said, gesturing behind me.

"Wait here," they told me, and they started the car to drive down to confront the three, who saw immediately what was going on and turned to sprint in the opposite direction. The cruiser picked up speed to pursue them in the universal rationale of the police: if it runs, it must be guilty. I turned the other direction, running until I hit the first intersection and then turning to careen down side roads in the attempts to lose both of my potential pursuers.

My breath came in even, short bursts, and my footsteps pounded on the pavement in the quiet Kampala morning, before the sun was even up, as I made distance between myself and danger. When I was well out of the Bugolobi neighborhood and certain I had not been chased, I sat on the curb to catch my breath and examine my options, which were—I realized—extremely limited. My employers, whoever they were, would most likely kill me. If I got lucky, I would die quickly. Not the end I had granted many people. *What goes around comes around, I suppose.*

As I sat there, I went down the checklist of my options. I knew without even finishing that I only had one option, besides fleeing into the jungles again, which would offer a modicum of comfort and which I had been carefully tending for months. Dominic. Didn't the Christians preach forgiveness? Weren't they always talking about the power of Jesus to forgive even the most abhorrent sins? Maybe Dominic had the answer. Maybe finally I was being led in the direction of the church. I had never had any faith, not really. I knew that. My relationship with the church was purely utilitarian. But who knew that?

"I need your help," I said. It was later that morning, and I was sitting in the overstuffed chair in front of Dominic's imposing wood desk in his grandiose office behind the auditorium of the church. He sat in his leather chair on the other side, under a picture of the blond, blue-eyed European Jesus that the white Christians love so much. There was no computer on the desk; Dominic thought they were the tool of the devil that made you waste your time and were portals to Godless places controlled by the devil. As he had told me a thousand times.

"What is the trouble?" Dominic said. He was wary this morning, which made me nervous. Something told me he was having a bad day, and if I had an option, I would have postponed this meeting until I saw that the big man was in a more forgiving mood. But time was one thing I did not have.

"I. I don't really know how to ... well, how to say ... I, perhaps, maybe ..."

"You have never been what you claimed to be. Although you claimed to be nothing," Dominic said. "I was not born yesterday, my good boy. But the time has come, it appears, for you to tell me your story."

"It is true," I said. "I have deceived you and God." Without further recourse, I began to tell him my story. I told him about the humiliation and powerlessness of the camps. I told him about the great evils of the rebels and the terrible violence that still permeated my days and nights. I told him about my theft, my flight.

"That's quite a story," said Dominic. "But I sense that's not everything."

"Can we just leave it there?" I pleaded. "Can we just say that I have sinned and need to be forgiven? That I'm ready for it?"

"No," he said firmly. "That, above all things, we cannot do."

I sighed and continued the story. I told him about Ruth, and he seemed somewhat sympathetic. Then, finally, I told him about my work, what I did to pay for the clothes I wore and the tithes I gave every Sunday and the food that I brought to share with the less fortunate. As I spoke of the violence, his countenance began to change, to harden somehow. He pursed his lips in a slight frown, and his brow began to furrow. I told him everything I dared, up to the previous night's encounter, but leaving out Ruth and the fate of college boy and making the story seem as if I had rebelled against the mobsters in a fit of guilt. I finished, and we sat in silence. And we sat, and sat and sat longer.

"That is it then?" Dominic said at last.

"Yes, that is it."

"What is it you want from me?"

I was startled. No kind words, no words of forgiveness, nothing about Jesus. I breathed deeply, steading myself, and responded, "I would like you to send me somewhere I will be safe. I would like you to give me work in a foreign land where I will dedicate myself to the service of God. I will be your greatest priest, your most committed monk. Your most valued soldier. Anywhere you want, I will go there. War zones, places that nobody else will dare. I am ready"—I took a deep breath—"to commit myself to the faith of Christ. You say people have moments when Christ talks to them, conversion moments. Well, this is my moment. I am Saul on the road to Damascus. I am ready to change it all."

I had made my pitch. I sat quietly while he contemplated all I had told him.

Again the silence extended, until he finally spoke. "Jesus once told a parable about a wayward son of a rich man. This man had two sons, in fact. One was committed and a hard worker and faithful to his father's land and labor. The other sun was a gambler, a swindler, a fornicator. A drunk. In a fit of wantonness, he went to his father and asked him early for his inheritance. His father, who loved his son, sold his assets to give his son what he did not deserve but was his birthright by tradition. The boy took the money and blew it on parties and girls and debauchery. But that life does not abide—it cannot prove lasting—and in time, the son returned to his father, repentant. He asked his father to allow him back into his house, in a position of a servant, somebody who would feed the pigs and water the mules. But the father was gracious, and he took his son back, throwing a grand party for him and reintroducing him to the family as a rightful member of the rich man's family."

As I listened to the story, I began to become hopeful. Perhaps Dominic would offer me the solution I so longed for; maybe I was to be saved. Perhaps there was something to this Christianity.

"This is the story that you pretend to tell me." Dominic's mood had not changed. His lips remained hard, his countenance grim. "There is a different story that Jesus also told. In the book of Matthew. He talked there about the false prophets. Those who carried out works in Jesus's name but who inwardly were wicked and evil. For a time, they did good works that were attributed to the power of God, but inside they were rotten like a fig that has fallen to the ground. Like a beautiful flower that is in fact a thistle. When the end came, they appealed to Jesus for entry into the holy kingdom. But Jesus told them, 'We know them by their fruits. Because good trees bear good fruits, while bad trees bear bad fruits.' Your fruits, Charles, are bad fruits. Despite that you pretended to do good things, your heart was full of wickedness and evil. At the end of this story, when Jesus finally spoke, he addressed these evildoers. He told them, 'I never knew you. Depart from me, you workers of lawlessness.'"

Dominic finished the story and said nothing further. However, I understood perfectly the message. I stood, bowing from the waist. "Thank you, Dominic, for all your kindness."

He said nothing, remaining seated in his chair, unmoved.

"What you have done for me, I will be thankful for it. Though now, at the end, you have proven what I always knew, that I am not good, not wanted in anybody's eyes. Thank you for confirming this. That I am not even worthy of forgiveness, that I am wholly a child of darkness. Damned and wretched forever." I turned my back to Dominic—the preacher—and started walking.

Yes, that is what I told that fat preacher those many years ago. However, what was really in my mind, though I did not have the words for it yet, what I should have said, what I have repeated to myself over and over and over again in the hopes of having it perfectly memorized should I ever see that man again, was, "And thank you, also, for adding some clarity to this thing you call 'faith' and 'salvation.' You see, I always doubted that the things which you so enthusiastically and skillfully extolled from the terrifying heights of your pulpit were in fact true. Scams and schemes I've known forever, and the little voice in my heart told me that what you preach about is in fact bullshit. Made to convince the weak minded to hand over money with which you purchase power and position. Thank you for confirming that for me. You throw me out to the 'weeping and gnashing of teeth'— yes, I listened when you preached. But what have I done that is so much worse than what you do? Sure, I am of the devil. You'll find no argument from me there. But the money I have taken, people are under no illusions as to why. They know very well what I'm up to, and if I come for them, they know exactly the reasons. But you. You are the greatest liar of all, demanding money from the innocent as the price of admittance to participate in a fairy tale."

And that was how, that fateful day, I lost my love, my religion, and my livelihood, the day I strode into the full waxing of my wickedness, slamming the door to the office in the back of the church on my way out. As I passed through the sanctuary, I overturned the altar, grabbed the sacramental wine bottle that was under the podium, and took a long, deep drink before hurling it behind me at the massive cross hung from the wall. I bet you think you've had bad days before, you who are reading this. Let me assure you, you've never had a day like that. It was a harbinger of what was to come.

So I started walking. North, because where else would I go? I could not flee the country. I had no papers, nowhere to go, nobody to receive me. I could not stay, hunted through the sewers and slums. I took the chance to return to my container, put on fresh clothes, and pack a small bag of everything I could carry. I hugged Dog; she wagged her tail and licked my face of the tears that were flowing freely at my realization that her, too, I must abandon. She would have followed me, but I knew that I would only bring about her destruction; like everything else that I touched, her continued association with me would cause her death. I had a wad of money in my pocket from my last jobs, and I took a taxi to the far end of the city and then started walking up the highway.

Several hours later, when I had some distance between myself and Kampala, I went off the road, found a tree that provided shade, and I wept. I wept for my wretchedness, abandoned by everybody, including God. I wept for the loss of everything I had dreamed could be, foolish dreams I now knew, but my dreams nonetheless. And I wept for my future, which spread out before me like a dark night, without even a tiny light to illuminate any path. I wept for Dog, the only consistent love I had known. I wept for the money that would no longer come to purchase basic luxuries, food—even the water I would drink. I wept for a past as barren as the future would be. But mostly I wept for Ruth. I wept because of what she had done to me, and what I had almost let happen to her. I wept at what we had lost, for a love that would never be, for a night, a single night that would be my constant companion forever. For the moments of sheer, perfect pleasure. Of abandon that was not reckless and her presence, which had been the only thing that filled that dark hole in my heart. I thought of her smell—her smile. Her eyes that twinkled playfully. Her beauty that knew no equal. I knew she would be fine; a fling is what she would call it. If she talked about it at all. With a boy from the camps, a criminal, an act of youthful recklessness. She would go to university. She would have children and eventually grandchildren. She would travel—see exotic places and learn about wonderful things. She would experience great moments, entertain epic ideas, and nourish lofty visions. She would have love. All of this she would have. Juxtaposed against this, the life I saw laid out before me was to consist of a series of endless struggles one after the other unto death. For all this I wept, and when I was spent, I lay down in the puddle of my tears, sleeping deeply and dreaming of nothing.

CHAPTER 11

⟨⟨◦⟩⟩

The first time I saw the line of uncut rock, I retched. Staring in disbelief at the piles of stones stretching into infinity before my eyes, something deep in the pit of my gut seized up, and I doubled over, squatting on my haunches to deflect from the panic while I choked back the bitterness, the despair, and the futility. That was the moment, I think, that I came to terms with the knowledge that it would never get any better for me, that I was to be forever a day laborer upon the fields of my betters, and that there was nothing for a black man in Africa. Not that up until that point my life had been easy. The road from the camps to the rocks had been heartbreaking, as you already have learned. And not that I had sought actively the path of darkness, as you also know. But it was from that moment on, I think, that I knew in my heart that the answer for me would not be found in attempts at work of any kind. Certainly not the work for which *they* had me destined. The tiny businesses of my peers, funded through ridiculous little loans given out by white people with cloth-knitted love-bracelets that they gave out to each other, holding hands and kissing in the corners, pawing at each other's questionably placed tattoos. Projects paid for by foreigners where the next in the endless line of pubescent long-haired boys or angry women lectured us for hours on why we were poor, before explaining to us how our lot would improve by selling their beads back to them in the forms of bracelets or necklaces, baubles that they would take back to their families as reminders of the days they helped out a poor black man in Africa. Trifling bags of vegetable seeds stamped garishly with the name of this or that charity on them, which we were supposed to plant in order to try to coax a paltry profit from a land that no longer gave generously.

But neither would it come from the work of the muscle, inflicting injury for profit, a fear peddler. Money earned through that dark profession drained away like ice guarded in a jeans pocket for safekeeping, only to realize when looking for it that it had long ago vanished in the African afternoon. The life of a thug was worthless, expendable, and anonymous. That life was over. I would miss the money but not the nightly visits of the ghosts, although little did I know that what was to come would be so very much worse.

All of that—at any rate—had been a long time before; it had been three years since I had walked out of the little office in the big church in Kampala. Three years since I had lost hope. The journey from the city to the road had been tumultuous and meaningless: working the harvests of others, life as a street vendor in a forgotten town, security guard guarding other people's money—ironically. All to arrive at the rocks, where I stood with a pick in my hand and an uncut row of rocks marching out in front of me in an unbroken line over the horizon. This job was, however, significant, because it was then that I met Frederich, who would prove my salvation. Twice.

"What wrong with you?" the Chinese foreman barked in bad English.

"Nothing." I breathed deeply once, twice, three times, swallowing hard to control the lump in my throat that no water would wash away, not that I had any.

"Good. Then you start here," and he threw a fist-size rock he'd been fingering at the large pile in front of me, kicking up small shards and a tiny plume of dust. Slowly I bent and picked up my tool, folding my fingers around the rough wood. It was heavy, substantial to lift. Decisive. I approached my first rock, contemplating the task at hand for a moment. It was light brown and smooth but with jagged edges, the size maybe of a wild river turtle that frequented the ponds where I used to swim naked as a boy, careful as I skinny-dipped lest the animal mistake my growing manhood for discarded fruit and rob me of my sons. I raised the pick high, the rough steel only reflecting the African sun at the very tip, polished as it had been through years of use; the rest was black, black as charcoal, black as the African night when there was no moon. I drew it back as my arm gave energy and purpose to the tool, bringing it down with determination upon a crease in the stone. To my satisfaction, the rock sliced neatly in two, with tiny splinters ricocheting toward my unprotected eyes as I ducked to avoid them. Slowly, starting with a tingle in the palms of my hands, the vibration journeyed up my arms, turning them to wax as it traveled into my torso and up my neck, finding at last my teeth, which chattered like the time I climbed the mountain in the north in search of the big wild goats after the rebels had murdered all our cows. "This is ridiculous," I said through the chattering, teeth still moving of their own accord as I threw down the pick.

"Pick up fucking pick," the Chinese foreman yelled, his pudgy yellow finger pointing down to where the instrument lay humming in the dust. The Chink was wearing a pair of new blue jeans—I had been a grown man before I had ever had a new pair of jeans, a brief flash, a parenthesis in my life of need—and a yellow shirt that matched his face, the two buttons at the top undone, exposing his hairless chest over which rested a thick gold chain. Above it all, a round straw hat.

"Yes, *Kichina*," I responded, tensing my fists and taking control of my tongue—myself—as I again bent to pick up the pick. The second blow was less of a shock, and as I learned to purse my teeth and loosen my arms at the precise moment of impact, the work became less painful, or I number. Resigned. This was what I would do. This is who I would become, a cutter of rocks. But how long could I keep it up? What would happen if I were injured? This was young man's work. What about when I aged? Idle questions without an answer. I brushed them all aside—as I always did. *I probably won't live that long anyway*, my only response.

Slowly the sun climbed into the sky as I worked; I noticed because the long shadow of that unfortunate figure with the pick had grown shorter and shorter and finally disappeared. Lift—swing—strike. Bend, move the rock aside. Lift—swing—strike. Bend. Again and again in a monotonous loop while the sweat dripped down my face and chest.

"Lunch."

Thank God. I rested the pick on the next rock and turned to accept the black plastic bag from the boy on the moto who had just pulled up. All the other workers—there were thirty of us on this piece of road—crowded around the box on the back of the sputtering old motorbike that spewed black smoke as we jostled with each other to find the coldest half-liter bottle of water. Lunch in hand, I walked alone to a tree farther than the others, its thin trunk supporting a wide cover and identical to the thousands of others that grow in the sand and upon the rocky ground of Africa's grasslands.

After satiating my thirst, I poured a little of the water over my head, letting the coolness wash away the dust, and then I opened the black bag. A boiled egg and half a loaf of French bread wrapped around *nyama choma*, mystery meat bought by the stick along the byroads of east Africa. I'd once as a child considered selling the meats on sticks pushed impatiently through the windows of passing cars, but I had been unable to raise the money to buy the old hubcap where I would roast it. I shrugged, biting into the sandwich but not gratefully. How could I be grateful for this life?

"Back to work," the yellow overseer shrieked. Why do they always sound so shrill? Why are they always so angry? So cold and surgical? So inhuman? I abandoned my uneaten food under the tree where a line of large black ants was eagerly waiting to carry it piece by piece underground. I slowly stood to walk back to my rock. I hefted the pick and again found my rhythm. Lift—swing—strike. Bend. Lift—swing—strike.

This was not slavery. Not really, I suppose. I could quit. I could walk away. I could spit in the face of the Chink if I wanted. That makes me *free*, right? The word made me laugh. Really? Was I? Where would I go? What would I do? There are not many places for an African these days, especially one on the run from his past. Who has no fancy piece of paper hanging on the wall of a clean house, just a group of angry men asking for his whereabouts. Who has no family in parliament and no friends in the government, just enemies in the police. Not even the church, usually the best place for an unfortunate African to get ahead. Profess to their faith, and the white people come running with buckets of money. But even that I had tried and failed. The famous forgiveness of their God evidently does not extend to people like me who have done what I have done.

White Jesus sure doesn't like the black man.

Which makes me angrier, because I now feel foolish. Memorizing the songs and singing them loudly—louder than the others. Repeating the gibberish Dominic said would bring me closer to God, rolling my eyes back in my head and thrashing about, spit flowing down my chin. They applauded me. They were excited. They dunked me in water and gave me a robe and put me in the choir to sing. But that was before the disgrace. I'd been denied access to their seminary, where they served three meals a day and gave us all a beer at night; where people slept upon laundered sheets only two or three to each room, which was swept clean every day and the floor washed down with bleach. I'd been denied forgiveness for my sins, thrown out into the cold. Literally.

I was still for a moment, looking again at the long line of unbroken rock that crested the hill in front of me, a straight line to the Sudan it seemed, and then lift—swing—strike. Bend. Lift—swing—strike. Bend …

I worked the remainder of the day on the rock pile until the waning light made our pick strikes more often miss their mark. We then mounted the pickup truck back toward the bunkhouse. I ate alone, huddled in a corner of the patio with a plastic bowl of plantain mash salted with dried fish, shoveled to my mouth with my fingers, drinking water from a plastic orange cup and then to bed. Tossing and turning, my back aching from the work and my mind with the emptiness of life. When I could no longer fake sleeping, my bunkmates' snoring driving me to anger, I slipped out and walked a ways from the bunkhouse into the savanna, where I sat on the cold ground.

"Can't sleep either?"

I pivoted my head to look behind but could only see a sparkling white smile in the darkness. "No," I said. "I can't keep my muscles from vibrating. And every time I'm almost asleep, they twitch and jump on their own, and I'm wide awake again."

"Ja," he said, eyes sparkling. "You'll get used to it."

"I don't want to get used to it," I mumbled. Bitterness.

"Nevertheless," he said. "You will. Just keep repeating to yourself, 'This too will pass; it is not the end.'"

"How long have you been doing this?" I asked him.

"Working the roads? Five years off and on. They usually stop during the rains, so I go back to my land to plant. When the harvest is finished, I sign back up." He had come to sit down beside me, and I could see him now. He stretched out his hand. "Frederich," he said.

"Charles," I responded and took his hand. I could barely feel it; my hand was still tingling from the day, but I could vaguely make out callouses and cracks. The hands of a worker, the hands of an African. Close by now, I noticed that he smelled of himself. It was not a bad smell but the earthen odors of humanity when it cannot afford to cover itself with spices and perfumes.

Side by side, we gazed out west for a time, out over the darkened Savana. There was no moon, and the stars twinkled in the blackness above, diamonds in a bed of tar that shimmered as the heat waves of the day radiated into the air above, releasing their grip on the land, at least for the short night. An owl hooted in the distance. A baboon shrieked somewhere across the flatness. The bats swirled overhead, their constant screeching as much a part of Africa as the ants big enough that I could hear their pattering at night when all else was silent. Back behind us, far enough away but still there, I could feel the looming presence of the warehouse that contained the implements of our work. Tractors, graters, the asphalt layer and the road rollers. Big barrels of tar. Bags of cement. But for us, piles upon piles of pickaxes. New ones to replace the ones that broke so often on the stones. Old ones, worn with time and baptized with the occasional tear by one of Africa's sons. Out back behind the warehouse was a long room with bunks where the workers rested, in front of a pit latrine and communal shower, beside the kitchen where we ate our evening meals in community. *Matoke*, that ball of boiled plantain so hot it burned my fingertips beside a little pile of the tiny fishes taken from the lake and salt dried, sold in orange cupfuls as the unit of measure and softened with tomato sauce, making a tangy-salty mix that flavored the plantain, although I would have preferred pili-pili, the hot spice that made everything taste good. Washed down by a beer, just one, along with a liter bottle of water. Blue plastic. The flatbed truck that had picked us up when the encroaching twilight had made work impossible was resting malevolently in front of the building.

127

"So," I said, looking over. My companion was close enough now that I could make out his face. He was older than me, perhaps forty to my twenty years. His arms were sinewy, and his hair had only touches of gray, cropped down more for cleanliness than for aesthetics. His white teeth were strong and full, displayed easily with his quick smile.

"Yes?"

"You are married?" I asked, fumbling around for a conversation.

"Yes, indeed. One wife only." He held up his index finger.

"Would you want more?"

"Alas, if I were a rich man perhaps. But women are a lot of work and expensive."

"And do you have children?" I asked.

"Yes, God has given me two boys and a girl. I had another boy, for a time. My first ..." he said, losing himself in thought for a moment. "They are eighteen and twelve—my boys. My girl is eight. My eldest boy is at university, thanks God. Studying computers, though how he understands all those things I'll never know. My other boy watches the goats and minds the farm, for now. And my girl helps her mother. They are all studying. I am the most blessed."

"Where is your home?" I asked. None of us were from this barren piece of savanna. All had come from far and wide upon contract: three thousand shillings a day, transport to and from work, three meals—such as they were, a bed, one day off a week. And three hundred thousand shillings to our families if we were killed. I didn't have a family, so I supposed if I died, the slanty foreman would buy an expensive whore on his next trip to Kampala.

"I am from Ankole. My wife is from Kitgum. We live in the west, where I have my lands."

"And how did you meet?" I asked. "The tribes from the south don't often go beyond the river." I spoke with authority as somebody from north of the river too. Nobody ever went there, not that I blamed them.

"Oh, she was fleeing the war," he said. "She ended up in Fort Portal, running until there was nowhere else to go. There was a camp there, and we met at the market. It was love." His eyes were twinkling. "She minds the children. We work the lands together when it is the season. Groundnuts, beans, maize mostly. In the off season, I pick up work wherever I can. For the last years, it's been here. Not bad, not really. It's better than sitting around drinking banana wine," he said, laughing. "I have no more cows, some goats only. We saw some hard years, my wife and I did. There was little rain, so little that we had to sell the cows to pay for food. Our great Ankole cows, it was hard to see them go. But we made it through. My son won a scholarship lottery from the president. We have some chickens and bought some goats and rabbits. Things will get better, are getting better, thanks God."

He did not ask me about my life. Most people don't, I've noticed. They are happy to talk about their problems and their dreams. I am glad of that. Mine is not a story I thank God for.

We sat for a time in silence. The bats still swirled overhead, churning the night sky into a vortex. Off in the distance, I could hear cattle snorting, or maybe it was a hippo. I lay back and tried to count the stars, as many as I could. I had never been great at math or counting. I knew enough to understand if I was being cheated on a pound of maize flour or the price of a pair of sandals in the market. But never enough to number the stars, the blanket of them so real, so close. A reminder of just how far away we were from the great cities of the south, from which I had fled. I shook my head, certainly not something I wanted to get into with Frederich. Those days were in the past, though what the future held ... Well, who knew that really? This God that they all talked about, I supposed I still believed in Him, despite all that had happened. If I were asked about it directly. But He was, well, irrelevant in my life. "His eye is on the sparrow," we used to sing. *It might be on the sparrow; sure as shit isn't on me.*

Oh well. Better not to think of those things again. It never helps. It provides no answers. It does not make me stronger to face tomorrow. And as I looked at the deepening night, I realized with a start that tomorrow would be coming all too quickly and that I was tired. To wield the pickax again—all day—I would need sleep. I stood.

"Good night," I told my new friend, Frederich. "I must sleep, if sleep will find me."

"Yes, me too, Charles. Come, we will go together," he said, and we walked back around the warehouse to creep quietly into the common room. As I lifted aside the bed net to lie on the hard board—covered only by a thin mattress—I heard a bump and a quiet curse in the darkness as my new friend tried to find his own. I smiled and, amazingly, drifted to sleep.

The days turned into weeks. Then a month passed. Each day blending into the next, the uniform patterns of oppression. Waking early in the morning as the rooster crowed to eat a hurried breakfast of bread and tea—one bag for each five workers—before piling onto the flatbed truck for the trip to the road, pickaxes in hand. Each day, the journey was a little longer but only ever so slightly. We measured our advance not in meters but in centimeters; the massive pile of rocks demanding cutting extended the great long savanna and over the curve of the earth. There was nothing to note our advance. Every tree looked the same; every rock was identical; every one of us slaves of the rocks was interchangeable. And every day was alike. Bread in the morning, matoke in the evening. *This too will pass. It is not the end.* I would repeat Frederich's words to myself when the moments of panic came or when the white-hot flashes of rage engulfed me, leaving me temporarily blind.

I tried to find fortitude in my increasing skill and strength. My precision was improving with greater power delivered at the precise moment to the weakest part of the rock. The rocks began to split like shale beneath my expert blows. It gave me some measure of composure when I needed it the most, imagining that my practice—my strength and discipline—would be useful in whatever came next. Not peace. I had only ever known that one night of peace, with her, with Ruth, just once before it had been wrested from me forever. But self-control. It was exercise, a workout. Learning to understand pain, to control it and harness it and use it. To enjoy it. Fat white men run in place in air-conditioned rooms with other fat men in the great cities beyond my access. In their ridiculous little shorts, bellies extended out, concealing from them their own manhood. Triple chins dripping sweat. It was fun to think of them as my muscles burned. Their efforts involved no pain and would not, therefore, reward them with strength. I had run into them sometimes—when I had lived in Kampala—walking hurriedly, self-importantly between the buildings in suits, huffing at the exertion, their expensive suits taunting me, "I'm in a hurry," and "Fuck off." My obsequiousness. My servility. My fury.

But it hadn't even been them that I hated the most. We are not born equal, we blacks from the camps and those whites who arrive to command us. We grow up with that knowledge, and it is always there in the forefront of our consciousness, never to be challenged. But the other blacks who hurled insults at me as I walked along, it was for them that my rage was preserved. And the Chinaman who enslaved me in my own land.

I was becoming thicker of limb. The youthful, sinewy resilience of my time in Kampala was being replaced by muscles I'd never known existed, the muscles of a man. I would look down at my arms as I swung the pick, swelling in all the right places, the veins protruding from under the smooth black skin. Often, I would stand shirtless in the sun, drinking water or filling my lungs with the scorching air while the other men would glance askance, admiring my flat stomach, ridged like a washboard and hard as a rock. Long gone were the days when with each blow my teeth would rattle in my head. Now, powerful jaws held them in place, the muscles of my chest absorbing the shocks easily. Raw power is respected by men. Hasn't it always been so? The greatest form of respect, above the studying and the praying and the dreaming—the oldest form of respect—comes from the fear of the physical. I'd been learning this. My time in Kampala taught me some. But back there, the fear had been mostly from association, not from my own, raw, carnal strength. Here, it was about what I could do to somebody if they crossed me. As I learned this, I became deliberately erratic and often ill-tempered, screaming into the silence or indiscriminately turning on a coworker. I never had to fight them. Men naturally seek an escape from violence even if it results in subjugation, my most important insight and my greatest advantage.

"What the fuck are you looking at?" I would scream, randomly and without warning.

"Nothing," mumbled this or that coworker.

"I should hope not."

But never toward Frederich. My friend, my mentor, my father, because my blood I had abandoned on that fateful day so far in the past—in the camps. Often, I would have competitions with Frederich: how many blows to shape a rock, how many rocks in an hour, who could lift the biggest rock. Invariably, I would lose, on purpose; respect for the camaraderie, old tribal ideas of deference to our elders. "First to the tree wins," I would say.

"Okay," my friend would respond, "but if you lose, you must give me your egg." I would lose on purpose, handing over the food expectantly, my pleasure childlike as I gave all I had to the *mzee*, the elder. I would look out for the particularly difficult rocks and break them when he was not looking. Often, I would send him for longer breaks, slicing through his rocks like butter quickly before returning to my own.

"Where is old man?" the Chinese foreman would sometimes ask, squinty eyes closed in the African sun, sweat sliding down his naked face and onto the collar of his shirt.

"Taking a piss," I would say.

"He piss a lot," the Kichina would say, cackling and moving away as my grip on the pick tightened. "He an ooooold man."

One day. My oath was silent but real.

CHAPTER 12

Our only respite was Sundays. Those were the days that Frederich and I were free to do what we would. We had become fast friends but also something more. My new elder, willing and anxious, well not necessarily to fill that role but perhaps to impart something, to be somebody to me when he must have instinctively known that I had never had anybody. To fill that void. And the old man seemed to be sensitive to that, a gentle soul. A kindly word when I became fitful, a soothing tongue when I thundered. He knew just what I needed, what I required to overcome the next in the long line of insults and injuries that we—slaves to the Chinks in our own country—must endure.

But all that was always for another day. Because Sundays, our days, were not for the work or the hate; they were days when we carefully stowed away our fury for the moments when we knew we would need it.

One Sunday, we'd both woken up early in the bunks behind the storage house. Rested because, while the others had left for a night in the nearby town, we'd instead watched the sunset, chewing on the cold maize that had been barbequed on a tire rim stolen from one of the disintegrating trucks beside the road and drinking orange Fanta, sweet with the bubbles tickling the backs of our throats, bought on our return from the rocks from a vendor who had no face, no name—no soul. Sunsets in Africa explode orange and yellow and sometimes green, turning to a deep purple at the advance of night. The mustiness of the dark hours creeps up, and the air becomes heavy with sleep. Bats, rats, owls. Other nighttime creatures begin their nocturnal dance, hunting for food, squawking at each other, seeking a mate. Screeching. After a time without talking, we'd returned to the bunk to sleep early in anticipation of the following day's exertion.

We met at the tiny hotplate in the corner beside the iron washbasin for a quick cup of tea, drunk in orange plastic mugs, sharing a single teabag. We then exited the tin shack. It was still early, the dew resting over the logs of the extinct fire, damp and moist. In the corner leaned up against the toilets, the malevolence of the tools of our wretched trade were piled in a dejected heap and covered by a spider web, the night's toil for the little arachnid who would lose its work at the hands of the Chinaman and his slave army. In the morning, the stench from those foul buildings had not begun yet to creep toward the dormitory.

The previous night, the Chink had taken the truck into town with a small group of his men, his filthy clan, those workers who didn't mind kissing the ass of a foreigner for some extra food or a more generous assignment in the shade. These had no families, and while other men had returned home for the day and some still slept in the bunkhouse, those who the Chinaman favored had spent their shillings on hookers and cheap Waragi. The evidence of their debauchery was strewn across the campsite. They had arrived late at night, when morning was tickling the stars in the east. I had heard them. How could I not? The truck had somehow come to rest against the side of the warehouse, as if abandoned in middrive by an unconscious driver, which it turned out was true. The screeching that I had heard in the early-morning hours, the racket that had woken me from sleep, turned out to have happened as it drifted off the worn path and coasted alongside the warehouse, leaving a painful scrape decorating the beast's posterior. The men had poured out of the truck, yelling in their drunkenness at each other as they thrashed around the camp looking for the latrines. But, evidently unsuccessful in their nocturnal quest, they had fallen one by one onto the compacted dirt around the fire pit, cold and damp, and passed out with the mostly empty Waragi bottles poking mischievously out of their pants pockets or held firmly in their deathlike grips. That's where I found them, still stinking of the moonshine, mixed with beer and cigarettes for those who had more money. Beside the pile of men, the Chinaman was snoring, his shirt untucked and a stain across the back of his pants as he lay on his side, arm extended toward the latrine as if he'd tried to crawl there during the night. Bile filled my mouth as the rage hidden away bubbled up, and I strode toward the spider web to lay hold of one of the picks.

"That, my good boy, is not the way," I heard Frederich say behind me, and I stopped, hand wrapped around the hilt of the tool that would have become a weapon, that might still someday. I turned to look at him, and he just shook his head slowly, smiling in a melancholy fashion, and he approached to take the tool from my trembling hand. Then he too looked around at the bodies strewn haphazardly and the acrid stench of the drink laying like a poison over the grass and the weeds. He sighed once.

"Come on," I said, grinning malevolently. "You know you would shed no tears."

"A small act of violence in a violent world goes unnoticed. If you want to leave your mark, you have to do something grand and unexpected. This," he pointed at the miserable yellow face, mouth open and saliva drooling down into the grass, "is not grand. Even in death."

I looked down. "Fair enough."

We both chuckled, and Frederich threw the pick back on the pile, the loud clang eliciting a collective moan from the fallen.

"Come. Today, we will fish," he said, leaning down to pick up the brown-fiber potato sack he had laid on the ground a few moments before.

"What's in there?" I asked.

"You'll see." And Frederich smiled graciously.

We started walking up the road, straight north. The rock piles—all I had ever known, at least so it seemed—lay haphazardly beside us in big mounds of impunity as we walked along. How I longed to leave the rocks behind, to never be forced to see them again, to never have to hear the crack of a pick or feel the shards piercing my cheeks, my forearms, the back of my hands as I covered my eyes. To leave my pick in the dust and walk away from the barked orders of the Chinaman in his infuriatingly high squeal. To lay it all aside and find someplace cool—cool, I hadn't felt the cool for so very long. The highway was a special kind of hell, the pounding African sun waxing until all I could think about was the heat and all I could dream about was a puddle, a pool, a stream or a river or an ocean. But the heat, I had to admit, was only degrees worse than what I had known before. The heat of the roadways of the big city as I sat waiting for the light to turn red to run with my broken-down bottle of diluted soapy water and an old rag to wash the front windows of the cars I would never afford—cars driven by other black men with clean little girls in the back making lewd gestures at me. That heat had been made worse by the exhaust from the cars that would fill my lungs until I would collapse, which I had often done, avoiding being run over by the grace of God and the protection of the other road urchins in my little gang. It was the same and at least not nearly as bad as the heat of the day when I would walk through the colossal piles of garbage in the dumps looking for something—anything—of value that I could sell to buy bread or strap to my naked feet that had blistered over from the burning roadways. Because in that heat, the refuse melted into such a toxic fetor of baby diapers and rotten vegetable husks and melted plastic that I would cover my mouth and nose with whatever I could find as my eyes watered from the waves that wafted over me as they shimmered into the sky above.

"What is troubling you, Charles? You've been silent for a long time," Frederich said.

"Oh, I was just thinking."

"About what?"

"Nothing, mzee, just unpleasant thoughts that have no place with us on a Sunday," I said, staving him off as I picked up my feet to move more quickly ahead. We fell silent for what seemed like a long time. I looked down at my feet. Each step stirred up little puffs of dust. In the distance, I heard a lion roar. The sky above was a shimmering blue, and for some unknown reason, I didn't even mind the heat.

"Life is not always fair, Charles. And the decisions we Africans must make seem especially so."

"I know."

"Things will change. They will get better. Life moves in fits and bursts, slowly for such a long time and then with great energy and purpose suddenly. But you must endure the tedium. If you let it drive you to make a rash decision, you will miss what is coming just over the horizon," he said, gesturing ahead.

"What if it never does?" I asked. "What if I'm just sitting here cracking rocks till my back gives out?"

"Nothing is written beforehand ..."

"That's the problem!" I said.

"Hear me out. You must be sensitive to the spirits: the wind and the water and our ancestors. They will guide you, if you are listening, and deliver you to your destiny." I thought about the camps, the celebrations to our ancestors, the bonfires where we honored the dead and the recently fallen in the latest attack, the latest accident. I could still feel the futility of my father on those occasions, that great Acholi patriarch reduced to waiting in the endless lines.

"That sounds all well and good," I said quietly, "but not practical. Not actionable. I like action. I've always been a man of action. One time, when I crossed the river the first time, I was young and alone and had nothing to eat and nowhere to go. My family was gone. I stood in the center of Masindi town. I did not know what to do. I just stood there, the traffic swirling around me with the gas fumes and the honking, the summer sun beating down heavily upon my small head. Then I saw it. A car with the window open, idling in the afternoon heat. I went quickly forward and saw that the driver, a woman, had her purse in her lap and was talking on her cell phone. I crept to the car window, and like lightning, I grabbed the purse and ran. And I ran, and I kept running until the screaming subsided. Down back alleys I did not know, in front of stores I had never seen. The pounding of feet behind me—I never looked back to see who—became quieter as I maneuvered the maze."

"That probably wasn't the right thing to do," Frederich scolded playfully.

"So you say. It's easy to say that here, now. We are both a long ways from that scared child standing in the street. But do you know what was in that bag?" I asked.

"What?"

"What else? Money. Enough money to pay for some food that made the growling in my stomach go away, at least for a while. And enough money to buy me a bus ticket to Kampala, where I was headed and which was the only place for me. Money. It's so simple for so many— pieces of paper that they throw around for food when they aren't really

137

hungry or a fifth pair of shoes that they will never wear. For me, it was the difference between hunger and purpose and starving quietly on the street corner. Have you ever been hungry?" I asked Frederich.

"Yes," he said. "We are Africans. We have all been hungry at one point or another."

"You said you lost your son?" I asked him. "What did he die of?" I realized the minute I said it how insensitive the question was. Yet he did not flinch. I suppose time heals old wounds.

"Malaria," he said. One word, a word that we all know.

"Well, I had a sister too, who died. In the camps, one summer, things were very bad. The food trucks had stopped coming for a while. Nobody knew why. The rebels were on the prowl, and even though it was planting season, going to our fields was impossible. So we all sat there, under the sun, getting thinner and thinner. Sure, I was already a little bit older and was desperately hungry, but that just made me angry. My little sister, she was tiny, maybe two years old. She just got tinier. My mother had no milk; she was hungry too but gave of her portion to my brothers. We only had just a little bit of corn-soy blend and some beans, and my father had to decide which children he thought should live. My little sister—she didn't make the cut. I watched her there, her arms getting thinner and thinner and the sparkle in her eye fading. She died on a Sunday like this one. Three months later, a charity opened a center in the hospital, giving special milk for starving babies. They said enough babies had died to prove to somebody in an air-conditioned room ten thousand miles away that they should do something about it, that the situation was urgent. I suppose my sister died to prove our desperation to the white people, to save the lives of others. But that is no consolation to me or my family. She had green eyes. Nobody knew why. So strange here in Africa. Green eyes, and they looked up at me when I was holding her that Sunday. They were beautiful eyes, and in them was forgiveness. How does a two-year-old know forgiveness? How can she have had such wisdom if her spirit had not been great? Who knows ..." And my voice trailed off.

Frederich was silent for a time before responding, "Life is not always fair. And the decisions we Africans must make seem especially so. I have no answer for your pain, Charles. You know, as well as I do, anything I say would be trite. A lie."

"No, I know. And I don't blame you. You, who breaks rocks with me, do not have the answer. But do you know who did? The fat woman with the purse. She had been getting fat all the while that my sister had been starving. We buried her in a cardboard shoebox alongside the others. Where is the sense in that?"

We had long since turned west, crossing over the streams and runoff from the seasonal rains and were headed in the direction of the great mountains. All of a sudden, we were through the plains and into a clump of trees that surrounded a small pool fed by a stream that meandered south in search of the great lake beneath the mountains. There Frederich stopped, finding a soft spot beneath the canopy of green to pull out his fishing line and hook. He rooted around in the mud, finding a beetle, which he hooked and dropped squirming into the placid waters. Without my own line and hook, and not really caring anyways—I was never much of a fan of fish or fishing—I took an armful of leaves and spread them out on a flat place beneath the great trees and lay down. Above, I watched two colorful birds as they chirped at each other in a delicate dance of love. I wondered what they were saying. Suddenly they were chased away by a brown monkey running through the treetops looking for food: eggs, insects, lizards. The sounds of the little stream trickling into the pond were soothing after the week punctuated by the maniacal rhythmic clinking of metal on rock. A fish splashed. Beside me, a hedgehog rooted around inside a fallen log. The coolness was refreshing, the wind rustling the leaves, all the sounds muted by the lushness around me. I drifted off to sleep.

I awoke to the sound of sizzling and the hearty goodness of frying fish. "Good afternoon," Frederich said.

"Wow," I responded. "How long have I been out?"

"About three hours," he said. "I myself drifted away until I felt a tugging on the line. Today's been productive." He gestured into the old iron pot.

"You lugged that all the way here?" I asked.

"I have a family; one learns to always be prepared," he said, and smiled gently. I approached to observe the fruits of the morning labor:

two catfish had been gutted and cleaned and were frying in their own fat above a small fire of wood collected from around the forest floor. The wood was still damp, and the fire was smoking, dark plumes billowing up into the leaves overhead. The wind shifted, and the smoke hit me in the eyes. It stung for a moment, but I didn't mind. Out of his pack, Frederich withdrew two potatoes, two tomatoes, two onions, and a large plantain that he sliced in half, throwing them all to stew together with the fish in the skillet. The pangs from my stomach reminded me that I was hungry, and I went over to drink from the cool pond, wash my face and hands, and then pick two large banana leaves from a tree to use as plates—and we ate.

"What was your great plan?" I asked at last.

"Huh?"

"Your great plan. The one that was gonna free you from this life." I gestured back toward the road. "The one that would give you the money to retire early and rest, to hold your grandchildren. To not have to break rocks."

He chuckled a little. "Let me think," Frederich said. "It's been a long time since I thought about that."

A cicada chirped under a leaf by my arm, and I swatted at it. A mosquito buzzed above my head, and I killed it between my palms. The trickle was a melodious background to this, our most luxurious moment.

"One time," Frederich finally said, "when I was a young boy, several years younger than you are now …"

"Yes?"

"I was studying at a secondary school in Fort Portal. I felt privileged; not many could study, but my father had saved and worked hard and bought me a seat. I had my uniform and my books and pencils, and at night—it was a boarding school—at night I would lie awake and dream about a life of work that did not depend on the strength of my back and my endurance and stamina. To work with our minds, isn't that the greatest blessing?"

"So what did you do about it? What happened?"

"Like I said, we weren't wealthy. My family wasn't. But my dad sent me to the school with the little money he could afford. And it turns out that at the school there were other boys from around the Fort Portal area. Some were sons of local councilors; others were sons of store managers; some state politicians, and even the son of the pastor in the city. Mixed in among us were some foreigners, three boys of a Pakistani family and the son of a white missionary. Sure, the Asians don't like us blacks in general. But there was one boy, Akil. He was my age, and we became close friends. We would take off after school to explore the rolling tea plantations, hiding from the plantation staff as we looked for frogs in the thick bushes. We would watch movies at the theater, hoping against hope for a flash of skin," he said as he grinned at me. "That adolescent search for the elusive naked breast." We both laughed. "Sometimes we'd go swimming in the rivers or take the trip down to Queen Elizabeth National Park to see the hippos, hitchhiking on the back of a truck piled high with bags of charcoal. A couple of times we even played hooky from school, something that his parents found out about."

"Sounds nice," I said. "I've never had a friend like that. Friends require money. I never had any. Nobody wants to hang out with a boy, orphaned, who shines shoes and picks pockets ..." *Except, of course, other boys who shine shoes and pick pockets.* I realized at once I was sounding whiny, and I shut up. Frederich didn't seem to notice. He had lapsed into memory, chuckling. And then he told me at great length of his friend and life in the days of Amin and the expulsion of the Asians. All the while, the sun drifted lazily overhead. I'd often wondered about Idi Amin, the King's African Rifle. Field marshal of the plains. Sitting here in the camps, my age gives me a lot of time to think. And I must admit, we Ugandans—especially we northerners—have a soft spot for this man they call a despot. Back in those days, the violence engulfed the whole country, not just the parts north of the river. Back in those days, we didn't just fight each other in the night, but we took our wars to Kampala. Blood. It's amazing how much blood the ground can soak up. You never know that, never think to think about it, to wonder when the ground will be satiated and at last cry out for an end.

"So what happened then?" I asked.

"I never saw my friend again. Those were troubled times, Charles. You asked before about my dreams. My dream had been to study, to graduate. I was thinking law school or perhaps a job in the civil service. I know, you think these times are also troubled. But you don't know what trouble is. Back in the days of Idi Amin."

"Is it true he was possessed by the devil?"

"Of that, there is no doubt," Frederich responded. "There is a special sort of evil that manifests itself in our jungles and rivers. The Pearl of Africa some have called it, and we are truly blessed. But there's something twisted that brings the malevolence upon us time and again."

"I agree with that," I said, remembering with distaste my days as a street beggar trying to shine shoes of people who thought they were too important. "Urchin," they called me. "Piss off" and "Nasty little bugger, don't touch me," and they would kick at me to force me to step aside. As if they too weren't Africans. As if they too didn't have the marks on their skin. As if they too hadn't done the rituals, hadn't eaten tilapia under the same stars and spoken with the same guides. As if their totems didn't still do battle with mine.

"Those were bad times," Frederich went on. "We couldn't find milk or cheese, couldn't buy anything really. The money seemed to melt away in our pockets, trickling onto the cracking sidewalks as we walked to the store to stare at the empty shelves. Nobody would buy our cattle and our leather. Hunger. That's what the expulsion of the Asians meant to us. I was pulled out of school. My father could no longer afford even the modest payments and so ended my dreams of a future. So I went to watching the cows with him and working where I could find something to do. And here I am," Frederich said, gesturing back toward the road we were building together. "So many years later. *He* destroyed my future too, although he himself was exiled so long ago and is dead now. Violence is like a fire; it burns black and white, good and bad alike, and consumes fine silk just as easily as coarse burlap."

"That's terrible," I said, genuinely sad.

"We are all made who we are by God," Frederich said. "And it isn't for us to second guess His plans."

"Meaningless words," I spat. The memory of the violence and the mention of God often set me off. "Taught to us by the missionaries, brought here by the British masters."

"You are young," Frederich said. "Soon you will find a girl and maybe make a house. You'll find that our lives too are not without meaning."

"Bullshit," I said, throwing my friend a disparaging glance before becoming instantly sorry.

He didn't respond.

The sun had descended closer to the horizon, and the mosquitoes were starting to become thicker in the evening air. "Well, we'd better get going. We have to get up early tomorrow."

We walked back in silence, the gentle Sunday mood disturbed by my outburst, as the oranges and purples crept into the sky, marking the end to another day, another meaningless day in Africa, the latest in a long line of meaningless days that extended backward in an unbroken line to the beginning of time.

CHAPTER 13

The days continued much the same. I would wake up in the morning, eat, shit, drink tea, and rush to the broken-down old truck to drive the distance to the road. Like a centipede crawling up the savanna toward the river, the new road slowly took form, edging forward inch by inch beneath our feet to reach the prize. The Nile. The boundary between south and north, Bantu and Luo, civilization and desolation, peace and war.

Lunch was a sandwich and water. Dinner in community, for what it was worth, eating whatever we were brought. Matoke, sometimes rice with beans. Slowly the seasons turned; the appalling heat of the African dry season slowly became more humid, giving way to the rains. But they didn't slow us either. Despite what I'd been told, we worked right through the wetness this year. "We must be under some deadline," Frederich explained. Sloshing around in the muck, rain flowing down our faces into our eyes as we tried to aim. Gales that pushed the trees sideways, and on we fought the elements.

Occasionally the monotony was interrupted by catastrophe. One day I heard a yell, "Watch out there," followed by a scream that turned the blood in my veins to sludge. I ran toward the sounds until I was standing beside two men, one from Rwanda and another a Tanzanian who had come to work the rocks. One stood still, straight, and tall with panic written across his countenance. His hands held fast to his pick, white knuckled while his eyes darted about in his head. "I didn't mean to," he blubbered. "It was an accident. I swear." I looked down at the

Rwandan who was facedown in the mud, the rain washing away the blood that was streaming from a wound above his left ear, fertilizing the ground with another blood sacrifice. "Honest, he slipped on that rock." The Tanzanian pointed over to a large rock with a red smear. His consternation was obvious. There had never been any love lost between these two men. Always competing to be the first, pushing themselves for more rocks, racing to receive the greatest lunch or be first to the pot over dinner. Only the night before, they had gotten into a dreadful fight over a card game, and long after everybody else had gone to bed, their voices could still be heard, insults flying as they attempted to outdo each other for the meager prize of a few waragi bags.

"What is problem here?" The Kichina marched over, squinting into the rain, his eyes slits, undiscerning, without wisdom or intelligence. Blind but not from lack of sight. "What you see here?" He turned to me.

"Nothing," I answered, not lying. I hadn't in fact seen anything, not that I would tell him if I had.

"Liar," he snapped at me, scowling for a time until he finally turned to the Tanzanian. "You—what you do?"

"I did nothing," the Tanzanian said. "He slipped. That is all."

The Kichina stood for a long moment, apparently trying to think—although none of us thought him of sufficient intellect to ponder anything beyond the rocks and the straight line of the road. "Aw, fuck it. We wasting time. You." He pointed again to me and said malevolently, "Help him bury body." And he pointed out over the savanna to a tree in the distance.

"But ..."

"No but. We waste time. Bury body."

"Shouldn't we call the police?" Frederich had appeared over the side of the crest.

"Fuck off, old man. This not your problem."

"Nevertheless," said Frederich, coming closer. "It is for the authorities to decide on these things."

He never saw the blow coming; the Kichina's hand flew up to deliver a wicked smack across the mouth. "You do what you told."

Watching the blow, as if in slow motion, I began to raise my pick high above my head, the muscles of my arms and my back rippling as

145

the latent power of hate and strength mingled. My mouth stung from the strike, although I was not its recipient. I tasted the blood on my own lips as Frederich wiped his. Humiliation rushed over me, making me shiver. I would have cut the Chink in half, but just as my feet gripped the dirt and the energy rushed up from my legs to my expectant arms, I felt a hand on my shoulder. "Charles." The soothing voice came as if from a great distance. "It doesn't matter. You do that, and he wins, even while he loses everything." He had switched to Swahili while the arrogant overseer stared in bewilderment, perhaps fear, perhaps panic, but overtop it all was always the loathing, the one abiding inclination of the Chinaman.

My shoulders slumped as I lowered the pick. Not saying a word, eyes downcast, I bent to lift the Rwandan under his arms while the Tanzanian worker quickly picked up his feet. We lugged the lifeless body toward the tree in the distance—defeated.

I buried the Rwandan in a grave, without even a prayer—without laying rocks above the grave to keep away the hyenas. Why should I care? All living things have to eat. Then I returned to breaking rocks.

"I hear that they eat their little girls," I said to Frederich.

"Now, Charles …"

"Tell me," I said, "have you ever seen a Chinese girl? Yes, we see their women sometimes in town. But have you seen a girl child?"

"No," said Frederich. "But that doesn't mean anything."

"I went down to the lake a few years ago," I said. "I was doing an errand and ended up going down a closed road to a building right on the lake. Inside that building, you know what I saw?"

"What?" Frederich asked, amused.

"They had been fishing. They had a huge pile of tilapia, higher than a man. One by one, they were slicing each carefully open and removing the stomach of the fish, throwing the rest to the cats while they placed only that one part in the sun to dry. There were so many cats—hundreds—fighting over the delicacies while these yellow bastards carefully preserved the intestines."

"So?"

"So? Who does that? Throw away perfectly good fish meat in order to harvest the unusable parts for their abnormal rituals?" I said.

"How do you know it was for their rituals?" Frederich asked, playing devil's advocate I suppose. "Maybe they just like the stomach."

"I have heard," I whispered, resting my pick on the ground for a moment and leaning on it while I took a drink of water from my bottle, "that they grind up the bones of their little girls and put them in the fish stomachs and then make their wives cook them into a stew." I looked around, as if somebody was listening, as if anybody cared what two black men with picks talked about in the African summer sun.

"Where did you hear that?" Frederich asked.

"Never you mind that. I know things too," and we both laughed heartily.

"Back to work, niggas." The Kichina had appeared out of nowhere and was approaching quickly. "I don't pay for you gossip like girls." I felt the vein in my forehead expand, and I picked up the pick, delivering a tremendous blow to the rock, shattering it under my feet—shards flying as far as the tree under which was buried another victim of Africa's endless struggle.

I thought often of Ruth with longing and anger, lust and a great deal of sadness mingled with jealousy. I wondered if she had made it to Europe, how she looked bundled up against a cold I had never experienced. Eating new foods, seeing grand old things, having discussions of significance bundled tight against the cold, in front of a fire or beside an imposing old hearth. I thought of her betrayal—of who was caressing her, placing his lips upon hers, touching her mouth, moistening her breasts. Though I tried not to, I kept returning to our times together, under the bridges or in the broken-down restaurants, laughing and careless. The words she whispered in my ear during our passion, which I knew now were lies. They were heavy memories—the heaviest of all being our night, our one night. That memory was an open wound, one that I did not handle often, lest it become gangrene for too much fondling.

And time flowed on. Occasionally we would vacate the bunk where we lived to find that another had been constructed many miles ahead. "Pick up your shit," we were told, and we loaded our meager possessions onto the bed of the truck to head the distance to our next identical billet. The wooden bunks three high. The latrines too close to the fire pit, the scent wafting into evening dinner. Light by fire and battery, kerosene lamp and flashlight. The stink of the same men, over and over. Water brought in on the back of a truck, bottles that were too few for both bathing and drinking. Dinners in the uncomfortable company of idiots, people I knew were my inferiors except for the frustrated realization that I was just like them.

One day as we clashed against the rocks under the sun, we heard a rumbling. Looking up, wiping the sweat from my forehead, I watched as the big asphalt layer and road roller approached. For days, we'd heard them behind us crunching and pounding and grating; then one morning, they were here. I choked as the tang of the tar was mixed into asphalt. The roaring of the powerful engines and the crunching as rocks big and small split into pieces under the weight of the behemoths. It was exciting, because something was happening. The arrival of the machines, they had caught up with us. That was important. Because it meant we were reaching the end—at least of this phase.

"They are here," Frederich said. "We are close. The work is almost done; we have almost arrived. The river." I could hear his voice crack.

"I haven't even paid attention," I said. "Did we really lay that much?"

"A hundred kilometers. Look back behind"—he turned—"back to our work, to our past."

I turned and looked at the tan canals to catch the rainwater, beside the black snake of road, freshly asphalted. Smooth and straight.

"Doesn't it make you proud?" Frederich asked. "The work of our hands built that. For a thousand years, this will endure."

"Proud? Not really. Bad work, hard hours, low pay. Proud certainly isn't the word I would have chosen."

"But there was nothing there before," Frederich insisted, "and now there is. An act of creation. Have you ever created anything else in your life?"

"No," I said, thoughtful. I suppose I hadn't.

"People will know we were here, not because of our names but because this"—he gestured behind us—"will last forever."

"I suppose. Although that doesn't really matter. Slaves build things. I've heard of the pyramids at the end of the river." I gestured north.

"They were built by slaves too. Nobody ever honors them—considers them—gives them their due. It is the pharaohs who are remembered, fat men drinking wine. The same will be said about this." I gestured at the road. "And it's just a road, after all."

We pushed forward, cracking our rocks with renewed energy. Only a few more days, and we turned the corner. The full view of the river offered itself up to us. It starts broad, the White Nile, meandering from the great lake far to the south. Heading north into the Sudan, into Egypt. Into the great water at the end of its journey. How much Ugandan blood had traveled the river upward to that expansive sea? From the days of Amin, of Obote, of Okello. From before the slave traders and the English, and even before them, the tribes fighting each other in anonymity, without history or a story. Always fighting. From the far side of my vision, it emerged from between two hills, a crystal line that looked like frozen ice. It flowed in a lazy arch, widening as all rivers do, and in the tranquility, a pod of hippos basked leisurely in the sunlight, only their snouts poking out of the deepness, their snorts reaching up even to us. Then from its rest, I could feel the river gathering energy, preparing. When it was ready, it hurled itself over Karuma Falls, the whitewater churning, raw power, purpose. It rushed over the rocks—which vibrated and hummed—and fell into a deep depression below, slowing again, becoming placid as it widened. The refreshing spray caught the wind, soaking me in a fine mist, and I breathed deeply. Strangely calm. Crocodiles waited at the bottom, to catch the confused fish or the battered body of a deer or horse or hippo that had become overconfident, had not considered the power of the water and had not escaped in time. Crossing the river, a thin band of rusted metal and wood, was the bridge. The connection of two worlds. The boundary between us and them.

"They are over there," Frederich said, pointing beyond the bridge.

"Who?" I asked.

"You know very well who. The Lord's Resistance Army, although what they think they are resisting is beyond me, and they certainly have nothing to do with God," Frederich said, crossing himself.

"Oh, yeah. I know. I am from the north."

"I know you are," he said.

"So I know about those people," I said.

"And?"

"And what?"

"Do you agree with them?" he asked.

"Agree with them? Let me tell you something. They were the reason I fled. Oh sure, I hate the government as much as anybody. Sitting there in their great white houses in Entebbe overlooking the lake. Flying around the world eating caviar and drinking expensive whiskey while I sip waragi under a tree. They will get theirs. They will pay—for sure. But those people," I said, gesturing across the river, "are not the answer. Raping our women, stealing our food, denying us access to our fields. Robbing our futures, erasing our past. I may not be overly educated in the strategies of war, but how can weakening our own tribe possibly help in the fight against our enemies? No. I am not friend of the Lord's Resistance Army."

Then we were there, at last—the Nile, all our work meeting us at the end in the great water that had forever divided my land from his. We were sitting together on a large rock beside the river, letting the spray cool us after our long months of hard labor. "What will you do now?" Frederich asked.

"That fucking Chinaman says they're gonna pay double to those who want to stay on and work the road. They're trying to go to Gulu—and even beyond to the border I hear," I said.

"You're willing to risk the war?" Frederich said.

"What else am I to do? I have no family, no career, no future, and no past really. All I have are these rocks and my complicated relationship with the Kichina." We both laughed, but it was bitter.

"And you?" I asked.

"No, I'm done—at least for now. It's been too long since I hugged my wife and family. Since I've seen the mountains and breathed the cool air. Your air up here is dry and hot; I want to go back to the green and the forests," Frederich said, but he wasn't looking at me. He stood up, and I followed suit, and we walked together to the group of lean-tos by the road. He bought me an ear of corn that had been roasted over hot coals, black and charred, and we ate together for a time, pulling the kernels off one by on and chewing on them, until the green matatu bus sputtered up the hill from the river belching black smoke and playing Congolese music. It stopped, unloading some passengers as a little boy yelled, "Kampala," from his perch, clinging to the side of the door-less cabin.

"That is for me," Frederich said.

"I know," I said. "I wish you safe travels."

"Thank you." We gave each other a firm handshake, and he rushed to the now-moving vehicle.

I returned to sit under the tree. Aloneness—it was not a new feeling. But this time it felt more desolate, darker, and with greater foreboding. I chewed the kernels without swallowing, spitting them into the hole from where the ants were coming—watching as one by one they grabbed the food and ferried it into their underground dominion. The sun rode lower toward the horizon as I pondered.

I must admit to you, those who are still engaged in my story, that was the moment of one of my greatest mistakes. If I had it to do over again—I would have forgotten everything and followed Frederich onto that bus, returning with him to clean latrines or pick tea or do whatever I could find. But I was angry and young, and the unfairness of the world was like an albatross around my shoulders that I could not shrug away—hard as I tried to make my peace with it. It was raw and sharp—my hate—a hate looking for retribution, to find solace in the suffering of others. Who knows what would have happened had I accepted Frederich's offer? Who knows anything really?

"Fuck you do here?" the Kichina asked, rousing me from my reverie. "We cross river tonight—to start early. You work better without old man. Maybe you focus." My hate burned clean and pure.

I woke up early the next morning, the river to my back as I faced north. Home—such as it was. It had been almost ten years since I had been back, since I'd seen the Luo lands and communed with my people. Flat and broad, great open grasslands perfect for growing plantain and groundnuts and millet. Farmers we were, had always been. The Ankole cows had been left below the river; nobody had cows anymore. They attracted attacks from the rebels. Even goats in too great a number was an invitation to destruction. We were able to farm—when we could make the perilous trek to our lands, that is. Even when we did, it was always in fear, with one hand around a bow and arrow, a machete, or even a gun if we could afford one. Not that the soldiers let us have guns, if they found out about them. We would bury them under the trees at our homesteads before returning to sleep in the camps. Anybody with guns they considered a rebel. Part of the Lord's Resistance Army. So there we sat—for generations—oppressed on one side by our own "freedom fighters," who were from our tribe and language, our tribal brothers who fought only us, leveling misery on their cousins. On the other, soldiers from the south who saw us all as terrorists, even though it was only we who suffered. That morning, I looked behind, at the river I had crossed the night before. The end of one life, the beginning of another, back home, the full circle of life. Choices. We all make choices and assume they are of no consequence, that they are all neutral. I felt the water pounding below me, reverberating through the steel. The spray from below felt cool, calming my tortured soul. I never second-guess myself; it is of no never mind what I have done, whatever I do. There is never another way, my future as immutable as my past. That is all. But something inside me told me that things had changed, were about to change forever.

I welcomed the sensation.

"Welcome to my world—nigga," the Kichina said, glaring at me malevolently as I arrived with a dozen of the braver, poorer workers. All of them I knew from our months of working together. All of them had nothing to lose. I ignored our yellow overlord as I went straight for my pick.

CHAPTER 14

"**P**ut your back into it," the Kichina screamed.

I said nothing.

"I said move."

"Why don't you pick up a damn pick and do some work," I said, trying to remain calm.

"That work not for me," he said, and wandered off. I gripped the pick harder, focusing my rage on the next rock. And the next. And the one after that.

The days were filled with heat as we pushed forward. No longer close to any town, we were guarded by a contingent of soldiers. But they didn't care about us; they were there to protect the machinery—it was expensive. A dozen bored soldiers in an old pickup truck, hats pulled over their heads as they slept their way through the hot north-Ugandan afternoon, the stench of unwashed flesh radiating in concentric waves from the truck. Occasionally they would swat a fly and then return to their slumber. We were not allowed to move beyond the "protection" of these idiots. There was no Sunday exploring, not that there was anybody to explore with. There were no trips to towns for partying, not that I would ever party with the fucking Kichina. There wasn't even any bunk to go back to; no fire was lit to advertise our presence to the unhinged men in the forests. We lay out under the stars upon mats provided by the company. Ate cold food from unmarked cans delivered weekly by trucks, escorted from the south by another contingent of soldiers—who would then relieve the lazy group who guarded us.

I hated the sun. I hated the flies. I hated the fleas that infested the mats upon which we slept our freezing, troubled nights. I hated the rain that pounded down upon us. I hated the food that was tasteless, and I hated my companions for their stupidity. Marginal people from marginal worlds—living on the fringes of society, not criminals. At least criminals had the audacity to do something, try something, anything. Shadow people who would pass through the world without even making the slightest of impressions. Even their breaths borrowed from the savannas and the jungles of lands that did not contemplate them.

But the purity of my hatred I saved for the Kichina, for the simple reason that he had come from the farthest away to enslave me.

It was on a dark night, when the soldiers had gone to sleep—except one who was on watch, who was also asleep—when I got my revenge. The stars were shining in a moonless sky. The mosquitoes were buzzing around my ears, echoing the snoring of the idiots. I had not planned to kill him. I had tried to think about what Frederich would have advised me, but Frederich was not there. The heat had gotten to all of us—I know—but that day I'd had a final fight with the prick.

"Work harder," he had said.

"I'm working as fucking hard as I can," I said.

"I don't care," he screamed, getting up in my face. "No talk back to me."

The sweat poured down my forehead onto my chest. "You crack a rock for a change," I responded, and shouldered him out of the way.

Then it happened—the Kichina wound up and slapped me across the mouth, as he was wont to do. As he had done with Frederich. "Learn your place, nigga," he said, and walked up the line.

Learn my place? It was then that I'd decided to show him his place—first six feet deep in the red African dirt, and from there down into the fires of hell, if such a place existed.

Late that night, I crept from my mattress under the tree to where our tools where stored. I quietly found my pick—the instrument of my slavery, my constant companion along the unending road—committed to making that one last strike, the one I'd been dreaming of for so long. I snuck silently across the makeshift camp, quiet lest I wake the dozing soldier, and approached the place where the Kichina was sleeping. Unlike the rest of us, he had a thick mattress and a mosquito net hanging from the tree above. He was snoring. I delicately lifted the mosquito net to hang it over the branch above the sleeping man, and he sputtered, reaching up to scratch a spot on his greasy head. I held my breath. He turned over, stomach down on the mattress, head laying to one side, and started snoring again. I lifted the pick high, my muscles rippling as I marshalled all my strength, and using the skill I had obtained during my time under the Kichina's dominion, I brought it down smooth and true, driving the pike through his temple. He perished instantly, without even the time to cry out. I left him there, head pinned expertly to the ground through the mattress that was rapidly soaking up his lifeblood.

I walked to the edge of the camp and turned to look around. There was my own mat. The pit where we threw our garbage. The bodies of my collaborators. A few cans of beer lying beside the sleeping soldiers. The pile of tools and the crime. It had been cold and calculated, not an act of passion but of determination, of liberation. I knew the soldiers would not follow me off the road, and in the bush, I would have time to plan my next move. I did not regret my actions. When you live for the next meal, to defecate in the bush and sleep dreamlessly only to rest your weariness for the next punishing day. When your life is that of an animal, with no past or future—only the ever-present pangs of now. When those were the plans of the yellow men, the white men and their benevolent God, the black men who had fought to free us only to deliver us again to slavery, our only legitimate response was to revolt. They wanted me as a pawn to their grand games? They wanted to deny me my own soul, while they so meticulously cultivated their own? I had made my decision; I wanted none of it. I was done trying to make my way in their world, striving for baubles that were always only denied to me. I would instead fight them—taking their lives, one by one if I had to, and as I could. Not just the yellow men from beyond the ocean but anybody who considered it their lot to rule and mine to obey. I stepped from the circle into the darkness. I hadn't thought about what would be next but walked instinctively in the direction of the forests.

That night when I looked back over the campsite seems so long ago now, but nevertheless itself at the end of such a long road. The body of a dead oppressor, head impaled to the ground with a pick. It was almost poetic, I suppose. Standing on the edge of the forest, the seam between two lives, three lives, four maybe—always a before and an after. I wanted you to know a little bit about my journey, what had brought me to stand beside a forest with nothing or nobody—hands stained permanently with blood. I wanted you to understand that I am not a monster or an animal, that I too am capable of great love, of ambition, and of dreams of peace and family and freedom. And I want you to admit, if only to yourself, that you might have done the same thing as I if you had been dealt the same hand as me. The decisions I made—despite their turning out so badly—were the only options in the limited life of a nameless boy from the camps. And I want you to acknowledge that my heart beats like yours does for the great things— even if those have always been beyond my grasp.

I want you to acknowledge all this because of what came next.

CHAPTER 15

That night, I stepped away from the encircling light of the Kichina's camp, walking resolutely west toward the forest. We were several kilometers north of the river, having passed Karuma Falls and the bridge a while back as we laboriously inched up the continent cracked rock by cracked rock. On the west side of the road was a combination of grasslands and forest, while on the eastern side were farmlands that extended away to Kenya and eventually the ocean.

I walked down the road that led toward Murchison Falls Game Park in Uganda. It was uneven, full of potholes, and appeared rarely used. Lounging by the side was an occasional troop of baboons picking at each other or rifling through a bag of garbage that had been jettisoned from one of the infrequent *matatus* on its way to the main highway. I walked along in silence. Slowly the sun began to rise as I put more and more distance between myself and my crime. By now, they would have discovered the Kichina, and they would have also realized that I was missing. It would not have taken the soldiers long—even those idiots—to discover what had happened. Especially with the unrelenting abuse that the Chinaman leveled in my direction from morning till night. I didn't care. An act of rebellion against slavery, that's all it had been. Insignificant in the epic struggles of a continent but existential for me, because where was I to go now? What was I to do?

I found a stream by the side of the road, somewhat rancid, but I drank from it anyway, knowing I had to take each opportunity as it presented itself. Slowly the terrain was changing, the jungles beside the road giving way to the savanna, punctuated by the acacia trees under whose shade rested animals of all sorts. The road became gravel as I inadvertently plunged into the heart of the park. Walking slowly forward, I came to an abandoned tourist information center, crawling with spiders and overrun by bats—a vestige of carefree times before the rebels had made the job of tending the park animals perilous. The haunted pillboxes beside the deserted buildings a memory of when park rangers had collected fees and welcomed tourists eager to see the animals. The buildings were pockmarked with bullet holes, weeds were growing from the broken pavement, and the roof had collapsed upon a shattered display that had once sold knickknacks. A skeleton washed out by the African sun grinned at me from where he sat, relaxing upon a bench under a faded sign announcing soda pop.

I passed under the rusted bar and began my walk into the heart of the park. I really didn't know where I was going, except I knew that I needed to get away from where people would probably be looking for me. You can't just kill a Kichina these days. They are worth more than our lives, and their deaths must be accounted for while ours pass without even a whisper. The gravel road had become two dirt ruts with waist-high grass growing in between. On either side, the old trees grew up into the African sky, vultures gazing down upon me in anticipation. A black mamba slithered across my path, surprised at my presence in a land that was her dominion. She struck out, but I jumped, and she slithered away, having made her point. I didn't come this far to die of a snake bite. I continued walking along the withered road west—in the direction of the lakes, the mountains, and eventually the Congo. The land was eerie, haunted. Nothing moved under the sun. There was no wind pushing the trees around. The blistering heat was a mantle that shimmered upward from the parched land. Spread out before my eyes were the endless prairies.

Death.

Lumbering awkwardly up to the road, as if having seen something else alive and desperate for some communion of any sort, was a lone giraffe. Legs bent, breathing labored, spots not the natural orange color but a sickly brown, neck hunched as he walked, as if carrying a great weight. He lowered his head to me in quiet supplication, and I stroked the nose and pulled some grass, which he chewed gratefully but unenthusiastically—as if only not to offend. The grasslands of Africa are difficult places—for humans and animals. Places of survival. I felt a kinship to this giraffe; like me, he was an outcast, far away from others of his kind. He had been marked for death long ago, but his will had refused to surrender to his sentence, and he struggled on. Lonely and desperate. For some reason, I thought about Ruth—her last look still burned deep in my consciousness. I took the giraffe's huge head by both hands and gave him a caress around the ears.

"You and me," I said, "are not that different. Alone in a harsh land. Solitary but undefeated." The animal grunted, and I grunted back and laughed a little.

Then I saw them, in the distance, coming fast and hard in our direction. Those of you who do not know Africa will nevertheless have heard of the tsetse fly. Yet you probably think it's like an annoying pest that crawls through your meals. At most, you will liken it to a horsefly, those huge things that buzz around bumping into things. You would be wrong. Because there's nothing scarier in Africa than the tsetse. They are about half the size of a horsefly, and instead of their wings poking diagonally out from their body, they lay one overtop the other on their backs. They are fast and travel great distances in enormous black clouds. That is until they land, at which point they plunge their stinger into the skin—not gently like a mosquito but instead like a nurse's needle—and they suck until they are so bloated they cannot fly, massive round balls of blood. The disease they carry—sleeping sickness—is the least of the worries if you are caught in the open by the tsetse. They have been known to suck animal or person dry in a matter of minutes, while the disease takes years to kill. Unbeknownst to me, this particular part of the park was the tsetses' domain, hence the desolation. Despite the greatest efforts to eradicate them, they did abide—here and in other remote locations of a continent not yet fully conquered.

The black cloud pressed forward toward us, sensing prey, and I began to search desperately for somewhere to hide. On the side of the roadway, there was a stinking fetid bog, green slime covering the top and bubbling in the summer sun, leftover from one of the rains or fed by some malevolent underground spring. I plunged myself into the pond, pushing deeper and deeper into the slime until I was covered, closing my eyes as I placed a thick reed that I had found growing by the side of the lagoon into my mouth and finally pulling my head into the sludge. The muck penetrated my ears and pressed upon my eyes and found my nose, and I almost gagged. With discipline, I breathed in and out and in again, counting my breaths for calm. Shortly I heard the muffled humming and the panicked grunting of the giraffe as he thrashed about in the throes of his predators. You cannot escape the damnable fly—and after a time, the prairie went silent again. Inside the muck, I felt something moving up against my toes and around my belly. I wanted to scream and run but could not risk the wrath of the fly. The pond was alive—parasites or snakes or frogs came poking around in curiosity, pushing and probing. All I could do was hope. Death from the pond was a possibility, but from the fly a certainty. Something moved in between my toes, and a pitiful scream escaped through my reed tube. I waited there for nightfall, bemoaning my wretchedness.

Finally, the cool drove the demon flies back to wherever they slept. When I knew they were gone, I poked my head from the mess and wiped some of the slop from my eyes with a few leaves from a tree beside the pond. It was night. There were stars twinkling above in a moonless sky. The prairie was oddly peaceful. It seemed somehow kind in the nighttime, until I saw off to one side the desiccated body of my friend, ostracized and left to die for who knows what crime.

I stopped for a moment, honoring him with a tear or two, and then walked forward, sticky and disgusted. After thirty or forty-five minutes, I found a small stream. There I stripped down naked and washed from my head to between my toes, inside orifices and under my nails. I found leeches—and one by one pulled them from my body with a scream, throwing them to die on the land. Finished, I moved my hands one last time over my entire body, making sure that there was nothing hidden or missed, and I turned to my clothes. Carefully washing them in the water took time, cleaning out the mud and making sure that there was nothing living remaining in the fabric, discarding pollywogs and baby snakes or eels and salamanders and other critters I didn't want to think about. Finally, when I was convinced too of their wholesomeness, I put them back on. I then examined the road and looked up at the sky. Five hours left, maybe, of the night before the flies would return. I drank some clean water, not too much to give me cramps. I knew I had to distance myself from the land of the flies; I would not spend another night in the muck.

I began to run. Not a jog but a marathon. I harnessed all the strength I had gained from my time moving rocks around, and I set out to follow the road deeper into the park. This had been a tourist spot, before rebel attacks had made it too dangerous. Under the assumption that the flies had been beaten back from at least some of the park, I pounded forward. I found renewed energy and momentum in my nocturnal sortie. Running under the stars was exhilarating; the pounding of my feet on the packed earth ricocheted up my body, giving my actions meaning. Around me, slowly, life started to return to the savanna. A large owl gazed down at me from the branch of a tree. A swarm of pigmy mice fled into the underbrush. I almost stepped on a huge cobra that was warming itself on a rock in the middle of the path. My wet shirt clung to my body, cooling me down despite my exertion, and I started to shiver a little bit.

After the hours, the tender glimmers of morning began to appear in the sky behind me. I was far from the fly lands, at least I believed I was as I emerged suddenly upon a T-junction that connected the path I had been on to a more-used roadway running north and south. I stopped there, catching my breath and hunting around for a stream or a trickle to satiate my thirst while I watched the savanna morning come to life. Rich white people often talk about safaris. Waking up early in their expensive bungalows, they dress in khaki shorts, many-pocketed vests, and hats or—worse—those round helmets over expensive sunglasses and drive off in their air-conditioned four-wheel-drive vehicles with their African guard carrying a rifle, to see the animals through the car windows. This is only slightly better than the colonialists of old, with entire teams of black errand boys erecting tents, making tea at odd hours, fanning the fat men when they became hot, and carrying them on their shoulders when they became exhausted or too drunk to walk. They call this "safari," Swahili for a journey. Tourism of the rich. At least the modern whites don't decimate the animal stocks like their forefathers did. At least they leave some behind for others to see, throwing a meager dollar tip here and there to their sweating servants.

For me, that morning as I walked northwest toward the river, I experienced the "safari" as just another African animal. Oh, I don't mean that in self-deprecation but as a simple fact. I was there, like them—another addition to their world. The gazelle had emerged from the forests to stand by the thousands upon the hard-packed breeding grounds where they eyed each other lustfully, waiting in stupidity for the lion that was approaching from under the tree where she had slept with her young, who were following a short distance behind, learning her steps. A group of buffalo looked up as I passed, returning disinterestedly to chewing at the high grass. A leopard lounged on the branch of a tree. It was quiet. Animals in their element do not make noise, unless they are the elephants or the hippos fighting one another for the attention of their mates or warning each other of upcoming dangers. None of the animals paid any attention to me. The air was still cool. The sun was not yet above the horizon as I walked. There were no safari tourists this morning, or any morning for a long time. The rebels were known to hold up in the park, regrouping from a loss or planning their next assault, and nobody wanted to risk the chance of falling into their wicked grasp. There were safer places for the rich to snap pictures.

I didn't really know where I was going; if I had to suggest a possible destination, I would have said that I was headed to the river. The Nile, after going east to west, the bridge over which I had crossed it then curved north to travel up Uganda's west side toward the Sudan and eventually Egypt. There, at that curve and under the mighty Murchison Falls is where life is held, preserved. It's the waters that make the savanna possible, and I knew instinctively that was the place where I would find the answer. Maybe a boat, perhaps a fisherman or a ferry to take me someplace safer where I could start anew. Who knows—who cares. In the act of living itself, I was finding defiance against everything that had never gone my way.

As I walked, the sun moved upward into the sky, and the animals began to slowly disperse, returning to hovel or cave or hole to wait out the heat until they would return to their nocturnal search for food when the sun was again below the horizon. All except the big game who would march down well-worn paths toward the river. I followed them—their avenues easily distinguishable after a millennium of feet and hoof destroyed all possibility of that land to recover.

I came over a crest to look down at the Nile below. It was teeming with life escaping the heat and returning to the waters for their salvation. At one end, the great Murchison waterfall propelled itself through a ten-foot-wide crack in the rock, foaming and thundering as it went down for almost a thousand feet. The rocks vibrated, even as far away as I was standing, at the sheer power of the water. Then it evened out into a wide, deep pool below the waterfall, where crocodiles waited for the bodies of careless animals that had slipped while drinking above and fallen to their deaths. A group of crocodiles was confronting a pod of hippos over one of their young, the monstrous animals roaring against the silent malevolence of the reptiles as the standoff extended. Then farther down in the water, a family of elephants played with their calf, refreshing themselves while chewing on the sturdy river grass that grew at the edge. It shimmered in the distance, antelope and elephant and even the occasional lion trying together to escape the heat—their eternal animas put aside for a moment as they lapped water side by side.

"You, stand. Who are you?" The silence was broken by a shrill adolescent voice speaking in the Luo tongue of my people. I turned to face a boy, twelve or thirteen years old. Ragged, oversize uniform hanging on his body—several holes stained with red, suggesting at the fate of its former owner—over blue plastic flip-flops. His eyes were bloodshot, drugs or alcohol; it smelled like alcohol, even from this distance. His breath could wither plants. His hair was in the beginning stages of dreadlocks, messy and with lice seething inside the clumps.

"I am Charles Agwok," I responded.

"What are you doing here, trespassing on our land? Are you a spy?"

"No, I am not a spy," I said, speaking slowly with the boy, but it was obvious that my words were not penetrating into the brain.

"Spy," he said, coming closer. "Come to see our strength? You work for the government?"

"Like I said," I responded patiently, "I don't—" But my words were cut off by a wicked blow from the back of his rifle—an AK-47, worn and polished with age and use—against my rib cage. I didn't even see it coming, and I doubled over.

"Liar. Spy. Come with me." And he grabbed me by the shirt and pulled me up over the hill.

In the tow of the child-rebel, I crested the little hill and realized that I'd accidentally wandered in pretty close to some sort of rebel facility. The installation spread out before me, taking up the entire hilltop. In days past, it had been called Pakuba, I know now, although I didn't then. Since then I have researched it, asking around a little. During the days of Idi Amin's self-exaltation, he decided that he wanted his own lodge to look out on the animals in his own park. He'd built Pakuba, sumptuous in its extravagance. Amin was a man with earthly allure, more a product of the rocks and the rivers of his land than any ideas imported from abroad or philosophies that were not rooted in the natural world around him. This made him a carnal man—in every sense of the word.

The first thing that caught my eye was the swimming pool, placed expertly for revelers to be able to float while admiring the mighty Nile. Amin had liked the Nile—its raw power, the thought that through it he could control the fates of nations, Sudan and even Egypt, mightier countries, older countries answering to him. That had appealed to his vanity. In Amin's day, the pool had been filled night and day with naked women, frolicking for the pleasure of the tyrant and his guests. Beside the pool had been a bar serving elegant drinks—Amin was an alcoholic. And the kitchen, hidden away behind the opposite hillock, prepared the simple but hearty meals that the dictator loved: meats and matoke and bread and potatoes. Sixty rooms, each with a unique view of the Nile and the savanna beyond, allowed him to hold court with ambassadors and ministers without the hassle of going to Kampala, a city that he hated. Amin was, after all, a man of the great wild north; no matter of responsibility or power would change that. Pakuba was his greatest effort to appropriate his former homeland unto himself. The rooms were sumptuous, decorated in the finest European designs and comfortable for the extended stay that Amin's court required. The second bar, inside the lobby, was always stocked—whiskey and rum and vodka and gin, expensive for the tastes of a man who was a Muslim only in name. The parties that lasted all night under the African stars were legendary: sex and alcohol, orgies and debauchery, waking the next day late in the afternoon. Oftentimes they would just power through, taking drugs or too much coffee, nursing their hangovers while they rolled their military jeeps recklessly through the grasslands to hunt the animals, decimating the once mighty herds of elephants, antelope, and even the lion prides. In the great hall, Amin would sit in judgment upon those he imagined had betrayed him, and as his paranoia waxed full, he would execute increasingly numerous perceived adversaries, throwing them to the Nile crocodiles who still to this day it is said have a taste for human flesh. The crocodiles, fat and lazy, were the only animals safe from the unstable man, because often he made great sport of throwing his enemies alive into the river, standing at the edge along with the horrified ambassadors from faraway lands and making wagers on who would live the longest, his arms thrown around his naked courtesans as he howled and jeered.

The place still stank of death and violence—and impunity.

It was the perfect hideout for the Lord's Resistance Army.

I recognized them, dragged into their midst as I had been by the adolescent minion. How could I miss them? There they were, the rebel army that claimed they wanted to rule Uganda by the Ten Commandments. To overthrow the dictator in Kampala and replace him with one of their own. But they were not an army, not even a rebel mob really. As they milled around before my eyes, they resembled more a swarm of the tsetse fly, and for the first time in many years, I was afraid.

"Where are you taking me?" I asked, only to receive a rifle whack again.

We walked by the pool, which was now half-empty. Gone were the naked girls. Now the green water was filled with frogs and the occasional rotting animal carcass. The elaborate rooms where Amin had fornicated with whomever he chose were now destroyed. The roof had fallen in from decades of abandon, and the rubble was still sitting atop the remains of what had been finely carved beds. Windows were broken out. The kitchen was a mess of bat droppings upon white tile, while the gaping holes that made the kitchen look like an old, toothless hag a testament to where the appliances had been before they were looted sometime in the past. The bar no longer had liquor, and the mirror shards had been pulverized into dust over the years, covering the floor in a glistening sand. There were tents for many of the rebels. Some were olive green, stolen from the Ugandan military after a victory, while others were makeshift, grass over mud. A few of the rooms were still miraculously protected from the elements, and there the senior commanders lived there with their young brides. Girls roamed the garrison, eyes downcast as they went about their work. Taking food in plastic bowls up to the rooms, retrieving others to wash them out in the swimming pool. Some had bruises on their faces. Others were pregnant. None looked over fourteen years old. These were the rebel "wives," spoils of successful raids against the camps. The place smelled of beans, rice, and sweat, overlaid by the excrement coming from over the hill where the rebels had turned a bungalow into a makeshift latrine. Death and frustration. The young child soldiers were everywhere, smoking and talking, washing out their one pair of clothes, eating something, or just gazing up into the sky. They were children, some even under ten, with the look of wild malevolence in their bloodshot eyes. They stared at me darkly as I was marched through the camp.

Occasionally I would see faces from my past, phantoms—boys who had been captured and had disappeared, had never existed really, girls whose names had been left off the lists that their families presented to the charities for food and nonfood handouts. If they recognized me, they did not indicate it. It was safer anyway. Nobody here was who they had been.

My juvenile captor marched me around the side of the lodge to what had been the front entrance. Several golf carts sat, disintegrated, their rusted remains a lasting reminder of the past. The double doors had fallen from their hinges, allowing entry of all manner of animals—wild and tame—as well as the rats, bats, anteaters, mosquitoes, and anything else seeking a respite from the sun's violence. We entered into the cavernous main lobby. The reception was on the right, old wood that was termite infested and crawling with worms. The polished wooden floor of yesteryear no longer shone with the luster of luxury but was instead covered in excrement of the animals and from the bats that hung from the imposing chandelier, which was itself hanging from two of the three chains, the third having been severed probably during a storm. The intertwined antlers that had hosted lightbulbs were now crawling with spiders, webs fastened from antler to antler as an intricate and elaborate artwork. The place smelled musty and dank. We walked down the hallway that had been carpeted but was now only rotten and fetid into the great dining hall—which was the command center of this, the most vicious rebellion in the world. There were tables with maps spread out upon them, some VHF radios and a few satellite telephones, a pile of weapons ranging from AK-47s to rocket launchers. In the back were cans of food and bags of rice and grains.

I walked forward through the rebel leaders that were milling about busily, dreadlocks flowing down their backs, reaching their waists, brown teeth rotten when they grinned at the new captive, fatigues on some fresh and pressed as if they had been issued yesterday and on others stained with sweat and time. At the very back was a sort of throne made of an old couch pushed up against the back wall, over which was nailed antlers in between two old guns behind a small table serving as a footstool. A man—whom I only could assume was the commander— was slouching back into the couch, his booted feet resting upon the foot table. He was the biggest man I had ever seen; his head was the size of a melon, with two lamb-chop-size sideburns parading down the sides, framing massive, swollen lips. His belly sat high, and as he looked at me, he was forced to stretch his neck to see over his own voluminous midriff. He stood slowly, breathing heavily from the exertion until he was on his feet, slightly wobbly from the effort. He was wearing fatigues and a tank top that exposed his man breasts. He had a scar on his shoulder and what looked like healed bullet wounds pockmarking his upper chest. He grinned, the smile turning into a cackling laugh while he jiggled, making me slightly dizzy—but I shivered in spite of myself at the macabre scene. The room had turned suddenly icy as his attention focused on me.

"Come here," he ordered, and as I was brought closer by the juvenile rebel, I felt the world closing in around me until it was only me and him and the shrinking distance between us. A wicked gleam sparkled in his eye. I was stopped three feet in front of him. With a careless wave, he brushed off my infant captor. "You may go." The boy stomped away, his faux marching too obviously for the benefit of his master. Our staring contest extended as he sized me up, probably trying to figure out who I

167

was and why I was there—and if I was a threat. Then, when finally he spoke, he said as much. "Who are you?"

"My name is Charles Agwok," I responded without emotion.

"Charles Agwok," he repeated. "Where are you from?"

"I am from Odek." There was no point in me lying to him; it would serve no purpose. Besides, I had nothing to hide. I was nobody. I knew this.

"Ah, Odek. That is a good omen. But what are you doing walking through my park uninvited?" His voice was almost kind, a ploy I knew as part of the dangerous game we were playing.

"I am simply on my way from one place to the next."

"But the park, it is out of the way for a traveler in search of fortune. Surely you heard it was ... unsafe?" He toyed with the word, rolling it around in his mouth before delivering it.

"Yes," I responded. "I knew that you were here, in the park. Sometimes our options are limited, and we must go where peril might wait."

"From one place to the next?" The rebel commander laughed deeply. "But with limited options? It sounds, my good man, like you have a story. I like a good story."

"Yes, of course," I said, and then decided to tell him everything. I suppose I figured I had nothing to lose, and there was no love lost between the rebels and the Chinamen building the road anyways. When in doubt, stick to the truth.

The commander listened intently, seating himself back on his couch with one of the dreadlocked rebels bringing me a field chair—two pieces of wood, one with the whole in the other through which the board rests, forming a V shape.

The story extended as I elaborated on the details, playing for my audience who was obviously enjoying the tale. I started from the camps and went through, only leaving out my time as a thug, not knowing what shady alliance the Lord's Resistance Army possessed in the underbelly of the capital. Finally, I finished with a flourish, dispatching the Chinaman with my pick. I even acted out the scene. This the commander seemed to especially like.

"Head nailed to the ground?" he asked, chuckling.

I, Charles, from the Camps

"Yes," I said.

"Well done," he said. "Those people are a plague. So you figured that nobody would follow you into the park?"

"Well, actually yes. I assumed that those looking for me would not dare to venture here."

"You are right," he said. "Here, we are untouchable. This is our land now."

"Yes," I answered.

"Well, Charles, I am in a bit of a quandary," the commander said at last.

"Why is that?" I asked. No fear anymore. You only have fear if you have something to lose. I, who had nothing, could not imagine there was anything else in the world that could be taken from me.

"Well, naturally, I cannot allow you to go. You know where we are. You have seen our troop strength and even some of our maps." He pointed to the tables where his commanders were placing X marks on the maps. "For this I was ready to slit your throat and throw you to the crocodiles, like Amin used to."

"So why haven't you?" I asked.

"It's a good question. Probably because, well, I like you. You were honest with me, and that took balls. You were decisive with the Kichina, and that took strength of will. You have survived working the rocks, and that took enormous physical strength. And you are from Odek. So I have made my decision. I will not let you leave, but neither will I kill you. You are now a soldier in the Lord's Resistance Army, to fight against the dictatorship in Kampala and for your people." He stopped, waiting for me to respond.

Naturally, there really wasn't much for me to say. I didn't have anywhere else to go, even if the commander would let me leave. I was being hunted. I had no friends or family. *God loves you and has a wonderful plan for your life.* "Yes," I said after a time. "I will fight with your army," I said.

The commander's thick lips curled upward, showing rotten stumps of teeth and emitting an odor that made me want to recoil, though I dared not. "Good decision! Naturally, I must warn you that if you try to escape, we will not only find you and kill you but your family as well, Charles from Odek."

"I understand," I said. And that is how I, son of the camps and victim of the longest civil war in modern history, became a rebel. It was not something that I had ever wanted. In fact, if you had told the young thief of yesteryear that he would join the rebellion, he would have told you he would rather die. But alas, were there any other options ... We all seize what life puts in our paths as we attempt to preserve the marriage of body and soul for as long as God allows. A rebel—it was as good as anything else, I suppose, and at least these were my people and this was my land. I reached out my hand, and he took it in a firm, meaty handshake, and the deal was sealed.

The first thing the rebel commander did was to give me a weapon and a uniform. Mine had been taken off a colonel in the Ugandan army not two days before and still smelled of him, of his odor, of his fear, and of his excrement after he soiled himself as he was cut down with a knife. I know this, because I had to sew closed the slit in the shirt, just where the heart is and which was covered in red blood that I tried to wash out in the pool, succeeding only in making the stain spread. I would go to the river, when I had a chance, to try to give it a more thorough scrubbing, but for now, I was, well, *abducted*.

"The rules are simple," said Thomas. He was a major in the rebel army, a boy of eighteen or nineteen, younger than myself, and slight of build with dreadlocks hanging all the way down his back. His stare was somehow vacant, but he was not evil, as I had imagined they all would be. The commander had assigned him to me as my minder, with stark warnings again of what would happen should I try to leave or refuse to follow orders. "Do what you're told. Don't stray from where I can see you. Don't try and escape."

"I understand," I said, resigned. And I started my life as a rebel soldier.

As it turns out, it really wasn't much of a life, at least not at the beginning. I woke early, Thomas as commanding officer walking through his platoon, reading off the day's tasks. We assembled early, standing in line to be inspected. "Rifles up" and "Shoulders out" and "Stop slouching" and the typical things you expect a superior to say, right out of Hollywood movies I'd seen in the camps, and I smirked a little bit. "What are you smirking at? Drop down and give me ten push-ups." And the like. Then I was assigned latrine duty, specifically digging a new pit latrine since the one that was being used over the hill was filling up and a new one was much needed. I spent the day with a shovel and a pick in the hard northern Ugandan soil, sweating profusely into the red dirt. For lunch, I was given an orange plastic bowl with rice and beans, and then back to digging the pit. My daily duties were finished when the sun went down, and I returned to the tent beside the pool where I swatted at mosquitoes as I ate another plate of beans. I stayed talking to my fellow abductees until the night blackened and the bats came out and the roar of the hippos from the river was softened as they too left the river to embark upon their nocturnal hunt for grass and leaves.

"So the commander, the man in the great hall ..." I said to one of my platoon mates.

"Yes?" He was immediately suspicious.

"Is he, well, is he *him*?"

"Ha!" The rebel laughed, his voice hoarse and cackling, and his breath almost knocked me over. "No—none of us have ever met *him*. They say he's a shadow or a ghost. He moves about at night over great distances, conferring with his lieutenants. He sees what is unseen. He knows things before they happen. He cannot be killed or even hurt, because the bullets flow off him like water. He knows what is in your heart and your deepest fears—your greatest betrayals. Be careful of what you think, because it is he who will come for you if he senses treason. Clean your spirit of any wrong, purge your thoughts of any doubt, or you will fall outside his protection."

Now before I go any further, I should clear something up. Like I said, I was born in Odek, subcounty of Gulu district, while the war raged. And yes, this is the same subcounty where *he* was born, although by the time I arrived, his story had moved into the shadows. In point of fact, none of us knew when he was born or the circumstances that made him who he became, although his old house still sits a few kilometers back from the camps, abandoned and haunted. There are legends, of course, parables and lore ancient and new. The vast plains of Africa spawn so many tales—some true, some false—wrapped in the traditions of our people and the realities of our hard lives; it is often hard to tell apart reality from the myths.

At any rate, the story that is most often told about *him* goes something like this. It is said that in the beginning there was a man. He was a happy man, contented to work his family farm out beyond the river. The house is still there, but nobody lives there anymore. It is haunted by ghosts—the braver of those who were killed, who challenge him in death as they never could in life. At any rate, this man was middle-aged. His teeth had not yet turned yellow from chewing the cane, and the sun had only just begun to wear a smooth patch at the top of his head. He was sinewy and strong and loved the work and the land. He had one little girl and one little boy, and they played together in the sun and swam the river, hunting the little crawdads.

Now, this man was wise. On Sundays, he would go to the village to help solve problems other families had. Maybe he was an elder. Maybe that's why the trouble started. It was one morning after a long day at the village and a walk home at night under the stars, when people could still walk under the stars. Before *he* came. Before people were afraid. That morning, he awoke feeling a little simple. He'd drunk too much, and his vision was a little blurry when he saw that the vegetable garden in front of his house had been dug up. Gone were the tomatoes, the potatoes, the beans, and the corn—and just before harvesting season. He cursed his luck, harvesting what was left or what was not damaged, to have his wife sell at the market. He still had the millet, and he would be fine, but it irked him, and he sat out at night for a while trying to catch the culprit, but nothing happened. After a time, he gave up.

A year went by, and another planting season came, and the man had forgotten all about the events of the previous year. Again, the night before the harvest, he spent out with his friends, but the next morning, he awoke to find that not only his vegetable field had been ravaged but also part of his millet crop. "Oh, woe is me," he said. "Last year, I hardly broke even. This year, I will become poorer." And the man wept. The years went by. The smooth patch on top of the man's head spread, his teeth slowly turned the color of the setting sun, and his chest started to tighten and sag. And each year it was the same. He did what he could to find what was happening. He stopped visiting the town, losing the place he loved so much as an elder. People no longer sought his advice; he was not a lucky man. His daughter and son became older, and as they grew up, they grew ashamed of their father. He began to sell what he had, and he sent one of his wives back to live with her brother. Each year, more and more of his fields were destroyed.

Nevertheless, he kept trying. He set up bonfires at night during harvest time. He had his family surround the fields. He brought warriors from the village. But try as he might, each time it was the same. Morning came, and the mayhem of his broken fields met his eyes, filled with despair. Finally, one night he covered himself in a thick layer of pond slime and slipped into the water. That night, he dug a root into his side to make sure he did not sleep, and he watched. At long last, there it was. A lizard, the size of a man, crawled out of the water down a ways to begin ravaging his field. The man waited until the beast was in full fury, and then he leaped out of the water, laying hold of the creature. They wrestled, and they fought, first on top, then underneath, then on top again until the light of the dawn laid bare the savagery of their contest. The beast leaped for the water, with the man seizing at the last moment its tail. The tail came off, and the beast fled, never to be seen again.

The man, who had become old, took the tail over to his house. His family was all gone, and he was ashamed. He put the tail in a basket and lit a bonfire with the remains of his field. That night, the fire raged, and he drank as he cursed the heavens and his life. The next morning when he awoke from his blackout, he was shocked to find a baby quiet and sleeping in the basket. He began to raise the child. But the child had a darkness to him. He was cruel to animals. He did not help with the work, and he refused to study or to listen. The bitter old man did not know what to do. When the child turned thirteen, the old man sat him down. He told him he was saddened but that he would have to leave. That he himself would be going to live in the village; there, at least he could beg for his food. The child's eyes lit with an unusual fire, and he stood, saying nothing. He turned and walked away. The legend says that as he reached the end of the man's vision, the old fellow swore to everybody who asked him that the boy descended to all fours, and a long, spiny tail extended out. It is said he went to the mountains and that he became—well, who he is now, he whom we all have known. Joseph Kony. Leader of the Lord's Resistance Army.

Now, it's not that I believed any of that, at least not at first. Like most people, I was naturally rational. But the stories kept coming. "He defeated the army in battle, sending a disease into their camps," and, "They shot him last night, but the bullets bounced back and knocked down one of their helicopters," and even, "He came to me in my sleep, told me I would be a great fighter." But beyond the magic, the rebel leader was known even more for his wickedness. This, more than the supernatural, buttressed his position in the hearts of his men.

One particularly gruesome tale kept making the rounds. I heard it many times as I sat by the fires at night. The rebel Thomas, who had become my companion, and I were sitting guard upon a wall. The night was dark, and a mist had rolled in from the river, making it hard to see even more than a few feet. It smelled like mud and fish, not unpleasant but distinct. "It is said that he caught his deputy in a betrayal," my friend said. "It was with one of his favorite wives, and his deputy thought he was being clever—that their affair was secret. Of course, *he* found out about it, so one day he called all his platoon to stand at attention in the parade grounds. Then he called his deputy to come forward and called his favorite wife from the tent. With a sharp knife, in front of all his men, he castrated the deputy, who just stood there through the pain without even crying out. And then he took a gun and forced his wife to go to the rebel and shoot him between the eyes. Then, in front of her, he killed all her children with the knife—one after the next, slitting their throats, saying, 'Because of your betrayal, I don't know which ones are mine,' and then he killed her."

All these things I pondered as I worked and waited for what came next. What came next was my first operation.

"On your feet, men!" Thomas yelled, jolting us all awake. It was still the middle of the night. Outside, the crickets still chirped, and the air smelled musty. We bolted to our feet, some naked, some with only underwear, and a few who slept in their uniforms—dreading moments like these.

"Inspection!" he yelled again, and we all threw on our uniforms and tied our shoes if we had them—if not, donning our flip-flops. Those who went barefoot, well, went barefoot. We tidied our beds, made mostly of piles of leaves or grass or straw with a blanket thrown over them, occasionally an old mattress that had been pillaged in a raid and that now pulsated with cockroaches and beetles and lice. We finished as efficiently as possible and stood beside them while Thomas walked up and down the line—imitating what we'd all seen in American war movies. "You, you're dirty." We were all dirty. "You, your uniform needs pressing." Our uniforms were a jumbled hodgepodge taken from the dead and dying. "You smell." He smelled worse. How could he tell? "Men, you disgrace me," he finished. "How will we win, with you at the front lines? No discipline, no spirit. No love of our commander." We sucked in our breaths. He'd gone too far. That offense was punishable by death. We would repeat often to each other our admiration for *him*, who would one day lead Uganda and institute a perfect system based upon the Ten Commandments. "Nevertheless, today—such as we are—we will strike out again. Rest is over. Now it is time to do battle for our commander's perfect vision. You will make yourselves ready. We march at daylight." And he walked out of the barracks. We spent the rest of the time before the sun rose preparing ourselves for the privation of the battlefield. Most of us had made bags or backpacks out of old cloth, into which we inserted the limited clothes that we had, the occasional odd bag of beans, pot or pan or orange bowl. Weapons we had, small arms mostly, AK-47s polished smooth during the waiting. The rebels' favorite weapon, one that fires in the rain, in the mud, does not overheat, and never jams. We trickled out of the barracks and assembled for our march.

There were thirty of us that morning. We marched single file straight north. Most of the small contingent were children, thirteen or fourteen years old. I had not gotten to know any of them—there was nobody to know behind the vacant, bloodshot eyes. The boys who had hunted lizards under the African sun and swam naked in the streams, who had played soccer with an old ball donated by some politician, who had made his seasonal trip to reap the votes of the caged—they were gone, those boys, replaced by entities without soul or spirit, who carried

175

out orders without question and when there was nothing to do simply sat without talking, staring into the night or the water or the jungle. Not thinking—it was better not to think. That's what the rebellion did to these children, teaching them that to think was to remember, and to remember—well, that was the worst pain of all. Not of what had been done to them. The human spirit is resilient and can recover even from the greatest violence. But what they had done. Been forced to do, to be sure, but what they had done after all. Some resorted to drugs or sometimes alcohol to wipe their minds clean for a time. The rebellion provided those free for their captives, when they had some. It was cheaper than food and assured a greater control over mind and body when necessary.

Some might ask why I joined the rebellion so willingly. Why my rage was not turned against my captors, as it had in the past. Why I became a guerilla. The answer, from the lofty perch of time, is I don't know. I suppose it was because always, at the back of my mind, my fallback option was the rebellion. It is for every Acholi boy. Why should I be any exception? And because I knew that at least I was enslaved to something that was mine—my people, cousins and uncles who spoke my same language and shared my same history. That this, after all, was my final fate after so long seeking something else. And it fit—it fit who I had become, where my viciousness would be welcome and my wickedness a calling card. I was home.

We marched in silence north. Thomas at the front, and I at the end to assure that there were no stragglers and no attempts to escape. I had not been abducted—had come willingly according to their calculations and was therefore of greater confidence than the youngsters who were always looking for a chance to flee. With us were four adolescent girls. Their jobs were to gather firewood and water, prepare the food for the fighters, and clean up afterward. They carried food in great bags on their backs or their heads. At night, they would be passed around the camp to fulfill the primal needs of the fighters who believed that the next day might be their last. These girls' eyes too were vacant, although they were the most likely to attempt flight. Not less than once a day, I found myself running through the bush after one or another who had gone to relieve herself or collect a potato she had seen along the way and did not return. I would find her and bringing her back but without violence—at least not yet.

At night, we would camp in a dale or under a wide tree, eating Spartan meals that consisted mostly of beans, some rice, tubers grown locally, the occasional maize if it was in season, thrown together with some local greens and boiled down into a stew of sorts. On a very rare occasion, we had meat—goat meat from one we had found along the way or stolen from one of our raids on a village or an ambush of a trading truck on the way to one of the bigger towns. Never did we have beef, because all the cows had been eaten years ago.

One evening, Thomas was holding what he called his evening briefing, a roundup of the day's events followed by announcements for the following day. It took place after dinner and after the chores of making up the camp were completed: spreading out bedding, dousing the fire, assigning watch duties. It was at these briefings that he would chastise those who had behaved badly in battle and mete out punishments, sometimes gruesome, to those who had not been obedient. He would issue orders he had received from the commander. None of us were ever let into the murky world of leadership. Thomas had with him a pocket-sized satellite phone that he kept charged by connecting it to a small solar tablet that he forced one of the girls to carry on her head all day in the sun. During dinner, he would slip away over a hill or across a stream to engage in a conversation, after which he would return to give us the next day's targets or movements.

As I fought with them, I gained firsthand experience of the rebels' sophisticated hit-and-run tactics, developed over the twenty years of rebellion. It was amazing really, the level of coordination by soldiers who were uneducated riffraff abducted from the camps and terrorized into fighting, led by an eccentric warrior priest who lived a country away and hadn't even been to Uganda for years. We would attack a single point, a weapons depot, a food shipment, a deployment of new recruits with shiny new weapons, in a coordinated fashion. From three sides, bands of child-soldiers would lay into their enemies, striking terror in the older, better-trained adversaries. Sometimes only a few dozen would send a platoon into a frenzy. We would move in, slashing with machetes and screaming, some half-naked, others with beads around their waists, and still others charging into the hail of bullets, somehow emerging unharmed on the other side to slide their knife into the platoon leader's lungs. We would meet up in the middle of the field of battle, rebels from my platoon and others who I didn't know, as we laid into our adversaries. As instructed, the level of brutality was such that all of our enemies—those who survived—would remember the battle. We would kill the soldiers, severing their heads from their bodies and hurling them at their comrades. We would castrate others, hanging their foreskins from our knives as we plunged them deep into the hearts of others. For those who surrendered, it would go worse—laying them down side by side and then hacking them all to thousands of pieces in a frenzy of machetes and saliva and blood, the field flowing red with their blood. Screams ricocheted off the mountains or the jungles or dissipated into the plains as we chased down our foes. Oftentimes, upon seeing us, the Ugandan army would turn and flee, running into the arms of another platoon of Joseph Kony's rebels. They would shred their clothes out of fear, dropping their weapons, and they would even sometimes fall upon each other in their panic as we watched, laughing.

Then, as quickly as we came, we would shatter and vanish—dissipating into the night like a vapor, an army of ghouls returning to the afterworld. The military would always send recruits, but they were cumbersome and lumbering like baby hippos. They would arrive seven or ten hours late, in time only to pick up the rotting bodies of their compatriots—we had left with everything we could carry, often leaving the bodies of the dead naked—and bury them in shallow graves, looking over their shoulders for a renewed assault by our army, but we were already long gone. I don't know how the commander controlled us, coordinated us. Maneuvered us to the exact place that we had to be to wreak the maximum havoc on our enemies. He must be a demon—as so many said—for the things I saw and experienced were not of this world.

Following dinner and his call with the senior generals of the rebellion as well as, I assumed, the commander himself, Thomas would arrive with new intelligence and often orders, some of which he shared with us; others he kept to himself. It was during this time that he would also offer an induction of sorts to the newcomers if the day had included a recruitment raid on a camp, village, or town. This always involved an initial, inhuman act of brutality. The theory—if theory it could be called—was that the best way to cement the loyalty of the newest wave of recruits was to induct them into the rebellion through an act of unspeakable violence. This way, the guilt upon their young minds would be such that they would be unable to shake the feeling of shame and filth and would be easily controlled. The act took different forms, and as my position of leadership increased in the organization— after Thomas was killed and I replaced him, and his superior, and his superior—I would often use my creativity to invent other, even more gruesome ways to guarantee the recruits' loyalty. For one group, we had them select one of their number by a vote, at which point we tied him to a tree, and each new recruit would walk by, taking a bite out of their former friend until he bled out. Other times, we abducted the sisters or the mothers of one of the strongest and forced him to rape her. Still other times, we would find a beehive, tie a child to it, and then have the others throw rocks until the child was swollen to almost double his size. I do not like to talk about these things because I am not proud of them, and I will not dwell on them, but they are part of my past, part of my story that I cannot deny.

"Men," Thomas said that evening as we were all sitting around after dinner. One of us was singing; another was playing cards. There was a desperate squealing coming from one of the tents. "We have our orders," Thomas said. "Tomorrow, we will hit the girls' school at Aboke. Our commander wishes to send a bold message to the tyrannical government that they cannot protect even their wealthiest girls. We march at midnight, to hit the school at dawn. Get what sleep you can." I ambled to the hole in the ground that I had softened for my own use and laid down my head.

I had become a rebel. It had not been my decision, but I had refused to run—and that act, or lack of it, would lead me deeper and deeper as I lost more and more of my soul in the process.

CHAPTER 16

We woke early to begin our assault on the girls' school. Aboke is a boarding school, one of thousands that British colonizers loved so much and left as one of their lasting legacies across Africa. It was home to several hundred girls, from primary school through secondary, six years to eighteen, the perfect ages in fact for the work that the commander had in mind for them. Cleaning, cooking, and screwing. "Our young men need wives, need women," Thomas had said to me, following his announcement to the group. "Else how will they keep following us? Young men have urges, itches they need to scratch. To fill them—that is what our commander cares about—to vie for the natural interests of his soldiers who are fighting for God. 'All is right in love and war,' as it has been said. Well, this is war, and our boys need love, small as they are, young, missing their mothers and their families. We will provide surrogate families." I had only nodded. With this, our assault was explained, justified, and given honor.

We marched in single file south, crossing a few tributaries of the Nile on our way with ropes that we had hung across the waters to facilitate our assaults and which the military had not yet found. Time stretched as the night deepened. There was no moon and only a few stars since it was rainy season and the heavens were cloudy. We all knew where we were going; this was our land, after all. Acholiland we called it, our homeland; nobody could best us here. We knew every tree, bush, and shrub, every village and watering hole and river. We marched without light—confident. As usual, I went last, although we did not expect any desertions. Before a fight, the children were given drugs such as we had or had grown. We didn't call them drugs. "They are a special potion given to us by our commander so that we can receive his protection during our battle. They will give us energy and fill us with a sense of his strength and greatness." This they believed wholly, without doubt or questioning; the minds of children are more attuned to the magic and do not require explanations but accept the ethereal as a natural part of the world around them. Occasionally, one would have a hallucination, which was then used to explain to the others of the special visitation that our commander had given to the boy, to underscore the importance of our mission that night. And the small rabble would be filled with hope and a renewed sense of purpose.

Slowly we passed the river and the forest into the farmland spreading out before us. We marched with impunity because we had informants who would advise us to the location of the military, so we knew exactly where they were at all times. It was the night they dreaded most anyway, and the government soldiers never ventured far beyond the bases, cowering in fear of us, huddling together like rabbits in the night while we were the mongooses, hunting them. The night smelled musty, dank. An owl hooted from a tree, scaring away a snake that slithered from beside the path where it had coiled a few inches from the feet of the boys who gave it not a second thought. The potion protected them from all harm—bullets or poison, it made no difference.

Slowly, carefully now because we were getting close, we scaled the small hill and crested the top, looking down upon a pristine little valley with the girls' school at the center. It was dark of night, but my pupils had adjusted, and to me it was clear. The school consisted of three buildings, set facing each other with an open square in the middle, which had an acacia tree, paths, gardens, and a playground area. The first building, imposing, was obviously the main facility where the nuns prepared the meals in the kitchen, and the girls ate in the adjacent cafeteria. It would have the school rooms, the library, and the offices for the administrators. Out back were two other buildings, one smaller, which would be the nuns' quarters, and one larger, two stories with many windows, each fitted with an air-conditioning unit. Those would be the girls' rooms and the target of our raid that night.

181

The regular puttering of the generator was the only sound, lighting a few lights in the courtyard. One of the windows in the nuns' building was lit—a sister reading her Bible early most likely. The girls' dorm was completely dark.

"Now," Thomas said, looking up at the sky. It was at its darkest, a short time before the suggestion of the sun would begin to insinuate itself in the east. It was when people were at their most vulnerable, when sleep was deepest and the ground was still at rest, unwilling to disturb its slumber to echo the footsteps of men. "We will divide into three groups of ten. You ten"—he gestured at the first group of ten, led by a rough adolescent named James who had been a fervent recruit since caught walking from his town to Kitgum to look for work—"will go down over there," and Thomas gestured left. "I will take my group, and we will go around there." He gestured around right. "You," he said, pointing at me, "will go straight in from here, creeping around the school building. Our target is the girls' dorm. We will take as many as we can. The signal for the attack"—he looked around, making sure he had his rebels' attention—"will be when I cut the generator. Then we move in from all sides. Kill the nuns. I don't care. Don't harm the girls. Our commander has need of an additional wife and has instructed that the finest of the group be sent to him. This is a sacred trust, choosing a wife for our great leader. We must take care to not injure any of the girls until I have made the choice. Any questions?"

Silence.

"Good. No talking now. The raid will last thirty minutes, after which we will reassemble here with as many girls as we have taken for our march north. Let's move."

We began our descent from the hill in three separate parties. First Thomas's, which had the longest way to travel around the west side of the compound; then the other led by James, and mine going last. "Let's go," I said when our turn arrived, and we began to creep delicately down the mountain. As the compound grew closer, I was able to make out additional details. The main building was actually two stories, with a fireplace emerging from its roof on one end. Large, wooden double doors were sealed against the night. It was surrounded by a chain-link fence and topped with razor wire, which had been invisible from the hilltop. We all knew how to deal with the fences, slicing through them using a makeshift wire cutter made of machetes, but it would slow us down. On we went, through the cornfields and into the vegetable gardens of the nuns. Tomatoes, cucumber, onion. I tripped over a ripe watermelon and bit my lip so as not to curse. Then I saw it, hidden from our view atop the mountain: a Ugandan army jeep parked on the far side, just outside the fence. Two tents—three soldiers, maybe four, protecting the compound. It was just where Thomas would need to come through, close to the generator, but there was nothing I could do except wait. He would see the soldiers and would have to dispatch them before the fighting began, but it was an additional complication that nobody had expected.

We waited, lying belly down in the vegetable garden with our wire cutters at the ready. A big dung beetle crawled into my loose-fitting pants, tickling its way up my buttocks excruciatingly as I tried to wedge it out, my hands deep below my crotch. Beside me, one of my soldiers let out an impatient whine, and I hit him with the butt of my gun across the head, a cold thunk that silenced the boy. Slowly, a storm was sneaking up on the dale, thunder chasing the lightning around the sky. A thin mist began to fall, drenching us all, turning our vigil into a soggy mess. Worms crawled from the depths of the rich black dirt when they heard the patter, writhing about in the puddles just under our noses.

Finally, I heard a sound, but it wasn't the sound that I was waiting for. Instead of the ceasing of the generator's soothing hum, what I heard was a rough command followed by a yell, the discharge of two rounds that ricocheted through the night above the storm, and then a bloody, gurgling scream. Then all remained still except the ongoing whirr of the generator. One by one, lights began to appear in the windows of the nuns' residences, and one elderly woman opened the screen door closest to where I was lying with my troops. "Hello?" she said, her voice nervous, shrill. "Is anybody out there?"

I swerved, barking an order to the boy I had belted. "Wait here. Don't move and don't say anything!" He just grunted at me, hate in his eyes, his hand still held nursing the side of his head. I put one elbow in front of the other, and the next and then the next, and started to slither around to the far side of the compound where Thomas was to have cut

183

the fence and disabled the generator. It took me fifteen minutes. By this time, all the sisters were awake, several standing in the doorframe of their group house, while a few others had braved the rains to rush to the entrance of the girls' dorms, making sure their charges were there, sleeping and unperturbed by what, the nuns knew not. Finally, I made it around the corner, sweating through the rain, and saw in front of me the mess. Two of the soldiers were draped across the seats of the jeep, lifeless eyes staring up into the storm. A third was lying on the ground entwined with—Thomas ... I jumped to my feet, running over to the stiffening body of my superior. I needn't have hurried. Thomas died the moment the soldier put a bullet through his heart and just at the same time as his own knife penetrated the liver of the soldier. Behind, cowering in the long grass a short distance, were Thomas's rabble, unable to move. Drugged and leaderless, they lay there, not in fear or indecision but simply as automatons awaiting orders that might or might not arrive.

In every life, there are moments that, especially when seen in hindsight, are of great significance. My life had many of these, and you who are reading this know them all. But what I did that stormy night will live in my nightmares until the devil takes me. I still don't know why; if there was any moment when I could have stood and walked away, it was then. Still of right mind, with only the limited sins of a rebel underling and a thug to weigh my conscience. I knew I should—I weighed the possibility. I thought about my options; in a split second, the mind can conjure many scenarios. I saw myself running east to the beaches of Kenya to drink beer and listen to the waves. I saw myself flitting away and following the river north through the Sudan, seeing the arid desert lands that I'd only ever heard about, maybe becoming a Muslim myself, marrying an Arab girl. I saw myself getting in the jeep and driving to the biggest army base I could find to tell them of the attack and become a soldier for the government. It was, however, as if somehow my spirit floated up out of my body to watch the unfolding scene emotionless and from a distance, without the weight of ownership and responsibility.

That fateful night, I stood, grabbing the makeshift wire cutters from my belt, and—no longer concerned with discovery—walked to the fence, slashing my way through with one powerful stroke. I strode through the hole and to the generator, lifting the panel and attacking the purring beast with my machete as oil and water and sparks flew everywhere. The great behemoth belched twice, sputtered, and ground to a stop while the lights flickered and went out.

Don't ask me how we could see in the utter darkness. Maybe it was an effect of the drugs. Perhaps the stories of our commander's magic were true, how he endowed us with the ability to prowl like the jungle cats he was said to commune with. I don't know. What I do know is that as soon as the compound was plunged into darkness, I bellowed the order at the top of my lungs, "Attack!" My voice ricocheted around the buildings and onto the waiting rabble, who threw themselves onto the wire fences and then into the compound, headed straight for the girls' dormitory.

"Stop!" one sister screamed, attempting to slow my advance, standing in my way and grabbing my arm until I cut her away with my knife.

"Please," another said, "they are just girls." And she too was silenced by a vicious kick. I was walking steadily as the pandemonium intensified around me. Some of the nuns had emerged from their rooms with kitchen knives or brooms, but they were easily brushed aside by my rebels.

My rebels.

I arrived at the door of the girls' dorm and entered without slowing, marching up to the second floor. I was not the first there; my troops had been going room by room, pulling the girls from their bunks—dressed still in their nightshirts—and pushing them toward the open door. I went in one room, and finding the closet door slightly ajar, I kicked it in and grabbed the two cowering teenagers by their nightshirts, ripping them as I threw them in the direction of my rebels in the hall.

"No!" yelled another one of the girls as I walked into a third room, and she leaped from the bunk bed upon me with her mirror held high, crashing it over my head. I only laughed, blood running into my eyes and my mouth. I licked it away—my teeth turning a sickening red—as I hefted her into the hall.

I kept walking. At the far end of the second-floor hall, a group of older girls had begun to barricade a door, stacking cots and beds and dressers and anything they could find against the other side in the hopes of buying time, praying out loud that we would leave, that we would not need them, that we would not take them, that we would consider it too much of a bother. But the hunt was in my blood now, and I leaned back, lifting my leg, and kicked against the thin door with the heel of my foot. One, two, three times. Again and again as the shards of splintering wood ricocheted around the hall. I was laughing maniacally but could barely hear myself above the screams of the girls behind the door. Slowly, the thin line of defense started to give way, and I could look into the room—four of the older, prettier girls, their eyes yellow with terror as they saw my bloodied visage and heard my cackling. I again withdrew the machete and began to hack at the meager defenses of the adolescents, taking my time while the girls stopped screaming—there was no point—and simply watched my advance in horror. Then I was through, falling upon one of them in lust and impunity while the others screamed again, throwing themselves upon me kicking and biting, but they were easily beaten back—and quickly taken as prizes by others of my more seasoned boys who followed my gruesome example with relish. When I was finished with the girl, I killed her, leaving her lying there on the floor as I strode evenly from the room.

The raid was over. The girls—as many as were left of them, a hundred or so I suppose—stood huddled together in the open area between the buildings. The mist had turned into a downpour, and they were all soaking wet, shivering in fear and in cold. I surveyed the situation. The sisters were all dead. Some girls were fleeing south through the farmlands. A fire was burning in one of the first-floor rooms of the dorm. Who set it, I didn't know, didn't care. My platoon was intact, sweating with smiles wide across their faces. The joy of the kill. Then from behind me, I was surprised by James, long knife lifted and brandishing his AK. "Where is Thomas?" he asked.

"Dead," I answered.

"Did you kill him?" he asked.

"No," I said. "It was the soldiers."

He was still for only a moment, then said, "Okay, then I am assuming command of this platoon."

"Like hell you are," I said, and before he could think, I delivered a wicked blow to his thorax—something I had learned when working as an enforcer in Kampala. He fell to his knees and then to the floor, eyes rolled up into his skull. I picked up his AK, turned the barrel to face him, and delivered a shot through the temple. Then I turned to face my rebels and the girls.

"You are under my command, and you will obey me."

Nobody said a thing.

"Now we march; girls, single file. I will lead, and you"—I pointed to one of the young men who I had become at ease with, although I did not know is name—"you will take the rear. If anybody tries to flee, shoot them. Understood?" Everybody nodded. I began to walk, exiting through the hole I had made by the generator, stooping to withdraw from Thomas's pocket the slim satellite telephone—my lifeline to the rebellion, my ticket to leadership—and I marched my rebels and our prizes up the hill and onward.

I'm sure you are wondering what brought about my behavior. Why I would have fulfilled the dastardly orders when my superior, my minder, the man charged with my obedience—who would have killed me without a second thought—had been killed? Why did I not simply flee, running east or west or south? Why didn't I turn myself over to the nuns, offering my protection in exchange for their leniency when the authorities arrived? Why didn't I take my soldiers—the platoon that was now mine—and start my own movement, fighting back against the rebels who had commandeered my obedience, or even creating a rebellion even more wicked in the hopes of greater spoils? The answer, again, is: I don't know. Each of us have moments in our lives when the road we are traveling diverges into two paths, and we must choose—for we can go one way or another but not both. Sometimes they are moments that are not even that existential—the choice between different jobs, between different spouses, where to live or what to study or who to fight. Choices—life is made up of many, and without adequate justification, we oftentimes, too often in fact, choose the rockiest of paths. That is my only defense, my only reasoning for embracing so completely my role in a rebellion that was not mine, that in fact had done me and mine such a great injury. You will probably say that moment was like so many others in my past. Like the moment so long ago in a camp when I became a thief; like the moment when I became a hired thug; like the moment when I killed the Kichina. That those were the reflections of my true nature, a soul black as the deepest night and unworthy of forgiveness or consideration. And I cannot say that I disagree with you; the evidence surely weighs in your favor. For this reason, I will not ask you for forgiveness. It is easy to commit acts of evil and then seek mercy after the benefits are reaped. It's customary upon being caught to cry out to the judge for leniency in remorse and sorrow. I will not insult you—or myself—by such a facile response. Therefore, I will say it again. I do not know why I chose the path I did, but while I do regret it, how could I not? I do not apologize for it. I can no more ask for release from you for having committed wicked deeds than you can obtain a pardon from me for my having been born black, a child of the camps, destitute and nameless. Both are facts of life, and there is no way around them. We are who we are, and damn those who say we can be other.

That night I had marched my platoon, thirty boys and one hundred girls, trembling and vomiting, barefoot in their nightdresses only—up into the hinterlands of Acholiland. I knew we had to keep walking. I could only assume that one of the sisters had radioed in the attack, either while it was beginning or after having survived us. Ugandan soldiers would be on their way, though it would take them hours to mobilize, organize, and deploy. By that time, we needed to be far enough away that the trail had gone cold, and into areas where the Ugandan military feared to go. I pushed them hard. The girls' feet began to bleed as they wept quietly, some holding each other for comfort. Only three collapsed, and we killed them to serve as a lesson to the others, lest we leave them by the side of the path and encourage other such behavior from the other girls. The rain was coming in sheets now. We were all soaked to the bone, but I didn't notice. Something electric was running through my veins, something I hadn't ever felt before, something new and dangerous and exciting.

We walked in silence, and as we progressed, the daytime insinuated itself in the east. "Harder, faster now. Or you will be punished," I said, words thrown over my shoulder not as a scream but that nevertheless still carried to every ear in the wretched procession. Behind me there was only silence, punctuated by the occasional whimper. We were going upward and west to a forest that was known, to everybody who needed to know, to be a hideout of the rebellion. I did not know if there were any platoons there, but whether there were or not, what I did know was that the soldiers would not follow us into the forest. One time, a unit of Central American jungle mercenaries had been hired to try to penetrate that jungle to kill the commander, but our boys had waited for them, catching them in the dark oppression of the jungle's interior and sending them into such fear and panic that they had killed each other in the crossfire while our rebels looked on from their perches in the branches. I doubted the soldiers would attempt a repeat of this for a few dozen girls.

The sun exploded onto the plains—the rains having tapered off— as we approached the jungle, and I stood by, allowing my parade of misery to pass as I examined the girls. If I'd been asked, which nobody had the courage to do, I would have said that I was looking over my prizes, to decide which was fitting as tribute to our commander. In reality, I was looking for a girl for myself. They came on, their white nightdresses blackened by mud, with the occasional red streak from a blow or where a leg had been snagged by a thistle or a thorn. Their eyes were bloodshot from their weeping, and vomit stained their fronts as they came trembling on, not daring to look me in the eye as they passed. Occasionally, I would stop one, lift her head by the chin, and open her mouth with my fingers, which still had the blood of James on them, and some of the girls gagged. Then I would lift up her dress for a closer examination and let her march along. The procession passed, and I stood looking backward, down over the valley to the tiny compound in the distance. I imagined that I saw movement, maybe the sisters cleaning up, sweeping away broken glass and collecting shattered wood. Maybe we had missed a girl or two, and they were together consoling each other. I thought I saw light glancing off a jeep's windshield and wondered how long it would take the military to mount their response. Such a thing had never been done—what I had accomplished. What I had dared. Rich girls from the Catholic school. Abducted in such numbers that it was sure to make the newspapers and embarrass the tyrant. It was sure to make our commander proud. I knew I had to get to him, to connect and inform him of my success before the story was told by somebody else who would spin it to my disadvantage.

It was later that evening at the hour that Thomas had always left the campfire out of earshot that I too took the phone that I had removed from the pocket of his corpse and walked to a clearing in the woods. We had made good time that day and were well away from the compound and free from immediate concern of a Ugandan military raid. I had given strict orders to my lieutenant that the girls were to be unharmed, fed with whatever we could give them, and afforded a place to sleep. Nevertheless, they were to be watched carefully until I returned; any escapes would be treated as the most serious of betrayals. I pulled the phone from my pocket and turned it on, waiting for the numbers to appear in orange on the small screen. I was not unfamiliar with technology, having lived as long as I did in Kampala and coming into contact with a great number of devices. With relief, I discovered that there was no passcode required and that it immediately connected with the satellite. I found the scroll button on the keypad and began scrolling down the previous calls. I discovered that there were in fact quite a few, not only once a day as I had assumed but several times a day, including one just before the previous evening's attack. Those numbers were all the same—but as I scrolled down, I discovered one from two evenings before, to a different number, and I held my breath as I hit the dial button.

Ring, ring, ring.

Finally, a voice answered. "You're late. You were supposed to call as soon as the raid was finished. I had two platoons standing by waiting for orders!"

"Sir, it's just that—"

"Who the hell is this?" the voice asked, interrupting me.

I cleared my throat but still squeaked out, "You might know me as Charles Agwok," I said, and continued with greater confidence.

"Charles, yes. Thomas spoke of you. Where is he, and why do you have his phone?"

With greater confidence, I told him the entire story, from the moment we marched down the hill to the arrival in the forest. When I was finished, I waited, and as the time extended, I became afraid that the call had dropped or worse—so much worse—he had hung up, when he finally said, "I see. Well, the loss of Thomas is bad. Nevertheless, you appear to have stepped up. I like that in my lieutenants. You say you have the girls?"

"Yes, sir. One hundred and thirty-seven, exactly."

"Are they of good stock, hardy and strong?"

"Yes," I said. "I inspected them myself. They will bear great children for Acholi."

"Good." The line went still for a moment. Then he said, "You are to march at first light back to Pakuba and deliver your acquisitions to my lieutenant there. He will know what to do with them."

"Yes, sir."

"And, Agwok," the voice said.

"Yes," I said, expectant.

"This day, you have earned Thomas's platoon. You are no longer Charles Agwok. Your new name will be Okot."

And that is how I became one of the lieutenants in the Lord's Resistance Army. As a territorial lieutenant, I was assigned the Kitgum theater of battle, managed from Lotuturu. As Pakuba was to Gulu, Lotuturu was to Kitgum. From there, I was untouchable as I commanded my child armies against the soldiers. Each platoon consisted of thirty to forty recruits, taken from the camps—although a few had come willingly, bored of poverty or frustrated by a life with no future. Volunteers received the preeminent spot in my affections and the command of one of the platoons. At any given time, I had fifty platoons spread out over the length and breadth of the Kitgum theater. Our mission—if we had one—was to wear out the government soldiers. Force them into ambushes they could not win; raid their supply lines where they were weakest; attack their camps at night, pillaging what we needed and killing who we could. It was a battle of attrition that I managed from my perch atop the mountain, seated in Amin's old throne as the reincarnation of evil that never seemed to release its hold on Africa's pearl. I also managed a network of spies in the towns of greater significance, who would call to inform of troop movements seen on the roads or orders overheard at some of the better bars where the officers drank—the Bomah Hotel, the Orchid, and others. These were all relayed to me through my satellite phone, which was paid directly by the Sudanese Ministry of Humanitarian Affairs in Khartoum.

"This is mine!" I said aloud, my words tumbling down the escarpment into the lush valley below. Nobody would challenge that assertion, for there was nobody who would dare come near me, which is exactly how I wanted it. Often, I would sit, at times for hours, looking down from Lotuturu over the high valley below.

Lotuturu.

Long ago, Idi Amin threw his gluttonous gaze across his country. At that time, it had all been his, and he built houses like outposts, as a physical representation of his presence, in every corner of his dominion. Entebbe, Kampala of course, Fort Portal, Murchison, West Nile. Lotuturu. Perched high atop the mountain range that divides Uganda from South Sudan, accessible by a narrow, rocky road that climbs through a forest—where he often hunted deer and monkey—Lotuturu was a collection of three buildings. Amin's residence had two rooms, one for his bed and one as a sitting room, with a latrine out back. A kitchen where his meals were prepared, for Amin was a voracious eater. And a guest house for when he wanted to bring ministers or allies to this place, although it was rumored he rarely did. His girls he kept with him until he had no need for them, and he either killed them if they had displeased him or gave them a house in Kampala that he had seized from one of his enemies if the parting was gentle. Finally, another shack sat far back down the road for his guards; he was also exceptionally paranoid. Inside, the houses were simple, the rooms small and austere with bare walls and rugs covering the floors, often with pillows or unassuming furniture to cater to Amin's unvarnished tastes. He would eat grilled meats and piles of potatoes or boiled bananas, the food of his people, prepared by a chef from his lands. His sophistication was saved for his drinking. Though reportedly a Muslim, Amin rarely prayed, never did the hajj or gave to charity, nor followed any other basic Islamic commands. More importantly, he was a heavy drinker, an alcoholic who would binge excessively, consuming huge quantities of liquor while engaged in sport both wicked and lawless. In front of his house, attached to the wall were three cement thrones, the one in the center larger than the other two. It was there where I myself sat that Amin would also sit for hours, calling for drinks over and over from the valet who stood quietly beside the rough bar attached to the kitchen as he—the self-proclaimed field marshal of the plains—would look out over his empire, occasionally pawing at his girls on both his right and his left.

Amin was said to have liked this place especially, for the same reason probably that I did. Legend has it that long ago, when Uganda was considered the Pearl of Africa by her British overlords, Lotuturu played a special role for the crown. It was at the height of World War II. Luo Ugandans were fighting as King's African Rifles from Italy to Algeria, Amin himself a private somewhere on the front lines. During this time, the British government began to be concerned about the potential overrunning of England by Nazi armies and the subsequent fate of their monarchs. The preservation of the royal line. For the British, the fate of their kings is always intertwined with the success of their civilization. It was rumored that British generals began looking for the most remote, faraway place for them to safeguard the bloodline. Not the queen, her absence would be too obvious. But duchesses and lords three and four steps removed from the crown in case something should happen to Elizabeth. In the survey of their empire, they discovered Lotuturu and established an outpost there fit for royalty: sumptuous tents resplendent with colors, silver tea pots and cutlery glistening in the African sun. Fine aromas of British cuisine wafting down the mountainside, prepared by chefs brought there from Europe to entertain the palates of the royals. Elegant men and women sipping Champagne or gin and tonics, playing cards, their white suits immaculate as they waited out the war. I am guessing, but I believe Amin liked this connection with royalty; occupying a place they had occupied gave him somehow more legitimacy. I guess this, because I, a boy from the camps, now held this place that had a history. I, a boy from the camps, now had a past. I sat upon the throne of a dictator upon a royal mountain. I, a boy from the camps, now had a name a new name, a nom de guerre. Okot.

In the morning, I would wake in the bedroom, a girl on either side.

I would go outside, drinking sweet tea from a thermos prepared by the cook, and then I would do my exercises—two hours of running, usually down through the forest that was eerily quiet, depleted of all animals from years of overhunting by one rebel group after the next. I would return, sweat pouring down my body, before I bathed with a cup drawing water from a green pail, water taken from the hand pump over a borehole that had been punched by the royal engineers. Then I would don my uniform and go into the second room in the lodge—this the war room. There I had painted on the floor a large map of the Kitgum theater, with the precise locations of all my platoons indicated by a red marker and all the Ugandan soldiers' bases and deployments in green. Each day, I would command my platoons via satellite telephone.

"There is a convoy of food going from Kitgum to Pader this afternoon. Join with Platoon 4 and 12 by the forest in ambush. Fighting should last only thirty minutes. Then retreat, taking what you can." And, "In Palabek, there is a new commander with new recruits who are not yet seasoned. Attack them at night but do not enter the camp. Just stay outside and snipe all night long. Flee before first light."

Occasionally, recruits would run low, or losses would become excessive due to unforeseen battles, and I would issue the order, "All platoons, each of you raid the camps closest and bring in ten new recruits. Send them with a trusted lieutenant to the training base."

Each night, before becoming drunk, I would call in to talk with our commander, who was doing the same as I was doing but for the entire war effort, encompassing the five theaters: Gulu, Amuru, Pader, Kitgum, and what he called Foreign Actions, which mostly consisted of attacks against the Sudanese rebels ordered by our Khartoum benefactors or the occasional incursion into Congo to keep that lawless country in play in case we had to flee there. Where the commander was, he never revealed. It was rumored he was in southwest Sudan, but others said he was in eastern Central African Republic, and even some others whispered quietly—for to say this was treason—that he was actually in Khartoum in a luxurious apartment provided by our benefactors. I didn't much care where he was; nor did we develop any rapport, no intimacy. There was nothing personal about our interactions. The telephone conversations were surgical, questions and answers short and to the point. In the American movies we would watch on movie night in the camps, military commanders are always drinking with their soldiers and giving powerful speeches about purpose and conquest. Communing with the men over their family news from far away, reassuring in the face of loss on a grand scale such as war brings. There was none of this with our commander. Not even any indication of the importance of the cause for the future of Acholi. The war was an epic endeavor that stood alone, not requiring justification or defense, nor even a great, overarching narrative. I imagine that at some time in the past there must have been one. Isn't that how these things always start? But, such as it had become, the war we were fighting existed on its own inertia, for its own sake; it was a fight for the sake of fighting, a desire to quench a bloodlust that seemed to be insatiable. We did not know what victory would look like. All talk of establishing a country governed by the Ten Commandments had ended long before I had joined. There was still the talk of our hate of the tyrant, but there were no efforts to oust him, to make him pay. Show trials to mock him. Monikers that made him seem less than he was, ethnic bile thrown against another tribe. Nothing. The hate meted out by our child soldiers was directed haphazardly at whoever was in our path—soldier or civilian, black or white, male or female, adult or child, Acholi and Buganda alike.

None of that bothered me. I had not joined for some great cause, some grand motivation, or some utopia that I had been sold by those who believed in such things. Mine had been an accidental membership born of opportunity and chance, of bitterness and anger. What I was given was much, much better—power, pure and beautiful, arbitrary and indiscriminate. My lust against their flesh; my hunger against their plenty; my past against their future; my knife—my gun—my rage; my whims against their lives.

As I said before, in the valley below Lotuturu, my third platoon managed one of our commanders' training camps for the new recruits. And we were constantly moving the young men and women through the process of subservience to the resistance and surrender of themselves to the commander. Some of the tactics I've mentioned before. I will not repeat them. I do not glory in dwelling on what I have done, but neither will I deny it. We did not seek to inspire their minds; we did not attempt to build a sense of community or a vision for the future. We did not give them the strength to endure the heroic or grand. Brutality—that was our commander's vision, subservience through torment—physical to be sure, but much more significant, the marks of the revolution permanently etched on the minds and the spirits of children. Through carefully crafted brutality, we molded them to our will—perfect fighters who had no sense of self, of their own place in the world. No future, no past, and no tomorrow. Only their tormented souls that cried out in the dark of night until they went silent. Forever.

And so I settled in to my new life, the life of a warlord. Not something I had planned, during the days when I had planned, sitting around the camps with no present but an active future in our young imaginations. I found my rhythm, the rhythm of battles without a purpose in a war without meaning. Abductions, indoctrination, fighting. Retreating, regrouping, and again sending the children out to battle against the government. There was no emotional connection for me to the war. The goal—well, as I said before, there was none to speak of. The soldiers—mindless children, automatons, not brothers in arms, not brothers in any way. Cannon fodder. A promotion, if there was such a thing with the rebels? No thanks—to flee my land, sit in some godforsaken bog with *him*. I couldn't imagine why anybody would want to do that. As long as I kept safe, as long as I had my privilege, my women, my food—my power. My Lotuturu. That was, for me, the most that life would ever provide. And it wasn't bad at all, for a boy from the camps of Odek.

Despite all that—what I had become—there was nevertheless a small part of me that still ached with sadness and itched for peace and, despite it all, still dreamed of Ruth. Not with love; that had died. But that feeling of possession, that which she represented to me, which I had not taken away even by murdering her college boy. That part, I knew, which would never die. Because, as I look back, far back along the length of my days, I realize now—like I realized then—that Ruth was the only dream I ever really had. But unlike the Hollywood films where the star-crossed lovers come together, old and withered but still in love, my story was different. Squandered and lost in a pit of violence and jealousy—and reality.

So I buried it under a putrescent pile of malevolence.

CHAPTER 17

Time flowed by like the seasons I watched crashing over Acholiland from my perch high above in Lotuturu. Black African storm clouds would roll over the valley like a mudslide, preceded as they always were by the musty heaviness of the upcoming monsoon. They would linger for a time, pondering their power before they unleashed the torrents. The dirt below turned to red mud, thick with nutrients running in rivulets to fill the rivers that turned the color of Moses's Nile. In those moments, I would stand atop Amin's throne daring the lightning to strike—almost hoping that it would. Naked, pounding my chest and raising my arms high and screaming into the gales as the wind whipped over the mountain in waves and my girls cowered in fear. I would curse the tyrant, curse the British who had come before, curse the soldiers and their administrators. But mostly I would curse the whites and their wretched camps. Then the storms would dissipate, fewer and fewer as the dryness came, scorching the earth below the harshness of the sun. The harvests would occur where men still dared to work, and we would raid them in their fields, carrying off the work of their backs in carts or buckets. Then again the rains. Nothing changed. The Acholi—men, women, and children—cowered in fear in their camps, afraid of me this time. Mostly the lands just lay fallow, growing richer each year of life and death of the grasslands, adding a layer to their fertility while the demigod they had known looked down from the mountaintop.

Crowded together in the camps, or protected in the few cities by the soldiers, boys went to school, going from classroom to classroom until they wandered away. They had sex, had babies, got married, and saw their babies crawl, walk, run, dance, and sing as they sat there under *my* shadow, in *my* dominion. Little girls grew, experienced their first period, their first moment of pleasure, had the babies that their new husbands would brag about. Births, weddings, and funerals. I watched all these from my perch—savoring the power over those far below who had once thought they were my betters, if they thought of me at all. Ah, but the monster on the mountain? They thought of him often!

I suppose I would have stayed on the mountain forever, perfect in my impunity. I was almost thirty, and five years had passed since I joined the LRA. I would have lived out my short life up there, looking down on my kingdom, had that fateful telephone call not interrupted my sleep early one morning. I jumped to attention, looking at the identification on the tiny screen, and blanched, silencing my women as I answered it.

"Yes?"

"There is a mission I want you to undertake." The commander never exchanged pleasantries, barking orders without waiting for a response.

"Yes, sir," I said.

"I want you to take four of your best platoons and head west. Northwest specifically. The road has been completed between the river and Gulu and has continued north, closing the distance between Gulu and Juba. It is close to halfway done. Our benefactors cannot have that road completed."

"Yes, sir," I said. And that was it. There was never any explanation either, but I knew that the Gulu theater commander had recently been overwhelmed by an incursion of an untested but freshly trained battalion of soldiers from the south who were attempting to secure the road to Gulu, and some tanks and other heavy weapons had been seen along that highway. I also knew that the benefactors were of course the Khartoum government, which had recently been enraged by the tyrant's decision to provide the rebels in the south of Sudan with weapons and other supplies, presumably in response for Khartoum supporting us, mixed with some misguided sense of crusade, keeping the Muslim hoards contained above the river. We didn't much care that Khartoum was Muslim, and they didn't much care that we were Christians. War is war and knows no religion.

I spent the day working with my deputy, a squirrely boy we had abducted a few years ago who was particularly adept at following orders and seemed to enjoy the significance that the war gave him. His brutality was more measured than my other lieutenants, who liked blood for the sake of blood, and he had a greater mind for strategy. We were engaged in a cat-and-mouse game with the soldiers over a particularly embarrassing incident that involved an attack against a humanitarian aid convoy meant to supply food and bed nets to one of the camps, which had fortuitously also had a group of foreign journalists on it from one of the Western news outlets. The journalists had, thankfully, been abducted by my trigger-happy soldiers. Most often, they killed white people, and I didn't complain. But these had been ransomed for a hefty sum after releasing some excellent footage of pathetic soldiers and the strength of the rebellion. To make matters worse, despite their misfortune, upon their release they had produced a scathing report on the Ugandan government's incompetence and even insinuated that our rebellion might have some merit and legitimacy. The piece included an interview that I had done, seated on my throne atop the mountain, an activity I had enjoyed immensely. For this reason, the soldiers were making a particularly ambitious push north of Kitgum toward the mountain, and my deputy and I were maneuvering our platoons to make their advance impossible.

That day, I also called the four senior-most platoon commanders and ordered them to assemble north of the town of Palabek, halfway between my location and the Gulu-Juba road. It took me only a few phone calls to identify the precise location of the road crew, as well as the numbers of soldiers guarding the workers, which were not as numerous as I would have assumed, them being deep in rebel territory.

I left early the next morning, leaving my women behind and my cook preparing my favorite dish—pan-fried pork with plantains—for my return. I fully intended to make quick work of this assignment in order to return to my orderly, quiet life, inflicting mayhem from the safety of my mountain and enjoying women and drink at night. I did not expect any trouble, nor did I think that anything would go wrong. The soldiers were like babies who screamed and ran, sometimes soiling themselves in the process as they fled for their lives. It was almost comical, if they hadn't left such a smelly, dirty, stinking mess to search through after they were dead, sending new recruits to clean out the uniforms that we needed. I don't know what I would have done if I'd known I would never return to Lotuturu. Over the months, the years, it had become my home and had given me comfort. Would I have defied the commander's order, risking immediate retribution? Our commander did not suffer dissent lightly, and his punishments were swift and final. Would I have broken off with my platoons and headed into Karamoja, fighting off the Karamojong—if it was possible to defeat those fierce cattle rustlers, considering it had never been done—to carve out a space for my own rebellion? Who knows. Life is like that, our perfect understanding of the past a tiresome companion when things go unplanned and turn out wrong. But such as it was, I donned my uniform, lacing tight my boots and kissing my women goodbye. While throwing my sack over my shoulder, I headed oblivious into the future.

My walk down the mountain and toward Palabek was quiet. I had chosen to walk alone. None would challenge me. There were no soldiers in the abandoned areas outside the towns. Occasionally, I walked by battle scenes, destruction from the decades-long struggle for Acholiland. Human cadavers bleached white by the sun, their uniforms rotting around them and their ghost sitting forlornly by their side or up in the branch of a nearby tree, smoking a cigarette, waiting for the time when they would be freed from the abrupt end and released to the afterlife. Worse still for me, though I don't know why, were the dead buildings sitting all around. A school, blackened by fire, doors kicked open, windows without glass or shutters, vacant sockets staring out across to the empty horizon. A bus, ripped open by a rocket-propelled grenade sometime in the distant past, laying on its side, looted of every part that had value, naked frame rusting to nothing. A ghost village, small cement buildings boarded up, spider webs hanging down from the zinc to the termite-eaten doors sealed with a padlock. Out back, the round Acholi homesteads overgrown with weeds, wooden doors removed under old, rotting thatch—now the home of snakes and wasps. An old church, once square and solid, was listing inward upon itself under a roof that no longer protected it from the rains. I stuck my head inside to see only the ravaged interior of the house of worship; no fire here, but all the pews had been overturned, some shattered to use for firewood or to make impromptu stretchers that we often used to carry our wounded from the battlefield. At the front, hands still tied to the pulpit, was the skeleton of what I assumed had been the preacher, head laying down almost peacefully upon a rotting old Bible opened to the book of Revelations. I continued on down the road, nothing living in sight except the vegetation. No animals, no people, not even any bugs. My land—my people. The past that we had lived, the future that was now dead and buried beside an unused church that nevertheless still resonated somehow with the presence of God—a God I no longer really believed in. I had seen so much destruction. And I had participated in my fair share, occasionally even leaving Lotuturu to engage in a raid or the sacking of a convoy when I felt my edge slipping, when I felt myself becoming complacent. Life and death in Acholiland.

All the while, I was thinking, not of issues of consequence but planning my assault on the road crew. The challenge with closing down road projects forever was that they were important to the government. We would plan the attack, make the raid, kill the workers, drive the soldiers back south, and burn all the equipment. Nevertheless, after a few weeks, we would find that a new road crew had been assigned, with new equipment and a new contingent of soldiers to protect them. We occasionally tried to destroy the road itself, but it was resistant to small arms fire, and even RPGs didn't make a significant dent in the asphalt. Any heavier weapons, artillery, or large-scale explosives were too valuable to be used on a piece of road. They were not available in the market, and we got them only from our benefactors; they were government-grade weapons, provided to Khartoum by the Russians. Those we kept for our battles against the soldiers.

This time I was planning something daring. Something I had taken from a story I had heard about Idi Amin sometime in the past when I was working in Kampala. You see, the southerners are superstitious. To be sure, the Acholi are as well, but nothing compared to those from below the river. Amulets and incantations and child sacrifices to appease their petty, vindictive gods. Amin, who was also from above the river, knew this. He knew that the powerful magic of the southerners could be easily used to his own advantage in his enduring efforts to subjugate his enemies. The southerners, the Buganda tribe of Kampala specifically, were central to the British colonialists' efforts at controlling the faraway territory. The Buganda were well organized, with their own tribal administration and organization. Their own parliament of elders, their own laws. These the British allowed to continue—to flourish. More than that, they encouraged them as they trained the tribe in public administration, in how to run the protectorate for the empire. As part of this effort, they built for the Buganda a glorious parliament building at the epicenter of their tribal kingdom, on one of the hills back behind Kampala. There the Buganda would debate and discuss, would honor their leaders, and would plan their support to the British. And it was from there that, during the waxing of Amin, they conspired against the dictator. One day, the Buganda parliament was in session, and the road to the building filled with trucks and soldiers, with Amin riding in his Cadillac at the head. Coming to stop at the front of the campus, they marched upward until they stood at the gate, knocking it down with a tank. But it was not the building or the parliamentarians they were after. Amin had learned of a natural cave under the building and went immediately there, striding arrogantly as he was wont to do, conferring with his generals and laughing raucously in the sun, so all could hear and fear. "This is it?" he is said to have asked when he arrived at the entrance to the cave. "Yes, sir," the answer. He walked inside for a few minutes and then emerged. "Yes, this will do fine."

Unseen by the parliamentarians who had kept their eyes fixed on Amin, behind the tanks had come several truckloads of unfortunates. Students, teachers, bankers, judges—poets and writers and musicians. All had offended the famously unstable Amin in some way, and all would pay the price. They were emaciated, smelled terrible, and had marks down their bodies and eternity in their eyes. "We'll offload them here," Amin had said, and the soldiers marched the men and women into the cave. There the torture was to continue, but first they were given shovels in order to dig a deep, wide pond across the entrance, which was then electrified, a moat to prevent flight. The screaming is said to have been heard throughout the subsequent session of parliament, after which the building was abandoned. Forever. It still reverberates with the misery of the thousands of souls who faced pain and then death there, and as is well known by the shamans of the southerners, the souls of those who die in torment abide at the place of their death, waiting for a time to find peace with their life in order to move to the other side. Revenge, a reckoning, only those who commune with the dead really know. And the Buganda packed their things and wandered off, defeated by Amin, their holy places destroyed, their culture soiled, their pride destroyed. It is still abandoned, that building; the spirits still have not found their peace.

I had been there once—to the cave—where I sat for a long time, listening to the story.

I would make this piece of land that was meant to host a road instead a place of great suffering—then a graveyard. The stories of my tortures would reach south as if on the wings of the African fish eagles. I would make sure of this. I would pick two witnesses, one laborer—the most articulate of the workers that I found—and one soldier, to corroborate each other's stories, and I would force them to watch what I would do to their friends, their brothers, their comrades. They would hear the screams and the pleas and the supplications and be able to do nothing. After finishing, we would then take what was left of the asphalt and pour it over the remains, right at the center of the road. A prominent mount of agony visible from near and far and haunted forever by the angry souls of those who had suffered and died in that spot. I cackled at my plan. If ever they were to finish the road, they would have to find a new route, scout out new earth, carry out new soil tests, level new hills. All the meticulous planning of the years would be for naught, because they would not be able to find any laborer to build the cursed highway, nor any contingent of soldiers willing to guard such a ghostly endeavor.

CHAPTER 18

own below me, the thin gray line of the road snaked effortlessly south, back to Gulu, to Karuma, over the river and onward. From where it had all started for me, so long ago. Immediately below, tiny as ants, were the laborers in their austere camp. A few jeeps with soldiers, one tank. Several dozen of the road crew beside a lorry, which I suppose transported them from here to there and back again. A makeshift shelter, looking like a lean-to of some sort that had been erected on the far side of the camp; I assumed it was a kitchen and storehouse. The workers all slept beneath the tree under the stars. It was the dry season, and they did not fear the squalls of winter for another several months.

I had positioned three of my platoons on the three extremes of the camp, one just north, one immediately south, one in the forests west, and one right below me. They had quietly taken their positions and were only waiting for the command to attack. It was not going to be a fight. I don't know why the commander had ordered four platoons to take on what looked like a meager few dozen soldiers below, but anyway, here we were. At least it would all fit neatly into the story that the two fortunate survivors would tell down south of overwhelming force and unquenchable brutality. My plan was to order the attack by two gunshots that would shatter the early-morning silence and simply overwhelm them. The trick was to kill as few as possible—at first. That process I wanted to last for days, even a week if we were lucky.

The sun rose slowly, and as the men started to stir in the camp below, I removed the handgun I always carried in my belt and fired two shots into the air. Pandemonium ensued. In the camp below, the soldiers deployed in a defensive formation around the little camp, crawling under jeeps, behind the trees, and beside the structures—awaiting the assault that they must have known was inevitable. My rebels, who were close at hand, charged from the four cardinal directions, engulfing the camp. The battle was short and unremarkable. A few soldiers fled into the bush and were hunted. Others threw down their weapons, and one turned his own gun on himself, unwilling to face us. Wise, I would say. The workers just huddled together in a pathetic lump of sweaty, smelly flesh. Some had shat themselves, and others were crying as I walked down from my perch on the hilltop to stroll among them.

"You are prisoners of the Lord's Resistance Army," I said.

Nobody said a thing. The soldiers had been lined up single file, on their knees, with their hands on their heads. Their eyes were yellow with fear and bloodshot from crying. I inspected them one by one as I continued my tirade.

"You have invaded our lands again, and again, and yet again. Each time, you have met us, but yet you still come. Stupidity it must be, I suppose. For I cannot understand why you fail to grasp the simple fact that every time the tyrant sends you here, you will meet us. And you will die."

The soldiers were looking down at the dirt in front of them.

"He won't die, your tyrant. He's safe and happy in his palace in Entebbe, which he built for himself with stolen money. Do you ever wonder what he eats for breakfast, while you prepare your slop in the morning? Do you ever consider his leisure, while you suffer the privations in an Acholiland that does not want you here? Do you ever wonder, at night when you are sleeping on the rocks, how many women are comforting the tyrant? Now, as you are about to die, do you think he is thinking of you? Of course not. Oh, sure, he will be angry. He will punish your senior commanders. He will rail against our cause, against our own commander. He will foam and froth and scream curses into the still air. But your names? He does not know you, and he does not care. You, who are about to die, will die in anonymity. And your families? Do you think they will get compensation for your sacrifice? Answer me this: When was the last time you were even paid, that would make you risk coming her to face me? Fools you are."

I stopped then, waiting for a time for my words to sink in. Sweat started to flow—the heat for sure but also panic as each of them came to terms with my intentions. The loss of hope is always intriguing to watch. All the while, I walked up and down the line, in front of the soldiers, choosing the soldier who would be the beneficiary of my mercy. I found him, just of age, glasses and clutching a rosary, repeating to himself the prayers of absolution that all good Catholics must repeat before they die.

"You," I said, and he blanched and then burst out weeping. "You, I have chosen for a special task." He looked up at me, who had stopped in front of him, not knowing what to think. "You will not die today." I could see the change in his eyes, instant relief followed by shame as he realized he was thankful, grateful, even though he knew all his comrades were not as lucky. I smiled. "Your job will be to watch what I will do to your comrades, your friends, your brothers. You will watch all of it, as long as it takes—days, a week. When it is over, you will go back south to tell the southerners what you have seen here, the level our resolve has reached, to assure that you stay forever out of our lands and no longer return here to cause us trouble. If you see the tyrant, you will give him my message. You will stand before him, look into his eyes, and say, 'You must give up, because the Lord's Resistance Army never will.' Do you understand me?"

"Yyyy ... yesss, ssssiiirrrr," the young soldier stuttered.

"You will tell him my name. Okot. The name I won when I took the girls—yes, that was me, so long ago. They are still with us. Two of them I still have, and they lie beside me at night to satisfy my needs and sometimes my whims."

While I had been talking, my men had also assembled the road workers in a similar line as the soldiers but behind them. There they were, kneeling in the dirt, fingers intertwined above their heads. I left the soldiers and turned to walk over to the civilians to address them as well.

"And you, who have heard what I have told the soldiers, know that you will not escape either. You have made a choice, to work for the invaders in their attempts to occupy our land and rob us of our birthright. You will also die, as a lesson to any other day laborers that there are easier, safer ways to make money. You have come here because you have nowhere else to go, nothing else to do. No other way to earn the simple handful of shillings you receive. I know. Long ago, I was in your shoes—working for a Chinaman, protected by soldiers as we pushed this same road up into the land that I now fight for. I killed my oppressors and joined the cause, something that you should have done." As I addressed these men, I walked down the line, from left to right, looking at each of them. "Now I will pick one of you, who also will ..." And my voice froze. Because it was then that I saw him, at the far end, kneeling with a look of peace in his eyes.

Frederich.

My mind was a blank. My words fled, and my mouth became instantly dry as an Acholi summer. I had stopped in my tracks, not knowing what to do, what to say. The soldiers were looking at me oddly, and my men were quizzical as my face contorted in agony as the battle for my soul that had been postponed for so many, many years was unleashed.

As I stood, time also seemed to stand still as my stomach seized up and I thought I would vomit or pass out or—or what I didn't know. It was then, looking into eyes that I had embraced in friendship and—yes, and love—that I realized finally how far gone I was. Frederich, who was looking back at me with what seemed like compassion. He surely knew it, and I became instantly ashamed. My own rebels did not think of me as a human, and the soldiers who were kneeling in the dust only saw a monster. And monster I was, but deep down in the depth below the scar tissue that surrounded my soul, something still beat. The boy who sacrificed for his family, the adolescent who loved Ruth, the young man who had dreamed of a future, the choir boy who had considered Jesus, and the hard man who had loved Frederich. They were all there, and as the veneer began to crack, my mind also started to reflect on the man I had become and the things I had done to make that man possible. Wickedness in the full light of the sun, subservience to evil pure and perfect. Helplessness to the demons who had seized my soul. Slowly, painfully, I put one foot in front of the other, and another and another—silent as I walked down the line to stand in front of Frederich.

He looked up at me as I swung my AK from my shoulder to hold it. The perfectly polished wood of my well-used weapon was comforting, the familiar weight in my hand a soothing reminder of what I had become. Slowly, I raised the AK to his head. My intention, if intention I had, was to exempt him from the torture that I knew I must inflict on the others. To give him the blessed gift of release. Then, randomly, thoughts began to flood into my mind. The river where we had fished for catfish. The early-morning walks to the waterfall. The contests—breaking rocks and laughing with each other at our agony. The truth, something I did not give freely—stories of life and love but also of suffering. Frederich's past—the Pakistani boy who had been his friend, his child lost to disease, his son studying computers. And then the final thought: three hundred thousand shillings, the paltry sum that would be given to Frederich's family. The price of his death; the value of his life, forfeited by my hands. How long would such a small sum last, if they indeed received it at all? If it didn't end up in the pockets of an expensive whore by a Kichina supervisor who didn't care? My finger started to squeeze on the trigger of the rifle, and as I looked into my friend's gentle eyes, I saw it. Forgiveness. I closed my eyes, and as I pulled the trigger, I let out a howl that echoed off the rivers and the trees, reaching to the mountains beyond as I felt myself spinning and spinning. A flock of sparrows took flight from where they had been resting, filling the air with their cries. The jungle monkeys screeched, and a hippo roared in response from the great distance of the river.

But when I peeled my lids open, I saw Frederich staring up at me from his position still kneeling on the ground, in his eyes a mixture of amazement, gratitude, and understanding. "Thank you, my friend," he said. And I looked around, shocked at what I was witnessing. Around me, a dozen of my rebels lay on the ground in pools of their own blood. From the other platoons, some of the children had fallen to the ground sobbing, while others had abandoned their own weapons in confusion and were running up into the bush or toward the jungles. The soldiers were still staring at me, kneeling as I had left them in the dirt, the fear having been replaced with confusion.

I did not respond to Frederich; I could not find the words. Instead, head still foggy as I considered my surroundings, I let my AK—still smoking and with the clip now empty—fall from my hands to clatter into the dust. I started to run, one foot, then another and another, as I pounded toward, well, toward nowhere, just away. I didn't look back. I half-expected a round to find me, square in the back, and put an end to my anguish. But the strides eventually became kilometers while the seconds, minutes, and finally hours ticked away, and I knew somewhere in my muddled consciousness that I was alone and unfollowed.

I don't know how long I ran or how far. Neither do I know exactly the direction, except that it was a different way from the one I had come, toward the mountains over which was the Congo. My mind was ravaged, a raging storm. What I had done, what I had become. Frederich, my friend, my mentor. My salvation. My destruction? I didn't even have energy to care about what would come after. Blinding white flashes of emotions that I could not identify—new feelings I had never experienced—ran together in my head like a reel-to-reel movie. I panted, out of breath, sweat flowing freely. At one point, I remember that I found a river, plunging through it without even bothering to wash or drink—the shocking coolness energizing me to run and run and run some more. I became colder. The exertion might have been harder—I didn't know. Until I finally collapsed, entering a deep, dreamless sleep where I fell, not knowing or caring if I would ever wake again.

I awoke from the cold on the mountaintop. I don't know what day it was, but what I did know was that it was evening time. I stood from where I had been curled up upon a small patch of long mountain grass beside a large rock on a cliff, and I stretched—reaching toward the skies that were darkening above me. It was cold, and I shivered as I looked down, far down the mountain and across the wide lake, into the dark green of the jungle that slowly tapered off into the muted browns of the plains of Acholiland so far in the distance. There was not much vegetation where I was, above the tree line on the narrow ridge— perhaps ten feet across—that divided one country from another, one set of problems from another, one set of rebels from another, one war from another. Far below in the distance, toward the south, I could make out the twinkling lights of Gulu town. The city preparing for another night under the siege of the darkness and the rebels who controlled the night.

I shivered again, my breath coming in short bursts of mist. It was cold up here on the ridge. The pass conducted the warmer air upward and over the lowest point, where I was standing, and as it met the mountain winds, it began to turn to fog, and quickly my views of Gulu and Uganda—my last view of Acholiland—began to fade. I started feeling around in my pockets for matches, a lighter, a knife, anything that I could use to build myself a fire or a shelter or something that would ward off the worst of the mountain night. As I searched, I was surprised to come across the satellite telephone in one of the pockets of my fatigues. For a reason I still cannot fathom, I turned it on to find that it still had enough battery life for that one last call. It was about that time, and I punched in the number that I had memorized by heart after so many calls—dialed and received, good and bad, praise and condemnation. It rang only once.

"You," the commander said, still without emotion—even after this. "I am surprised that you called."

"This will be my last call," I said stupidly.

"I know that," he said. "Why did you call?"

"I don't know," I said.

"You have betrayed our rebellion, our cause. And me," he continued, still measured, although there were twinges of fury in the insinuation of the words. "I will find you, and I will kill you."

"You won't find me," I said.

"I ask again, then—why did you call?"

"Because," I said, beginning to understand, "I wanted you to know that I was free of you. But more importantly, I wanted *me* to know that I am free of you."

"You may think—" he said, but I interrupted.

"No. No more of your lies. Do you know what I have done for you? What we all have done for you? Not even of our own accord, at least for most of us—abducted and forced to murder. For a time, I thought I could make peace with it, but I guess we both know now that was not to be. Your war, it has been nothing but ashes and dust. Violence for violence's sake, hate for—well, for nothing at all."

"You are over—Charles Agwok. Yes, I use your real name. I have withdrawn the one I gave you, as I have withdrawn from you your titles and my protection. I will hunt you. I will alert my sponsors to you. We will not rest, and neither will you," he said, and then he went on. "But let me answer your assertion—that you will be free of me. Because you will never be free of me. As much as you might blame me for what you have done, it was you who abducted those girls so long ago. Yes, right now I am seated beside the one that you sent me. She has borne me children, who are themselves growing up to learn to fight. You did that. You will not be free of me, because those new lives were created because of you—and they will be fighters. Every time you see a child, you will think of them. And you will not be free of me, because of what you did each day, each act that you bragged about on our calls. Each terrified woman crying under your lust. Each little boy curled up around his machine gun, afraid of the dark and crying himself to sleep with songs his mother taught him on his lips. Each skeleton staring vacantly into the Acholi afternoon. All of those things you did—and you alone. I know why you did them, even if you do not. And now that you forsake the mission and the calling, the full weight of your actions will come down upon you, and it will crush you. So if you think you will be free of me, let me assure you—you are only just beginning to contemplate me."

"You …" I began, but before I could respond, the line went dead. I looked down; the battery had been spent, leaving me with the last words—my last retort—stillborn upon my lips. I screamed in anguish and hate and bitterness—and I have been told that throughout the length of the country, north to south, east to west, young men in the bars lifted their heads, night watchmen clutched their guns tighter, mothers walked quietly to their children's doors to peer in upon their babies, that the entire country heard my anguish and was shaken.

I took the telephone and looked at it for a moment before stepping back and hurling it as far as I could down the mountain in the direction of Acholi. Spent, I curled up on the mountaintop with the long grass as a bed and again fell asleep.

So that is my story, my manifesto and my motivation, such as it is. The rest is of no consequence. My path down the mountain into Congo. The flight down the length of the Kivus, avoiding detection using Kiswahili, our common trade language of East Africa, blending in among the rivers of refugees always on the move, a torrent flooding that land from one side to the other and back again. Traversing the great lakes as I sought a place where I would not be known, having buried Okot upon the ridge of a high mountain overlooking Acholi. My arrival at Kigoma, the greatest of all Congolese refugee camps in Tanzania, where I could hide nameless among so many thousands who arrive every day, fleeing misfortune.

And it is here that I have lived these many years. It is fitting really, finishing out my life back where I started, in the camps. Camps I tried every way I could to escape: sacrifice, love, violence. Rebellion. But now, at the end, I know that it was all folly—vainglorious attempts at significance that are never meant to be for those of us from the camps. You might be surprised to know that I even married here, though she doesn't know who I am. Sometimes she looks at me anxiously when I awake in the night screaming, covered in sweat. When I turn the other way at the sight of a soldier or yet another in the endless line of white men, who I now know I will never be free of. When I stay tuned to the BBC on my small radio—listening in an English I pretend not to know for news about Africa—and when my eyebrows turn up at the mention of Uganda. When I refuse to attend the Pentecostal services even when she begs me and when I occasionally get drunk and rage against the church and their white Jesus.

We have had children, my wife and I. More mouths to feed from the camps. They do not know either who they are or what wickedness has been passed to them through my blood. Not that it matters. Congolese, Ugandan, Tanzanian—Kigoman. It is all the same for us Africans from the camps. Homeless, landless, deprived of our past and denied a future. I teach them not to hope, not to struggle, not to dream. I teach them to focus on little things that are achievable—a few liters of banana wine sold at market, several kilos of potatoes from a good harvest. Flirtations with a local girl who knows the camps and does not expect more. I teach them that ambition only brings a greater darkness—that we as shadow people must accept that we are such because the gods do not forgive attempts at triumph.

So there you have it. I have reached the end, and I pen this for you upon a ream of paper I stole from the offices of a charity so that you may know that I lived and that I struggled. That I was not only a shade that drifted from camp to camp—a frail flame to be extinguished at the end without ever having blazed. That we Africans from the camps also covet, dream, lust, and sorrow—that we also feel. And that we also fight. I am not proud of what I have done, of who I became. I don't know if there is a god or, if there is, if He will forgive me. I surely would not, if I were Him. But I can tell you for certain that it is not easy being born a black man from the African camps. So before you judge me too harshly, you who live with plenty, I ask you one last time to examine yourself first.

Would you have done any differently?

CPSIA information can be obtained
at www.ICGtesting.com
Printed in the USA
FFOW02n0843260418
46377191-48076FF